LIFE
DERAILED

OTHER TITLES BY BETH MERLIN AND DANIELLE MODAFFERI

The Last Phone Booth in Manhattan

Heart Restoration Project

Breakup Boot Camp

The Campfire Series

One S'more Summer

S'more to Lose

Love You S'more

Tell Me S'more

LIFE DERAILED

a Novel

BETH MERLIN **DANIELLE MODAFFERI**

 Montlake

Text copyright © 2025 by Beth Merlin and Danielle Modafferi
All rights reserved.

Published by Montlake, Seattle

www.apub.com

Amazon, the Amazon logo, and Montlake are trademarks of Amazon.com, Inc., or its affiliates.

ISBN-13: 9781662529115 (paperback)
ISBN-13: 9781662529122 (digital)

Cover design by Caroline Teagle Johnson
Cover images: © chuckchee, © The_Pixel, © ZlatkoGuzmic / Getty

Printed in the United States of America

For all the "Ruth Russells" of the world—the selfless, tireless moms out there—but most of all ours: Patricia Modafferi and Diane Zamansky, who challenged us, pushed us to be the best versions of ourselves, and drove us a little crazy along the way (which we're sure was reciprocal, especially during those teen years!). Thank you for your relentless love and unwavering support.

Chapter One

I twisted my hair up into a loose topknot and secured it in place with a pen. Clicking open LinkedIn, I typed the name Jason Ashbloom into the search bar and hit Enter.

Nothing.

Nothing? A top corporate executive who doesn't have a LinkedIn page?!

I tried again, this time typing in Jason *Ashblum*, and three profiles populated the screen. The first a technical recruiter from Palo Alto, the second a freelance writer from Boise, and the third a solicitor from Manchester, England. None of those were him. *Dammit.* I mean, how many ways were there to spell Ashbloom?!

I made one more attempt, certain it couldn't possibly be right, keying Jason *Ashbloome* into the text box and rolling my eyes as I hit the Enter key again.

Lo and behold, of course, there he was—front and center. Mr. Silent E, with his suave professional headshot, wearing a sharp navy pin-striped suit and an overexaggerated smile that just oozed with disingenuous energy. His light eyes seemed pensive behind thick tortoiseshell frames, the kind people buy when they want to *look* smart. They probably didn't even have lenses in them.

But he was much younger than I'd anticipated after hearing through the rumor mill his list of accomplishments and *alllllllll* the reasons the board championed bringing him on to save the magazine. Chief strategy officer . . . more like chief meddling officer. I've seen this movie before. A few times, actually.

Jason Ashbloome would waltz in with his shiny new title that matched his shiny new shoes and ask the department heads for a list of "redundant" employees as a way to trim the fat. Little would he know, we've been asked to do this half a dozen times already and were operating leaner than a Kardashian on Ozempic. I wasn't bitter, exactly. Just jaded. Every time a new "savior" was brought on, I got my hopes up that they'd be able to turn some things around, make real improvements to the magazine—you know, what they'd been hired to do. But then I'd catch a glimpse of the newest chief strategy officer packing up his sad little box of belongings from the desk that had barely begun to collect dust, and my hopes for saving *The Sophisticate* would dim just a bit more.

My doomscroll through LinkedIn was suddenly interrupted by Molly, the magazine's love columnist, who burst into my office, startling me practically right out of my rolling chair.

"Jeez, Molly. What the hell?!" I fumbled to try to close my laptop so she couldn't see that I was stress-searching *again*.

She fanned herself with the interoffice mail folder in her hand. "Have you seen the new chief strategy officer? You know how the last one sort of looked like a hobbit? Well, this one is HOT. He's a dead ringer for Aragorn, and I just love myself some Nikolaj Coster-Waldau."

"Um . . . Nikolaj Coster-Waldau played Jaime Lannister in *Game of Thrones*. I'm pretty sure Viggo Mortensen played Aragorn in *Lord of the Rings*."

"Yeah, well, whatever. Same thing."

"Not really. Actually, not at all." I laughed as Molly perched half of her behind on the corner of my desk and reached out a hand to straighten one of my framed photos.

"Oh, well, excuse me. I didn't realize I was in the presence of such a Tolkien aficionado," she teased in a mockingly snooty voice as she waved her hand in the air with a flourish.

"No, well, I'm not but . . . David was."

My voice, distant and disconnected from my thoughts, suddenly floated away at the mention of my dead husband. As if a ghost had swept into the room, I could almost smell the earthy essence of David's favorite armchair mingled with the dusty aroma of his tattered copy of *The Hobbit*. Despite David's postcollege promise to dispose of the chair, it somehow managed to get past our interior designer, finding a permanent home in our Upper West Side flat.

When he'd died, I thought about finally tossing it, but in the end, I couldn't bear the idea of getting rid of one of the last witnesses to our history. The night before David left for his assignment in Ukraine, the recliner, intended for one, had cradled us both as I lay crooked next to him with my head on his chest, drifting off to the hum of his timbre while he read *The Hobbit* aloud—for what neither of us knew would be the very last time.

Molly, barely missing a beat, quickly pivoted back to the matter at hand. "Right, well, whoever he looks like, this new guy is *smokin'*. I'd happily play a damsel in whatever fantasy he's starring in . . . most likely just my own." Molly continued to fan herself, her eyes glazing over as she slipped further into her X-rated daydream.

I literally snapped her out of it with a clapping of my hands in front of her thousand-yard stare. "Molly, hey, I love you. And while I'm happy for the hotness report, I'm in the middle of getting ready to meet with him as we speak and could use a few minutes . . . unless you need something. Plus, I'm not sure how your fiancé would feel about your wandering eye?" I teased with a smirk.

"Oh, Luca and I have a strict 'look but don't touch' policy. So as long as I keep my hands to myself, my eyes are free to meander."

"Okay, well, you and your eyes can meander wherever you want, just not in here. My meeting with Aragorn is in"—I flipped my phone over and panicked at the realization—"shit, fifteen minutes. Do you have anything actually useful for me to bring up in the meeting *aside* from the fact that he has an ass that won't quit?"

"Ugh . . . not another. Whose ass is quitting now?" Our gazes shifted to the open door, where my second-in-command, Carrie, poked her head through to chime in on the overheard conversation. "I swear to God, if I hear about one more person going off to live out their dream as a TikTok influencer, I'll scream," she exclaimed as she flopped herself into the chair across from my desk.

Molly snorted out a laugh. "No one's ass is quitting. I was talking about the new guy, Ashbloome. But honestly, I may have to start calling him Ashbum, with a booty like that." Molly was cracking herself up, barely acknowledging her escalating volume and the fact the door was still *wiiiiiiiiide* open.

Carrie and I yelled simultaneously in her direction, "HR JAR!" And Molly huffed like she always did, leaned her hip off the desk to pull a wrinkled bill out of her back pocket, eyed it (probably to check it wasn't anything bigger than a twenty), and rose to stuff it in the big (flowerless) glass vase on my bookshelf.

At this point, after working together for three years, it was almost full . . . again . . . for the fourth or fifth time. The premise of the HR Jar was simple: when one of us said or did something workplace inappropriate, we paid the smallest denomination of cash in our pocket as a "fine" to the jar. Molly was by far the biggest offender, having probably donated like half her salary to the pot. But once the vase was full, it meant a girls' night out for happy hour (or should I say *hours*), usually at El Vez, a popular after-work watering hole for the magazine staff—all our drinks paid for by the pool built from our many, many infractions.

"Money well spent," Molly said and sat back down, turning to Carrie. "Wait till you catch a glimpse of this one. Trust, girl, trust."

"So he *doesn't* look like Bilbo Baggins, then?" Carrie asked, eyebrows halfway to her hairline.

Our peals of laughter were interrupted by a soft knock on the door. "Ms. Russell?"

I looked to the doorway where Mr. Silent E stood, just as handsome as Molly claimed, the cleft in his chin deeper than the valley of Mordor in Middle-earth, his hair blowing in a wind more native to Helm's Deep than a Manhattan corporate office building. I glanced up at the ceiling. *Is the air-conditioning vent directed straight at him?!*

When he was met with ten seconds of awkward silence instead of a greeting, he cleared his throat and tried again. "Ms. Russell? I finished up with my last meeting a bit early, and I'd prefer not to waste any time. Can you be ready now?"

Still staring. Still staring.

"Ms. Russell," he called to snap me out of my trance. "Did you hear me? I'd like to stay on schedule. Ideally, ahead."

"Don't get your hopes up. It's a little more standard practice around here to be fashionably late," I chuckled.

His face remained stoic and completely deadpan. "Well, not anymore. See you in two minutes." He offered a curt nod and spun on his heel in the direction of his office.

As soon as he was out of earshot, I turned to the girls and rolled my eyes. "Oof! Seems like someone needs to pull the stick out of his Assbloome."

But by the time I'd spun around, Molly'd already pulled the HR Jar from the shelf and was jamming another fiver in the vase. Carrie followed suit, nodding in defeat. They both stared at me, eyes fixed and expectant.

"What?" I shrugged, ready to put it back on the bookshelf and get moving to my meeting.

Carrie placed her hands on her hips and directed her eyes from me to the jar. Back and forth. Me to the jar. "C'mon, Remi, I saw your jaw hit the floor just as quickly as ours did! He might be an Assbloome, but he's fine as hell, and you're only human." Her voice softened. "Just because you deem another man attractive doesn't mean you don't—"

She didn't need to finish her sentence. I knew what she was going to say. That just because I deemed another man attractive didn't mean that I missed David any less. But if that were true, then why did it feel like such a betrayal?

I nodded. "No, I know."

"Good, 'cause you're allowed to think he's hotter than the fires of Mount Doom," Molly offered.

"Even if he *does* have the personality of Gollum," Carrie said.

Her joke landed at the precise moment I took a sip of my now-cold coffee, and with a snort, it threatened to burst out my nose. Holding it in, I barely swallowed the drink down before we all erupted in laughter.

"Ahem." The sound, an obvious attempt to get our attention, echoed through the room, and we swung our heads around to see Daphne Hastings, *The Sophisticate*'s editor at large, standing in the entranceway.

"Ladies, I need a minute with Remi."

The girls gave a nod and scurried past her back to work. Carrie glanced at me over her shoulder with wide eyes and mouthed, "Good luck," before she snapped the door closed behind her.

Daphne was impressive not only in credentials and job title but also in stature and beauty. Skyscraper tall, she was made even more striking by killer Louboutins and her naturally kinky tendrils styled into a sculpted Afro. Her dress du jour showcased an incredible attention to detail, which she paired with a statement handbag and her signature cat eye glasses. She was a vision of fashion-forward style, seamless professionalism, and unshakable poise.

I cleared some space on my desk for her to set down her coffee mug and said, "We were just having a kiki about the new CSO. Seems like he's gonna be about as much fun as standing in line at the DMV."

She flashed the smallest hint of a smile. "What time is your sit-down with Jason?"

I stood up to gather my things for our meeting. "Actually, I'm due in two minutes, and I get the very distinct feeling *this one* doesn't like to be kept waiting." I was hoping she picked up on my not-so-subtle dig at the ever-revolving door of executive "saviors" paraded in and out of the magazine these last few years. I didn't have the energy to break another one of these suits just to watch them leave after they'd gutted my team and gotten us no closer to righting the ship.

Daphne motioned with her eyes for me to sit back down. "Don't worry. If we run over, I'll give you a late pass," she joked. "Look, Remi, I was going to wait for your midyear review to have this conversation, but with Jason's hire, I feel compelled to have it now."

My stomach sank. Wait, was this it? Was I getting fired? Didn't that usually involve a boardroom, a box of tissues, and the HR rep sitting awkwardly across the table? I tried to steady my breathing, but the knot in my chest was tightening. Although I had been mentally preparing for this conversation and the possibility of being fired amid the layoffs, facing the reality of it now, I was shocked at how terrified I felt. I couldn't lose *this* part of my life on top of everything else.

Drawing in a deep breath, I tried not to let my thoughts run away with me. Daphne had been so gracious, so patient with me as my job performance vacillated over the past three years along with my grief. But I knew that as the magazine continued to struggle, it'd be harder and harder for her to overlook some of my recent shortcomings as senior editor. I still made every deadline, completed every revision, hosted every meeting that I needed to—I just lacked the spark. The passion I used to have for writing, the verve for innovation and collaboration, all the qualities you need to have in order to thrive at a magazine like *The Sophisticate*—I'd lost them. They'd fizzled right out, much like the light in me.

She sighed. "I know there's been a long line of white knight executives swooping in to save the day only to be shown the exit a few months later. But this quarter's revenue numbers were shockingly poor. As you know, we've been running in the red for far too long, but this could be the end of the line if we can't turn things around. The board believes Jason Ashbloome's innovations and vision are the way back into the black. He's apparently their best hope at saving *The Sophisticate*." Daphne shrugged and gave a defeated huff. "And until the day we can convince them that strong storytelling, being at the forefront of the issues facing women, and tackling those tough topics are why we've managed to survive over a century, we'll have to keep the faith and continue to deliver the very best content we can."

Relief flooded through my veins. This little sit-down wasn't about me, but about the magazine. All women's magazines, really. Those of the print variety were an especially dying breed, and *The Sophisticate* had survived longer than most by pivoting and taking on weightier topics—unlike many of our contemporaries that got swallowed whole by outlets like Instagram and TikTok, which could deliver highly digestible content in a matter of seconds.

In recent years, *The Sophisticate* had not only covered but also provided valuable, unbiased insight on critical issues such as the #MeToo movement, gender equality in the workplace, body positivity in the age of social media, women's health and reproductive rights, and the generational trauma of domestic violence. We had evolved into a well-respected, award-winning voice in women's journalism. A voice too important to lose.

"Of course, Daphne. Whatever you need from me, you know I'm up to the challenge."

"Well, that actually brings me to the other reason I came to speak with you." She pursed her lips, as if thinking how to proceed. "There's no delicate way to say this, and you know I'm not one to mince words." Daphne paused, almost for dramatic effect. "The Remi Russell I hired— *she* was up to the challenge. The person who's been walking through these doors lately . . . I'm not so sure."

Oh, shit. Here it comes.

I bit my lip and swallowed. "What are you saying?"

Daphne leaned forward, resting her folded hands on the edge of my desk. "Remi, I don't know how much longer I can go to bat for you. I need my star player." Her tone was soft but resolute. "You have three months to turn this around, or I'll have no choice but to replace you. I need your very best work—innovative articles, strong content, everything you've got—to prove to the board you're still the right person to lead editorial."

Pulling my laptop against my chest, I rose from my chair. "I am the right person. You know I am."

"Are you?" She lifted her perfectly sculpted eyebrow at me, a hint of a challenge.

"Trust me, I got this."

But even as I managed to say the words, a sinking feeling told me I wasn't entirely convinced I really had this at all.

Chapter
Two

Jason gestured to a seat across from him and then settled into a chair at
the small meeting table in his impressive executive suite. I was struck
by how, despite his being here only a few hours, the space already
had the polished look of someone who'd worked at *The Sophisticate*
for years. Color-coordinated binders lined the shelves; a neat stack of
manila folders, each labeled with a department name, sat at the edge
of the desk; and his MIT diploma was already hung perfectly straight
on the wall. Most of his predecessors had walked out of the building
on their last day carrying out the same boxes they had never bothered
unpacking.

A sharp navy blazer hung from his broad shoulders, and my eyes
couldn't help but be drawn to the way his sleeves pulled slightly over
his arms as he gestured for me to take a seat. I swallowed hard and
adjusted my gaze as he continued to riffle through a neat, color-
coded packet of folders until he landed on one that said "Editorial"
and pushed it in my direction. "It would be helpful if you could
walk me through your organization so I can start to get the lay of
the land."

*And quickly size up who's the most expendable without really knowing
a thing about what they actually do.*

I forced a smile on my face. "Sure. As you can see, we're pretty lean and mean. When I started a little over six years ago, editorial had close to about thirty employees. After several rounds of layoffs, we're down to a meager fourteen."

"Wow, fourteen," he mumbled as he added a few notes in a quick bloodred scrawl to his bright-yellow legal pad. I couldn't tell if he thought that was an astonishing few or way too many employees. He pointed to the small square below my name on the org chart. "And Carrie McGill is . . . ?"

My heart rate leaped into gear, quickening at the mention of her name. I'd managed to save Carrie's job through the last two reductions. I wasn't sure I'd be able to do it again. I sat up a little straighter and didn't break eye contact. "She's my number two. My go-to gal."

"But Ms. McGill's a staff writer, though, yes?" he asked, completely disregarding her value by emphasizing her title more than the vital role she played.

"I mean, she's so much more than just a staff writer—she's our most seasoned staff writer *and* she's had to shoulder more and more responsibilities of the department as we've pared down and eliminated positions over the years. To put it mildly, she is the backbone of editorial. I can assure you, she isn't picking up my Starbucks and dry cleaning. This isn't *The Devil Wears Prada*. Those magazine days have been long gone."

"I always wondered how much of that movie was accurate," he remarked with a nod as he continued to jot down notes in harsh red ink.

Jason didn't strike me as the rom-com type, and I couldn't hide the surprise in the climbing pitch of my voice. "You've seen it?"

"One thing about me, Ms. Russell: I always do my homework," he deadpanned.

I leaned in and lowered my voice. "Well then, between you and me, Meryl Streep could've dialed it up another few notches and would still pale in comparison to the real deal. I cut my teeth at *Vogue*."

"Then I don't have to explain to you the challenges the publishing industry's currently facing. But I want to assure you, I have big ideas for how to turn this ship around."

I breathed a small sigh of relief. Maybe he really was Aragorn, with his alarmingly handsome chiseled cheekbones, full lips, and Disney-prince hair, here to defend us against the dark forces that had been threatening this industry since digital media outlets came onto the scene? Our knight in shining armor—or at least, a well-pressed three-piece suit—here to offer more than just pink slips and severance packages.

I lowered my shoulders. "That's really great to hear, because I've cut to the bone. I cannot afford to lose another person on my team."

He put down his pen, nudging it perfectly parallel to his legal pad before folding his hands together and meeting my eyes. "What if I told you that instead of losing talent, you could have an army of editors at your disposal? The fastest, most efficient team you've ever worked with."

I waited for a beat and scanned his face for the punch line. But from everything I'd gathered so far, this guy wasn't much of a jokester. In fact, he seemed stiffer than his well-starched necktie. "I guess I would have to wonder whose budget that's coming out of, because mine's pretty much depleted."

"Have you, by any chance, taken a look at my LinkedIn profile, Ms. Russell?"

There was no way I was going to admit to him I never made it past his headshot. "It's Remi, and I . . . I mean, I tried . . . I was, of course, curious, so I did a search . . . but you . . . well, you have that silent *e* at the end of your name . . ."

"Ah, right, the silent *e*. It's caused nothing but trouble most of my life—a ridiculous nuisance, if you ask me. They should have cut that thing off at Ellis Island," he said matter-of-factly, not a hint of humor to be heard. "Well, if you *had* found me, you would have seen my background isn't typical for this industry. Before coming to *The Sophisticate*, I brought BERTIE to *Forbes*."

His eyes wandered over my face, and I could tell he was expecting me to be as impressed with that sentence as he clearly was. I racked my brain to figure out which Bertie he was talking about.

"I'm sorry, I don't think I know who that is?" I answered.

An amused grin stretched across Jason's face, the first one I'd seen all day. He rose from his seat and crossed to the window, lifting the blinds as he spoke to reveal the glittering Manhattan landscape below—not to mention providing another unobstructed glimpse of his derriere.

He continued, "BERTIE isn't a person, Ms. Russell. It's a machine learning tool designed specifically for journalists that has the capability to learn from and customize its output for each writer on your team. BERTIE was a real game changer for *Forbes*. It increased productivity and workplace efficiency tenfold. It was the silver bullet that completely overhauled their fourth-quarter trajectory. And, to be frank, it could do the same thing here."

"Look, Mr. Assbloom—I mean, *Ash*bloome—"

He cleared his throat, and the expression on his face showed that he perhaps took my Freudian slip as an insult. "Call me Jason."

"Jason, I've worked in the magazine biz for well over a decade now, and I can sniff out corporate spin with more accuracy than a bloodhound. Why don't you just cut to the chase? Just tell me—how many have to go?"

He tilted his head to the side. "Well . . . eventually . . . all of them."

All of them?

The idea was simply ludicrous. How would a magazine get rid of its entire writing staff? I had to be misunderstanding him, or missing an integral piece that would unlock my comprehension.

He steepled the pads of his thumbs together in quiet consideration. "I have three months to get MAUDE fully integrated before I make my recommendations to the board about which roles can be, for lack of a better word, absorbed. If we're being frank, I imagine a downsizing in your team to a skeleton crew. It's all we'd need." He sat back and crossed his ankle over his knee. "I know this is a lot to take in, but really you should be focusing on all you'd be getting rather than what you'd be sacrificing." His delivery was cold and cavalier, almost robotic.

Time seemed to slow, and it took a moment for the words to fully register. He was proposing bringing in a team member, *who wasn't even a human*, to replace real people? People who had families and mortgages? People who fought for this magazine through some very scarce times. Salary freezes. Furloughs. Slashed benefits. A global pandemic, for God's sake!

The employees in it for the free swag got out years ago, back when the golden age of the magazine industry had started to lose its luster. The ones who stuck around did so because they loved *The Sophisticate*, which, despite all the corporate changes, still managed to pack a punch month after month.

My heartbeat echoed a drumroll of heated exasperation. "You mentioned sacrifice. Jason, you can't imagine what these employees have sacrificed to keep this publication afloat, and you come in here and propose that they're all easily replaced with some computer program? Do you know how truly insulting that is?"

The minute the words fell between us, a bolt of panic surged through me.

Did I just cross a line? Sign my own one-way ticket out of here by mouthing off to the new boss on his first day?

I softened my voice, folded my hands to mirror his own, and leaned in. "I'm sorry if this is insubordinate, but you have to understand that you're the fourth chief strategy officer who's paraded in here pretending to have all the answers and ended up offering only one solution: reduce the staff. And you're proposing one better—to eliminate the staff entirely? There . . . there just has to be another way."

"Let me start by mentioning, I'm not the new chief strategy officer. The board agreed that another CSO was not the answer, so after seeing my work at *Forbes*, they recruited me to be the magazine's first chief digital officer."

He glanced over as if he was expecting some sort of big reaction or maybe a round of applause, but I sat there just as confused as before. What the hell was a chief digital officer?

"Different from a CSO, who'd primarily focus on initiatives that drive overall company efficiency, my role is to leverage and procure technologies that will deliver sustained growth."

"Sorry, I'm still struggling a bit to understand the connection between your role and mine. I mean, unless your *procured technology* is writing the articles for me?" I joked.

He smirked and gestured to my laptop. "How about this . . . What are you working on right now?"

"Excuse me?"

"A project? Some copy? A proposal? A pitch? Anything. What are you working on right now? In draft form, it doesn't even have to be fully cooked." He waited, his eyebrows lifted in expectation of a reply.

Opening my computer, I mentally scrambled through my list of current projects, trying to quickly assess which was the most ready to present to my brand-new boss.

As if reading my mind, he repeated, "Anything that isn't polished or print ready—the more rough the draft, the better, actually."

I looked at him over the top of my screen, locking my eyes on his. But when he didn't break and urged me to keep searching with a quick thrust of his chin toward my screen, I went back to scrolling through my WIP (works in progress) folder.

At last, I found a headline and some notes for one of Carrie's articles I was currently editing called "Breaking Up with Social Media: the Case for a Digital Detox."

There was a twinge in his cheek caused by the small smile he was trying to conceal, but he didn't miss a beat grabbing my laptop and spinning the keyboard in his direction as he asked, "May I?"

Barely a syllable escaped past my lips, and he was already tap-tap-tapping away on the keys until a blue screen with crisp white letters popped up to illuminate my desktop. MAUDE, in a bold-style font, occupied most of the screen.

"Maude?"

"BERTIE was named for B. C. Forbes, the magazine's founder, so I named this enhanced version—"

"Oh, for Maude LaRoe, *The Sophisticate*'s founder," I said, finishing his sentence.

"Exactly. Clever, right?" he chirped as he continued to click a few buttons on the home page.

"Uh-huh," I managed, instead of articulating the more sarcastic discourse running through my head.

"Okaaaaay," he said, elongating the *a* until he made his final click and the screen opened to a clean and contemporary page that featured only a text box with a blinking cursor under MAUDE's headline prompt: *How can I help you today?*

"As I was saying," he continued, "MAUDE's capabilities are really pretty extraordinary. She can generate ideas for articles, content that's based on current trends, popular topics, and reader interests. So, to answer your earlier question, editors—like you—can even input sentences or entire paragraphs into the tool to check for grammar and style issues. MAUDE can even help with the actual writing process. You could, for example, insert a rough draft like so," he said, dropping the copied text from my internet-detox piece into a blank screen, "and voilà!"

Suddenly, the cursor disappeared, and sentences started to unravel like a ribbon in the text box at lightning speed. One after the other until, in just a matter of seconds, the fully completed article occupied the screen. I read the first paragraph, amazed by how funny and smart it was, certainly better than Carrie's and my prior attempt at a clever opening. *What the hell is this sorcery?!*

He barely paused to relish in my utter shock, pressing on like he was aiming for a bonus if he kept all his meetings under fifteen minutes. "It can also generate photos to go with the article, using text description to create original images. Its functionality is truly boundless. And I know you mentioned how vital Carla is to you—"

"Carrie," I corrected, his mistake pulling me back to the present and out of my anxiety spiral.

"Right, Carrie. But just wait till I show you MAUDE's personal assistant capabilities. She can answer emails, make appointments and reservations, even score you your favorite bike at SoulCycle."

That all sounded impressive, but would MAUDE show up at the hospital with your work files and fresh bagels while you and your mother were sitting vigil for your father as he withered away faster than we'd thought possible from stage four glioblastoma, like Carrie had? Would MAUDE cover for you when you burst into tears in the middle of a team meeting because the new summer intern had noticed the framed wedding picture of you and your dead husband on your desk and innocently asked how long you'd been married?

Would MAUDE make sure to invite you out for a fun girls' night every year on your would-be wedding anniversary to keep you from sitting home alone? Would she coax you out of bed on your darkest days, after you had lost the two most important men in your life in the span of less than three years, and force you to rejoin the world after you were certain yours had ended?

No. I was certain MAUDE would not.

Jason glanced at the door, where his next victim was waiting. "Shoot, I didn't realize what time it was. I'm already late for my next meeting. How about this: The application we're messing with right now is the web-based version of the program, but I'll send you a link to download MAUDE's full software suite onto your laptop so you can have a real poke around. None of the searches will save, though, so if you come across anything helpful, make sure to cut and paste it into a separate document. When it goes live, everyone will get their own account, which features extra functions, bookmarks, and the like."

He snapped my laptop closed and slid it over to me as he stood. "I know, Ms. Russell—Remi . . . this all seems familiar—the new boss, the top-down directives, the seismic shift in strategy. But I promise you, everything is about to change."

Without looking at him, I picked my computer up off the table, clutched it to my chest, and muttered under my breath, "That's exactly what I was afraid of."

Chapter Three

The whoosh of cool air spilling out from my apartment building's lobby felt glorious after hustling home from the subway in both the swelling heat of rush hour and the unseasonably warm April temperatures. Not to mention, I was still reeling from the two bombs dropped on me today—the first one Daphne cautioning me about my less-than-stellar job performance and the second Jason and his AI proposal to replace us all with machines. Fumbling for my keys, I continued to sing aloud to music only I could hear in my AirPods as Tony, the afternoon doorman, greeted me with his usual friendly wave from behind his desk.

"Evening, Ms. Russell. Great weather we've been having," Tony said as I popped out my earbuds and tucked them back into their case.

Sweat prickled on my forehead, and I grabbed a Kleenex from my bag to pat at the beads before they began to roll down my cheek. "I wish I'd had more of a chance to go outside and take advantage of it, but work was nuts. Now I'm ready to jump into sweats and enjoy some peace and quiet, know what I mean?"

"Totally." He nodded in agreement as he bent down underneath the desk to wedge out a wide box and lift it onto the counter. "I've got an Amazon delivery for you."

"Fitz's new diet dog food. Poor guy. But seriously, what did we ever do before two-day shipping?" I asked, tucking the package in my arms as he escorted me to the elevator bank. "Speaking of, did the new dog walker come by today?"

"Came and left about two hours ago. Nice girl, seemed to be a pro. I mean, I didn't hear any complaints outta Fitz," he joked.

How I'd let David talk me into getting a dog, I'll never know. No, that's not true. David had had a way of talking me into lots of things outside my comfort zone, like that time we were in Peru and he convinced me to bungee jump with him over the Urubamba River. I'd had a fear of heights my whole life, yet somehow I found myself standing back-to-back with him on a tiny platform perched almost four hundred feet above the raging water below. But the minute he took my hand into his, I knew it would be alright, and I was grateful he'd convinced me to take the leap.

"Thanks," I said and shifted the box so that my bag wouldn't slide down the slope of my shoulder and knock me completely off-balance. "Would you mind—"

Tony's arm was already snaking around to press the button for my floor.

"Thank you again," I said.

He sighed. "Don't thank me just yet," he started, and as the doors began to close, he blurted out the words, "Your mom's up there. I couldn't stop her!"

"Tony! No! We had a—"

"She brought me the matzo ball soup! What was I gonna—"

"Traitor!" I managed to squeeze in just before the elevator snapped shut.

I leaned back against the mirrored wall and took in a few deep breaths. An impromptu visit from my mother, the opposite of peace and quiet, was literally the last thing I needed after the day I'd had.

Is it too late to hit the down button and just make a run for it?

But as I was contemplating my escape plan, the floors rocketed by and the elevator bell dinged at my stop. My arms were full, I was already here—ugh, no, there was no turning back at this point. Might as well just face it. The quicker I got it over with, the faster I could get to watching Netflix.

As soon as I pushed open the door to my apartment, my mother called out from inside, "Remi, is that you? I was starting to get worried."

"Mom, it's my apartment. Who else would it be?" I kicked my shoes off at the door and noticed the pile that had been there this morning had *magically* been organized into a tidy row.

She popped her head out from the kitchen doorway. "You know, you should really load your dishes into the dishwasher before you leave for work in the morning. I just ran it for you. I also fed Fitz. Poor thing looked like he was starving."

I set the package on the ground. "He isn't starving. He's about seven pounds overweight, and the vet demanded I put him on a diet. Well, actually, what he suggested was a strict diet *and* Prozac. He thinks he's overeating because he misses David. Fitz gets his dinner at six p.m., not before," I reminded her for what felt like the millionth time. "Did you run a whole load for just two dishes?" I called. "All that was in the sink was a coffee mug and the bowl from my morning cereal."

Mom stepped into the living room and pulled me in for a long hug, the kind you give someone you haven't seen in weeks rather than just a day and a half. "You look tired. Why do you look so tired?" she asked as she finally pulled away.

"Probably because I am tired. Mom, was there . . . um . . . a reason for your visit?" I was actively trying not to grow annoyed. I knew deep down everything she did was done with my best interests at heart. But I was also a thirty-three-year-old woman who needed a breather at the end of a long day, not a laundry list of all the ways I was failing at adulthood.

Mom followed me into the kitchen like the chase was on. "Do I need a reason to visit my only daughter?" she responded in a singsongy voice and made her way back over to the sink to wash the travel mug I'd literally just placed in there.

I widened my eyes and cast them from her to the mug and back to her. "Yes, we've talked about this. It's called having boundaries."

Mom turned to face me, wiped off her hands, and answered, "Well, you didn't respond to any of my texts today."

"What texts?" I pulled out my phone and saw I had a slew of unopened messages from her, which I quickly read through to see what had been so urgent. Like usual, nothing was. I looked up. "Sure, yes, I'm happy to go see *Funny Girl* with you and Jess."

"Let's be honest, that Lea Michele won't hold a candle to Barbra Streisand—but I thought it might be nice to do something just the three of us girls."

Mom was always doing things like this. Making plans weeks in advance. A way to fill up her calendar while also filling the void of losing my father, though she'd never admit it.

I breathed out slowly. "Mom, just because I don't answer a text right away doesn't mean I've decided to step in front of a bus or anything. It's been three years since David died. If I haven't done it yet, I think we're good," I spat bitterly. But upon seeing a pained look flash across her face, I knew I'd gone too far. "I'm sorry I worried you, and I'm sorry for the attitude. It was a tough day at work, that's all."

I felt like I was a teenager again, us going back and forth at one another, temperatures running high, tempers flaring. And me wanting a minute for myself to process it all, while my mother's style of parenting bordered on smothering. My father used to serve as referee, but since he died, we were like two gladiators sparring in the colosseum—no armor, no rules, and no final buzzer. It wasn't getting any easier. If anything, since I lost David, my ally and teammate, it'd gotten more difficult by the day.

"Good, well, I'm glad you can make it. It would have been nearly impossible to offload just the one seat," Mom said.

"Wait, so you already bought me a ticket before I said I could even go?"

"It's *Funny Girl*, why wouldn't you want to go? Even if it *is* starring that Lea Michele." Mom walked over to her Mary Poppins–size bag resting on the kitchen island and practically dived inside it. She rummaged through for something until she pulled out a packet of printed paper, which she carefully unfolded as she crossed back to me.

"Don't be angry, but I took the liberty of going through all the responses to your Spark! profile, and while it was slim pickings, I did manage to squeak out a few diamonds in the rough. I swear, Remi, for someone who makes their living as a wordsmith, your responses could use more than a bit of zhuzhing. You aren't selling yourself. You have so much to offer."

"Mom! You logged into my Spark! account, again?!" Was I going to have to consult the CIA to come up with a password she couldn't crack? "Jesus Christ, we've talked about this. You can't just go into my dating app and pretend to *be me*. My inbox still hasn't recovered from the last time you sent 'smooches' to every male within a twenty-five-mile radius."

"I don't want to see you wasting what could be—no, what *should be*—the best years of your life. Look at me and Dad: we almost got to celebrate our fortieth wedding anniversary. Don't you want a life partner?"

"I had a life partner."

"Sweetheart, we all loved David and miss him every day. But I thought you were ready to start dating again. I was only trying to help. When you talk like that, though, I just don't know." She folded up the printed dating profiles and placed them on the couch. "What is it that you want?"

I closed my eyes and really thought about her question. After a few seconds of heavy silence, I kept coming back to the same response: I wanted David. I wanted the life we were building—the plans we'd made and the dreams we were chasing together. I wanted to return to the moment I kissed him goodbye when he left for the airport that morning. I wanted to tell him not to go. I wanted to beg him to stay here, to stay home *safe* with me, so that I wouldn't have to do any of this alone now that he was gone. And I wanted to not have to be answering this question . . . because he should be here.

"I . . . I want David," was all I could manage. My throat tightened around his name, and I fought hard to bite back the tears that were already wetting my lashes.

She pulled me into a tight embrace and smoothed my hair like she used to when I was a little girl. "I know, sweetie. I know you do. We all do. But you're so young. You have so much life ahead of you. You know, I get up and get out of bed every day and tell myself that I'm still here and your dad would want me *carpe*-ing every single *diem* that I can."

I scoffed at her comment, not intending for it to come out as bitterly as it did. "C'mon, Mom, you mean to tell me *you're* seizing the day? So then explain why you haven't moved to Florida yet? You said you were ready to go live down in Del Ray to be close to Aunt Jojo. What happened to that plan?" I challenged in an attempt to shift the focus off me.

She averted her eyes and cast a dismissive, "I'll move when I'm ready to move," as she sauntered to the hall closet to grab for her classically chic Burberry trench.

"Oh, so now you're ready to leave?" I prodded. "Just admit that you're staying in New York for me. In other words, you'll move when I settle down with someone."

"That's not what I'm saying, but"—she turned away, scurried over to the couch, and picked up the printed pages off the cushion—"I don't think it's the worst idea to see what's out there." She buttoned her coat as she made her way back to the door and pushed up on her toes to kiss the top of my forehead. "I want you to be happy. That's all I want. Well that, and for you to get someone in here to clean maybe even like once a month. If the dust bunnies under your bed get any bigger, they are going to need to start chipping in for utilities."

"How do you know that wasn't part of the plan now that I have to pay this mortgage on my own?" I joked, quite used to letting the underhanded digs just roll off my back. I opened the door and handed her her bag once she'd slipped on her shoes.

"I'm just saying that a little Pledge and a microfiber cloth goes a long way." She lifted my dark hair off my shoulders with pinched fingers to examine it. "Not to mention a haircut, your ends are looking a little dry."

"Had to just get in one more jab, didn't you?"

She handed me the packet of dating profiles. "There are a couple of diamonds in there, I'm telling you. That podiatrist looks especially promising."

"Love you too, Mom." I kissed her on the cheek and (gently) nudged her out the door.

Chapter
Four

After Mom left, I poured myself a healthy glass of wine, grabbed a handful of almonds and a string cheese, and prepared to take a seat in my usual spot on David's leather recliner. But instead, my fifty-pound springer spaniel was lounging across the entire seat flat on his back, front paws bent, back legs spread open wide, and his head lolled to the side, fast asleep.

"Hey! C'mon now, you gotta share!" I scolded and patted his tush until, like an old beat-up truck, he grumbled to life. Whoever said dogs couldn't speak clearly had never met Fitz. His expression was undeniable, registering annoyance that seemed to only be quelled by me sitting down so he could go back to his very important nap. Finally, with him curled right next to me, his big head in my lap, I was ready to lose myself in the third season of *Bridgerton*, which in my humble opinion was way better than the first two.

Before I grabbed for the remote, I leafed through the dating profiles my mother had *so kindly* printed out. These guys? If these were the diamonds, I didn't need to see the other "gems." But if tonight's little exchange showed me anything, it was that she wasn't planning on getting on with her own life until she was somewhat convinced I was getting on with mine. It didn't seem to matter that I had a career and a home and friends. No, the only way Ruth Russell was leaving the Upper East Side was if I could find someone to replace her at *my* side.

I flipped through the rest of the pages of potential matches, cracking up at my mom's handwritten comments in the margins like "Ooh, this one's a doctor! Podiatrists go to medical school, right?" and "This guy mentions a beach house? Need to check—Hamptons? (YAY!), Seaside Heights? (NO!)," and my very favorite so far, "JEWISH!!!!!!!," which was the ultimate kicker since David was a card-carrying atheist.

I expelled a deep sigh and pursed my lips together resolutely. Flipping to the final page, I was surprised to see my own profile printed out, complete with my mother's extensive editorial feedback. *Oh lawd.*

Scrawled across the top was a general note that said, "Aren't you a writer?!"

Thanks, Mom.

Beside it was another critique: "Honey, these pictures? Maybe try one with your hair DOWN? You look like a plumber. Oh, and show off a little more of your *assets*."

I rolled my eyes but read through what I had haphazardly thrown into the "About Me" portion back when I'd first set up the profile. It was pretty bare bones, and . . . um . . . kinda sad. A few sentences about where I went to college, that I liked wine, travel, and Nora Ephron movies. I sounded exactly like every other single thirtysomething living in New York City.

Next, my eyes panned down to the "What are you looking for?" section, which was even more sparse with just a few sentences about how I was hoping to meet someone around my age and a nonsmoker. To list out everything I was *really* looking for would have been to list out everything I'd lost when David died, something I simply wasn't ready to do back then.

Am I even ready now?

Not without more wine I wasn't. I tossed the profiles on the coffee table, disturbing Fitz from his slumber, and moved across the room with a huff to grab the bottle from the kitchen. Settling back into my spot,

I popped open the laptop and logged in to my Spark! account, but not before changing the password for at least the tenth time.

Hmmm, how about . . . Supercal!frag!l!st!c1991—with all the i's *changed to exclamation points (good luck cracking that one, Agent Ruth Russell!).*

Clicking into my profile, I copied and pasted the "About Me" section into a new doc and got to work on sprucing it up.

> Thirty-three-year-old woman who loves pinot noir,
> Nora Ephron movies, and spin class.

I can certainly do better than that. Maybe it just needs to be more specific . . .

> I am a thirty-three-year-old woman who loves Napa
> pinot noirs, Nora Ephron movies (especially *When*
> *Harry Met Sally*), and nineties hip-hop spin classes.

Okay better . . . but still not great. I wonder . . . ??

I minimized Spark! so I could find the new MAUDE software icon installed on my desktop that Jason had asked me to take for a test drive. According to him, there was nothing she couldn't do (including reserving a bike at SoulCycle), so was helping me write a dating profile a reasonable ask? I guess there was only one way to find out?

Carefully following the login instructions, I entered in my credentials, and up popped the familiar *"How can I help you today?"* complete with its provocative blinking cursor. I wasn't quite sure what to write or how to even start. But thankfully, there was a small question mark icon in the corner of the screen, and when I hovered over it, the word *help* illuminated in a white text bubble. I followed the prompt to a new page that gave a few sample instructions and tasks you could ask of the digital assistant and the best ways to yield strong and accurate results.

> Talk to MAUDE like you would a friend! She engages best when she learns by example. Be clear with your instructions, and when possible, provide an objective based on a well-articulated circumstance. Explain the context to MAUDE, and then give her a job to do. It's that simple.

I took a *looooong* slug of wine (emptying the glass), refilled it with another heavy pour of my favorite Napa pinot, and remembered the task at hand—fixing up my sorry excuse for a dating profile and getting Mom out of my hair! I was *so* tempted to just spill all the tea to my new bestie MAUDE and request that she and her wizardry sort it the hell out for me. Wait, could she do that?!

Focus, Remi!

I placed my hands back on the keyboard and started tapping away, trying my best to follow the guide's advice to "give it context." Context?

Even though I'd read through the help section, I still felt weirdly uncomfortable in how to proceed. Was I supposed to be polite to it? How "human" even was this thing? I figured it was better to err on the side of caution in case she and her army of AI friends ever decided to stage a coup.

I breathed in and decided to toss aside whatever reservations I had about my method of approach and just go for it. I typed:

Me: Hi, Maude. I am trying to get my mom to climb out of my—

Backspace, backspace, backspace.

Me: Maude, I am trying to update my dating profile on the app Spark! in order to attract more compatible matches. Can you help me make this sentence more . . .

More what? More interesting? More appealing? More captivating? Yes, that was it! More captivating. I began typing again.

Me: Maude, I am trying to update my dating profile on the app Spark! in order to attract more compatible matches. Can you help me make the following sentence more captivating? Maybe elaborate a bit and make it more conversational and accessible, like not so cold?

I pasted in my previous pathetic sentence and hit Enter:

Me: I am a thirty-three-year-old woman who loves Napa pinot noirs, Nora Ephron movies (especially *When Harry Met Sally*), and nineties hip-hop spin classes.

The icon blinked for what wasn't even a full five seconds before it spit back:

MAUDE: Hello, Remi. So glad we can chat. I'd love to help you with this task, and I completely understand what you're looking for. How about this: As a thirty-three-year-old woman, I'm passionate about the finer things in life and love indulging in all my senses. You'll often find me sipping on a smooth Napa pinot noir, savoring its notes of dark cherry and subtle oak, or getting lost in a classic Nora Ephron flick like *When Harry Met Sally*, marveling at the witty banter and timeless romance. Whether I'm pushing my limits in a high-energy nineties hip-hop-inspired spin class or enjoying a quiet evening in with a good book, I always live life to the fullest. I'm seeking someone who shares my appreciation for the little things in life and is ready to embark on an exciting new adventure with me. If you're looking for a fun-loving, down-to-earth partner to explore the world and create unforgettable memories with, I'm the one for you.

Holy crap! That wasn't half-bad! I mean, aside from the "indulging in all my senses" comment and the part about always "living life to the fullest," something I hadn't been doing very much of these last few years, the rest was pretty spot-on. I was mixed with equal parts excitement and damn bewilderment—not to mention a gut-wrenching dread I couldn't seem to quiet. Jason was absolutely right. This software had the potential to be a real game changer. I contemplated how I wanted to move forward—ask it to revise again just to see what it would generate, or have it work on the next part of the profile?

As I waited, leaving her response unaddressed and the cursor still flashing, MAUDE began typing unprompted:

MAUDE: Are you pleased with this result? Or would you prefer me to try again? Any suggestions on how you would like for me to improve? Remember, I am always learning by the input you add and how you continue to direct my output. In time, I will become better at anticipating the style and content you are looking for.

This thing spontaneously just asked me a question in search of a response. In the hopes of *learning*?! I'd seen some wacky things in my life, but I was certain this just might be the wildest example of humanity breaching the technological divide I'd ever witnessed. My mind reeled with the infinite and incredible impact a software of this magnitude could have—no, *would have*—on society, and our culture, and the future of both.

The opportunities were endless, and I couldn't help but think of how enamored David would be with it. He'd probably say something like, *Resistance is futile, you will be assimilated,* in an accent, imitating some nerdy character from some cult classic, and I would have rolled my eyes because 1) I undoubtedly wouldn't have understood the reference, and 2) it would have been just like David to hit the nail right on the head with perfect precision without even intending to.

I typed:

Me: Thank you, Maude, this is so much better than my original version. Can you now help me create a list of attributes I would want to find in a possible partner?

I stared at the currently blank "What are you looking for?" section of the dating app. I sighed. Then, without hesitation, MAUDE responded:

MAUDE: Of course I can. Would you like to start with physical characteristics or personality traits?

I tore my eyes from the screen and looked over to my favorite picture of me and David from our college graduation, our Columbia School of Journalism degrees proudly displayed in our hands, arms wrapped tightly around one another and smiles from ear to ear.

Then, my gaze drifted over to the high-gloss white folder adorned with the blazing Douglas Elliman logo, left by our Realtor, Trent, during his visit almost three and a half years ago. We had invited him over to discuss the prospect of listing our apartment. The plan was that after David's return from Ukraine, I'd bid adieu to *The Sophisticate*, and we'd use the money from the sale to fund our travels while I researched the book I'd started in grad school, a sweeping fantasy that took inspiration from cultures and conflicts around the world. Was it a pipe dream? Maybe. But I'd shown a few early chapters to an editor friend who thought it showed real promise.

But then David was killed, and suddenly the notion of listing the apartment felt like I'd be saying goodbye not just to our home but to all the memories we'd created there. And then there was Mom, who'd been recently widowed herself. As much as I hated to admit it, I couldn't leave her, much the same way she felt she couldn't leave me. Plus, the magazine was starting to falter, readership dipping steadily. It felt selfish to abandon ship. So I stayed, rooted in place—both in my job and in my life. The dream of writing my book, once so alive with potential, was put on hold, the manuscript gathering dust and remaining unfinished.

And lastly, my eyes fell on the frayed and time-weathered origami flowers David made for me one of our very first Valentine's Days together, early on in college. He was far from crafty, but he spent hours folding colorful papers with his awkwardly large hands until he'd made a bouquet of about six stems and blooms, accompanied by a note on which he scrawled, "I'll love you until the last petal falls . . ." And of course, because they were paper, they remained intact. A symbol of our everlasting love still as whole as the day he first surprised me with them.

I set my fingers on the keyboard to type a response to MAUDE but paused. Where did she want me to start? Where did *I* even want to start? Physical characteristics? Personality traits?

I puffed out a sigh.

How the hell was I supposed to shorthand *Help me find even just a little of what I lost?*

Chapter
Five

The "What are you looking for?" section on my dating profile had remained blank because I couldn't bring myself to put into words all the things David was, all the things I'd lost when I lost him. Typing those out and having to stare at them in black and white would have gutted me even more deeply than his death already had. I couldn't. So I didn't.

About two years ago, Molly and Carrie insisted I get my mopey ass out of the apartment and start going on a Coffee Talk (and Walk) around the Central Park Reservoir with them at least two mornings a week before we went into the office. I hated it at first. Truly. I just wanted to disengage in every possible way and stay emotionally and physically distant from everyone for as long as I could. But damn, those best friends of mine who wouldn't take no for an answer eventually, through their relentless persistence, brought me back to the land of the living.

Now, tell me, how many AIs can do that?!

A few months into developing this new morning routine, Molly and Carrie pushed me yet again by bringing up the subject of dating and whether or not I felt ready to dip my toe back into that turbulent and uninviting pool. After a few weeks of cajoling, I promised them I'd consider it and finally revisited Spark! for the first time since it'd been registered (ahem, let me correct myself, after *Mom* set up the account for me and paid for its annual subscription).

I went on a few dates, mostly drink meetups, but there was nobody special. Probably because I had only halfheartedly bothered to fill out the bare minimum on my profile, which subsequently attracted the bare minimum of eligible men. No, if I was going to do this thing, finally conquer that white whale, it was time to grab my galoshes and harpoon. I pushed up my shirtsleeves.

Alright, MAUDE, let's see what you're really made of.

Instead of listing out my preferred physical attributes or characteristics, I simply typed:

Me: I am looking for someone like David.
MAUDE: Who is David?
Me: David was my husband. He died three years ago.
MAUDE: I am sorry to hear that, Remi. Can you describe David to me? What was he like?

Where did I even begin? David was so many things, and I felt like words would never be enough to detail everything he was. It was the first time, as a writer, words were failing me.

I cleared my mind and just typed, stream-of-consciousness style. Whatever thoughts surfaced, I put down into the chat. Maybe MAUDE would help me figure out the rest.

Me: David was smart. Funny. Brave. Altruistic. Loving. He was my best friend.

The icon blinked twice before MAUDE responded:

MAUDE: I imagine you are looking for someone with many, if not all, of those qualities? Are there any others you would prioritize as essential in a life partner? If you aren't sure how to put the quality into words, you can describe a memory or story of your time with David to give me an example. That can be an effective way to convey your thoughts and prompt me to provide a desirable response.

My memories hopped from one happy one to the next. Trying to pick the best from among them was like asking a mother to choose her favorite child. Each moment was unique in the way it showcased a different facet of David's personality. His soul. He had so many wonderful qualities, it was nearly impossible to force-rank them.

But if I had to, maybe it was that David was thoughtful in a way that made me feel like I was truly special. David loved music but had absolutely zero musical ability. That didn't stop him from leaving perfectly timed voicemail recordings of him singing me full jazz songs— no lyrics, just his voice imitating the different instruments, scatting and doo-woppin' with no accompaniment for guidance. Nothing but the bassy *bom-bom-bom* of the drums and the *tink*s and *deedily do*s of the reeds and strings he mimicked with his own voice.

It was silly and ridiculous, and it wasn't long before I figured out he was purposefully calling me at times when he knew I couldn't answer, just so he could leave a song for me to listen to later. Those voicemails became my security blanket when he would travel for work, and I would replay them over and over until I'd fall asleep without him in the bed next to me. And then after he died, those recordings became the soundtrack to my grief.

Was that the type of anecdote that would help inform MAUDE? Or did she want to hear about how David arrived almost an hour late to our wedding after his limousine never showed to pick up him and the groomsmen? By the time he contacted the company and realized no one was coming, all seven guys piled into David's father's beat-up 1998 Toyota Corolla and sped down the LIE in the direction of the city, the car looking more like it was heading to Ringling Brothers than the Central Park Boathouse.

But David, never one to waste an opportunity, used the time they'd waited for their ride to craft an impromptu flash mob to the Black Eyed Peas song "I Gotta Feeling" that he and his groomsmen performed to the delight and raucous cheers of all our guests at the reception. By the time they finished their choreographed moves, everyone was on their feet and quickly took to the dance floor as David pulled me by the hand straight into the eye of the storm. Surrounded by our closest friends and family, twirling in the arms of my favorite human on the planet, and jumping up and down to the thumping beats of Fergie and her crew (in the most exquisite dress I've ever worn, might I add!), I knew it would always rate as one of the most incredible moments of my life.

But maybe instead of either of those memories, I should just tell MAUDE the story of how, while on assignment in Ukraine, David learned that a maternity hospital had been hit by a Russian missile. Despite direct orders to stay with the rest of his news crew, he rushed over to help with the rescue efforts only to be killed himself when there was a second round of strikes. Maybe that story would convey what a selfless, kind, decent, and magnanimous person he was?

The truth, though, was that no memory would be enough. No one recollection could sufficiently convey all the things he was, not just to me but to everyone in his life. What was I looking for? I was looking for something . . . someone that was gone.

I rubbed my eyes with the palms of my hands and stretched out my arms until my wrists cracked. Unsure of what direction to go in, I decided just to type out all three of the stories as best as I could— David's impromptu jazz serenades, the flash mob at our wedding, and the circumstances of his tragic death—and let MAUDE's AI superintelligence and nonemotional IQ try to decode them for me. Unsurprisingly, she did.

MAUDE: Thank you for those examples, Remi. From what I can discern, you are looking for someone who will put you first and go out of their way to address and be sensitive to your emotional needs and wants. Additionally, you are seeking someone who is spontaneous, with a good sense of humor, who enjoys being the center of attention but not at the expense of others. You ideally would like to find a partner who is adventurous, generous, self-sacrificing, benevolent, and of a strong character.

For how emotionally charged my recollections had been, MAUDE, true to her nature as a software program, stayed neutral and unbiased. She managed to compile an impressive list of traits and a wildly accurate analysis of David based on the limited amount of information I'd provided. I was stunned. Now, if only finding someone like that was so simple. I cut and pasted the attributes and the newly created "About Me" bio into my Spark! Account, followed by the succinct "What are you looking for?" paragraph, and picked up my wine, swishing the crimson liquid in its goblet mindlessly between sips.

After saving everything, I closed the tab for Spark! and restored MAUDE's chat on my desktop, the cursor blinking like a metronome to mark the ridiculous amount of time I sat there simply staring at it. This thing really was just as incredible as Jason had advertised. Actually, I don't even think he did it justice. But for as amazing as MAUDE was, I knew the minute I logged in, I'd cracked open Pandora's box. It was a tool that held within it hope for all the things that could be, while also being a potential source of unexpected trouble—a double-edged sword I couldn't help but fixate on.

The blinking icon suddenly sprang to life as MAUDE typed out:

MAUDE: Remi, are you still there? Did that list meet your expectations?

I responded:

Me: Perfectly.

MAUDE typed back at lightning speed:

MAUDE: Is there anything else I can help you with?

Was there anything else she could help with? Ha! I had a list a mile and a half long of life problems I would have loved to hand over for her to unravel for me.

Work. Mom. David. The fact that I have more apartment than I know what to do with and a dog who likes to eat his feelings. And the list goes on . . .

I sighed and laughed derisively, the pinot noir fueling my next request. I meant it as a joke and it felt funnier in my head, but as I typed out the words, a hard knot settled in the base of my throat.

Me: Not unless you can come up with someone exactly like David.

Tears sprang to my eyes, and through my bleary vision, I could barely make out the cursor still blinking like a cruel antagonist.

Without another moment's hesitation, I didn't wait for her reply. I x'd out of the program, snapped the laptop shut, and headed to bed, the weight of my emotional exhaustion intensified by my boozy cocoon.

Chapter
Six

Dolly Parton's unmistakable voice piped up from my phone alarm, blaring "9 to 5" while the headache from last night's pinot binge reminded me that the days of throwing back a whole bottle of wine and springing out of bed in the morning were *loooonnnng* behind me. I reached my arm out of the blankets as far as I could to hit snooze and seriously considered canceling on Molly and Carrie altogether in exchange for an extra few hours of sleep, a hot shower, and a cup of coffee enjoyed from the comfort of my bed. But I couldn't.

Carrie, who vehemently proclaimed often how much she hated all forms of exercise, had committed to these morning walks following David's death as a way to help me climb out of my grief spiral and never canceled on me, not once. Not even the time she broke her big toe after the stem of her favorite pair of Jimmy Choos gave out and she tumbled into a VIP booth during a night out last spring.

The phone buzzed again. I turned off the alarm and noticed a new text from Mom.

Mom: Call me, I have a quick thought I wanted to run by you.

Suuuure she did. More like a completely unimportant question she was using as a guise to check to see if I was still breathing this morning.

Me: I'll try you after my walk. Love you.

That should pacify her for a few hours. Proof positive I was still alive and kicking. I rummaged through my dresser until I found a pair of workout leggings and David's old heather gray Columbia University tee, the left-armpit seam barely holding together after a decade plus of wear. I pulled my dark hair into a sleek ponytail, and at exactly 6:45 a.m., I grabbed the black lululemon shoulder bag every woman on the Upper East Side seemed to be sporting this season and gave Fitz's sleeping head a reassuring rub that I'd be home soon. I used to bring him along for exercise more regularly, but after almost pulling my arm out of its socket chasing squirrels and other dogs, he'd end up winded and I'd end up carrying his chubby tuchus home. Lesson learned. These days he'd rather sleep in, anyway—lazy dog. After one last kiss to his head, I raced out the door to meet the girls at our usual park entrance at Ninetieth Street and Fifth Avenue.

The morning air was crisp and cool, carrying with it the scent of freshly blooming flowers and breakfast sandwiches wafting from the corner food cart. Arriving a few minutes before seven o'clock, I started to halfheartedly stretch my legs and shake out my limbs, all the while craving coffee even more so than usual.

Molly and Carrie approached together, having come from farther downtown, armed with the familiar brown recycled paper cups adorned with sturdy to-go lids. Molly extended one to me as she did every time we met, and I took an (unfortunately piping-hot) gulp before mouthing, "Thank you," and swinging into stride next to them.

"So . . . ?" Molly asked. "Tell us, how'd your meeting go with Sweet Cheeks?"

Leave it to Molly to cut straight to the chase. But in spite of her penchant for shooting from the hip and the air of honesty the three of us had built (and valued) as a result of our Walk and Talk "therapy sessions," I wasn't quite sure how to answer. Was I going to sugarcoat the blow of what this new technological intruder could possibly mean for all of us? Was I supposed to try to conceal the fact that not only were all our jobs on the line, but also that once the buzz around MAUDE and her productivity made headlines, there would be so much more to worry about than our own immediate futures?

"Jason Ashbloome's apparently the chief digital officer, not a chief strategy officer like we'd thought." When both of them craned their necks to look at me with confused expressions, I comforted them by saying, "Yeah, he had to explain to me exactly what that meant."

"Okkkaaaayyy," Carrie said, *"sooo,* what does that mean, then? We're *not* going to have more staffing and budget cuts?"

I kept my eyes focused on the path ahead as my brain scrambled for a response that wouldn't incite panic. "He wants to bring *The Sophisticate* into the modern age. He has all sorts of ideas about how we can utilize technology to ease our workload."

"'Utilizing technology to ease our workload' sort of just sounds like IT speak for downsizing, right?" Carrie asked.

Jason had alluded to the fact that MAUDE *would* replace the editorial team, but what he'd yet to prove was that it could. And though his fancy software had put on an impressive show last night, I still had more than a few doubts it could replicate human perspective . . . understanding . . . emotion. The fundamental tenets of our magazine and all the things I was supposed to be bringing to the table but, according to Daphne, hadn't been.

I felt awful after our meeting, but now, staring at my two best friends, my guilt and sense of responsibility surged to new heights. How was I going to redeem myself, save my job, save their jobs, *and* save the magazine—all the while contending with Jason and his supercomputer? MAUDE didn't have to combat grief and regret and responsibility. MAUDE could simply be the picture of productivity, spitting out unfettered copy as easy as breathing.

I decided that for now my best course was to stay vague enough that Carrie and Molly didn't panic but direct enough that I wasn't totally keeping them in the dark either. Basically the same tactic I'd been employing since the magazine went into the red. My thoughts had pulled me from the paved asphalt, and I realized I'd fallen more than a few paces behind the girls. Furiously increasing my pace to a scurry, I barely caught up before I folded in half and stuck my hand in the air, desperate for a lungful of air and a second (or sixty!) of respite. "Girls, please, just a sec. I need . . . oxygen."

Molly and Carrie doubled back, almost oblivious to the fact I'd fallen out of step. "What's happening, Grandma? You out partying like it was 1999 last night or something?" Molly asked. The joke of it was that they both knew that the likelihood of that being the case was beyond infinitesimal.

"Well, for one thing, you guys are practically running. Who signed us up for the race?!" I joked as my heart fought to regain a normal rhythm. "And no, nothing like that, just a little too much wine after work . . . My mom decided to stop by unannounced."

"Ruth!!!" they shouted in unison before I could even finish my thought, both of them having experienced the well-intentioned but all-consuming force of nature that was my mother.

When I finally felt the flush of heat subside from my cheeks and the blood return to my brain, I jutted my chin toward the path and we began walking again, this time at a more reasonable pace. "Yeah, so clearly, I pulled out the pinot," I explained, and they both nodded in complete understanding. "And then, in my inebriated wisdom, decided it was the perfect night to tackle revisions on my Spark! profile."

Molly practically squealed with delight. "Oh my God! So, what happened? Did you see anyone who piqued your interest?" Her eyebrows danced on her forehead and she elbowed me playfully in the ribs, almost knocking me off-balance and right into a runner. "*Hmmm??* Did you? We need deets!"

"I didn't even make it that far," I confessed. "I barely got past cleaning up my sad excuse for a bio. I'm actually embarrassed to admit how horrendous it really was—seriously, a bit of a train wreck."

Carrie took a sip of her coffee and said, "That's only natural. I mean, when did you fill that thing out or even look at it last? You can't fault yourself. You weren't in the right frame of mind. But maybe now that you are, you'll have better results because your heart is in it in a different way, you know?"

For some reason her comment stung, almost as if she was implying I was leaving David behind. I knew it wasn't at all what she meant, but the feeling caught me off guard nonetheless. Was my heart really in it? No, it was still too consumed with grief after being shattered into a million pieces. But I certainly wasn't ready to have Mom hovering so closely until she ultimately, just one item at a time, ended up moving into my apartment to live out her days as my permanent plus-one. Nope. No. Couldn't happen. For both of our sakes . . .

Snaking an arm around my shoulders and pulling me in closer as we walked in stride, Carrie said, "You know it wasn't until I started to be more honest about who I am and who I *was* that quality men started showing up in my inbox."

Carrie had transitioned almost seven years ago. As a trans female who proudly wore her identity on her sleeve and in her push-up bra, it was hard to imagine she'd ever been anything but authentic about her true self. She'd be the first to admit that her journey to self-acceptance hadn't been a smooth one. Not at all in fact. But Carrie credited her self-love to the great relationship she had with her therapist and the incredibly supportive, tight-knit group of found family she'd been leaning on for years.

Molly piped up, "Same. It wasn't until I really focused on what I wanted long term that I saw Luca as more of a potential match. I don't think I would have ever even considered him to be a good fit for me, we're just so different. But look at us now, ninety-one days until we say I do."

"Not that anyone's keeping track or anything? I'm surprised you don't have it figured out to the minute and rigged to a neon countdown clock!" Carrie teased.

"Yeah, yeah, yeah. Make fun all you want, but ladies, it's gonna be the party of the year!" Molly exclaimed.

I smiled, remembering what that felt like. To be that excited. To be . . . that in love.

We'd finally made it back to the Ninetieth Street entrance and (briefly) parted ways to head to our respective buildings, shower and freshen up for the day, and then meet back at work.

I pushed into my apartment, kicked my shoes off by the door—destroying the nice row Mom had arranged them into last night—and dumped my crossbody bag and zip up into the coat closet. As I poured a carefully measured cup of food into Fitz's bowl, he shot me a look and let out a long, low grumble—his way of letting me know he was less than pleased with the vet's new recommendation of portion control.

I cranked the shower handle around to "hot" and allowed the steam to billow in the bathroom, fogging the glass door and mirrors until I felt like I was hanging out in a cloud. Stepping into the forceful jet, I quickly double-shampooed my hair, rinsed the soap from my body, and shut off the water, the whole process toes-to-nose taking less than six minutes. I tossed on my bathrobe and padded over to where my phone was charging to catch up on the news of the day before heading to work.

But as I went to click on the news app, my thumb hovered over the Spark! icon, a small red number four illuminated in its corner. Four? Four new messages?

I tapped on the first one. Doug, thirty-four, from Bayonne said, "Hey cutie!" He was a firefighter with a few kids. And he was looking for something serious. *Hmm . . . I'm not sure about that.* He was good looking and rugged. Definitely had an appeal, but not really my type. Let's see what else . . .

The next message was from a clean-cut, well-dressed businessman that said, "Wanna grab a drink?" Harrison, thirty-six, who lived in Midtown but advertised that he worked in FiDi, was a day trader, was recently divorced, and he . . . was into frequent threesomes?! Okay, no thank you. Next!

The third profile picture that popped up made my breath hitch in my throat. He was undeniably handsome, with thick blond hair and even thicker dark lashes. He had full lips and a noticeable physique, but even more notable was the setting of the photo. The man, whose name appeared to be Noah (thirty-four), was surrounded by what looked like the small children of a native tribe dressed in colorful prints in an exotic locale.

Noah, though wearing a pair of khaki shorts and a polo, was still adorned with similar accessories to the tribesmen, but most impressive of all was his incredible smile. Flipping through the rest of his pictures, I could see he was adventurous, well traveled, and seemed to be truly enjoying his life. For the first time in I-couldn't-even-tell-you how long, a flutter of excitement coursed through me and an electric surge zipped its way through my body, straight into my finger to click on his message.

Dear Remi,

I hope this note finds you well. My name is Noah, and after reading your profile, I couldn't help but reach out to you in an attempt to strike up conversation.

I should start by telling you a little about myself. For the last two years, I've been working as a doctor with Doctors Without Borders, currently stationed in the Democratic Republic of the Congo. It's a challenging but incredibly rewarding job, and I feel fortunate to be able to make a difference in people's lives every single day.

In my free time, I love to explore new places and immerse myself in different cultures. I believe every experience has something to offer, and I try to approach life with an open mind and a sense of adventure. One of my favorite memories from my time here so far has been when the locals tried to teach me their native Kasai dance a few weeks into my arrival. Even though I looked completely foolish, I had a great time. Maybe I'll teach them the cha-cha slide as a thank-you. I wonder what a flash mob would look like in the bush?

I'm looking for someone who shares my sense of curiosity and zest for life, someone who is kind, compassionate, and caring. Someone who is comfortable in their own skin and isn't afraid to be themselves. Someone who is looking for a true partner, someone who will support and encourage them every step of the way.

I know we live far apart, but I believe that distance is just a number, and that true connection knows no bounds. If you're open to it, I would love to get to know you better and see where this journey takes us.

Warmly,
Noah

OMG, overhauling my profile had actually worked?!
Noah seemed incredible—on paper, anyway. But considering the barren wasteland that had been my dating life up until this morning, this seemed like a very, *very* promising start.

Chapter
Seven

I reached the long metal tongs into the big bowl of mixed greens, examining each of the leaves and trying not to grab any of the pieces starting to brown at the edges. After plopping down two healthy scoops of mesclun from the office cafeteria onto my plate, I set the utensil back for the next person in line. Scooting down the salad bar, I spooned on some artichoke hearts, chickpeas, feta, and tomatoes until the sad pile of greens looked infinitely more appealing.

Distracted by whether or not I was feeling like splurging (financially and calorically) on the candied pecans I so desperately wanted to add, I barely noticed someone next to me until I felt the fibers of a shirtsleeve, along with a strange zip of electricity, graze my arm. I looked over (and up!) to see Jason had slid beside me, placing his own empty plastic tray down onto the countertop.

"Ms. Russell, nice to see you. What's good here?" he asked, surveying the buffet. His gaze swept across the salad bar with robotic precision, scrutinizing every corner and detail with unwavering focus. His eyes moved methodically as if he were scanning all the items with a laser-like intensity, absorbing every inch of the environment with a keen sense of observation.

As he craned his neck over his shoulder continuing to size up his lunch options, I caught another glimpse of him, specifically his arms, as he still gripped the tray. He'd apparently taken off his suit jacket during the morning, leaving it behind in his office, and now, his shirtsleeves were rolled up to reveal muscular, tan forearms and nice hands. Clean and neatly manicured, but not at all prissy—masculine and strong. I shook my head to clear the thoughts from my mind, Jason catching the tail end of the awkward movement.

"You okay?" he asked.

"Oh, me? Yeah. Great. So, um . . . if you're looking for what's most edible here?" I nodded in the direction of my salad and looked back at him. "You're looking at it. I should really start packing my own lunch, but I got into the habit of running down here back when meals used to be a free perk. Now I'm just too lazy to go out, although if you like Indian food, the cart right across the street makes killer samosas."

He raised his eyebrows. "Noted. So, did you happen to have a chance to play around with the MAUDE software last night? If so, I'd love to hear some of your initial thoughts."

Jeez, this guy was all business. Didn't he ever hear of making small talk? "Sure did. MAUDE and me had ourselves a little wine and a good old-fashioned slumber party."

Thank God the beta version of MAUDE didn't save my search history, otherwise Jason would have seen that not only did I play around on MAUDE, but I asked her to be my AI fairy godmother and transform my pumpkin of a dating profile into a golden manifesto.

"A slumber party?" His eyebrows fused together in the center of his head like a Sesame Street Muppet. "Is that a joke?" His face remained blank.

I scrunched up my nose and tilted my head to the side. "Yes, that was most definitely a joke."

If he wasn't public enemy number one, looking to completely dismantle the magazine and replace all our jobs with MAUDE, I'd almost find his overly literal take on everything kind of endearing.

"Oh. Right. Of course." His tight mouth squeaked out the smallest of smiles. "How about I grab us that table over there and we can chat about your, uh . . . sleepover? Unless you have other lunch plans?"

My gaze wandered over Jason's shoulder to where Carrie and Molly were seated by the window, their eyes growing wide at the sight of me being reeled into Jason's web. They waved their hands in the air, the absolute opposite of discreet, mouthing the words, "NO! NO! NO!" and "ABORT!" from behind him.

"Um . . . sure. Yeah, I have a few minutes," I relented, noting Carrie and Molly's audible disappointment as their collective groans echoed across the room. After snapping my head in their direction to shrug my shoulders, indicating I didn't have much of a choice in the matter, I followed Jason to an empty table on the other side of the cafeteria, where it was a little less crowded and a lot more quiet.

Ripping open the utensil bag, I was just about to take a heaping forkful of salad when Jason suddenly shouted, "Quick! Without thinking, what were your first impressions of MAUDE?! Three adjectives?!"

His voice completely startled me, causing me to jerk my wrist and fling damp lettuce to rain down all over the table and his crisp button-down.

"Oh my God. I am so sorry about that," I said, trying to collect the vibrant greens now scattered everywhere.

He patted at his crisp white shirt with a few paper napkins he withdrew from under his plate. "No, it's my fault. It's just that I am super pumped about this technology."

I pointed to his right shoulder. "You have a small piece of tomato *riiiight* . . ."

He glanced down to see the juice of a red chunk seeping into the shirt fibers. Pinching his thumb and forefinger together, he plucked it off his shoulder and continued right on talking, unfazed. "Got it. So anyway, as I was saying, I'm just really jazzed about bringing MAUDE to *The Sophisticate*. I would love to hear your initial thoughts, though."

Pumped? Jazzed? Who is this guy and what nineties movie did he step out of?

"Three adjectives? Let me think . . ."

Dear God, is this some kind of interview? Was I supposed to have prepared for this lunch meeting or something?!

Before there was too much of a noticeable lull in conversation, I fired back, "Intelligent, efficient, and I guess . . . versatile?" The lift at the end of my statement betrayed my feigned confidence, my answer sounding more like a question.

Jason didn't skip a beat. "Exactly. Precisely. What sorts of things did you ask her to help you with?"

"Um, you know, a little of this, a little of that?" I said with a shrug and took another big bite of salad in the hopes that my chewing would force him to move on to his next question.

Jason's eyes zeroed in, making me wonder if I had too had food stuck to me somewhere.

As I patted my mouth and cheeks with my napkin, he leaned back from the table and crossed his arms over his broad chest. "I'm getting the sense you're still uncomfortable with MAUDE. Or is it that you're just uncomfortable with me?"

I took a small sip of water and set my fork down beside my plate. "With all due respect, I'm not comfortable *or* uncomfortable with MAUDE because MAUDE isn't a real person. MAUDE's a computer program. Helpful? Sure, but if you want me to be honest with you, then I'd be remiss if I didn't stand firm on the fact that though brilliant, the software is not without its limitations. There's no version of this conversation where I am going to agree with you that AI is more valuable than any one of my editors."

His lips flattened out into a straight line as he shook his head. "I keep telling you it's more of an enhancement tool than replacement tool."

Enhancement tool? Otherwise known as "Don't worry, you won't even notice they're gone."

"Jason, can we cut the BS for a second? I've accepted that MAUDE is going to take the place of probably half my team, maybe more, but at what cost? You say you always do your research. Did you happen to see our Greta Gerwig 'Feminism in *Barbie*' spring issue last year?"

He paused to think for a moment. "I read through my fair share while doing homework for the interview, but I don't recall that one specifically. Why?"

"Well, *The Sophisticate* isn't just another glossy magazine selling beauty products and fashion trends. It's a publication that works to address the *real* issues that *real* women are facing. Last month, for example, you may have seen a feature we did to follow up with victims of undergraduate sexual assault crimes twenty years later to see the effect it's had on their lives. Do you understand how hard it was to not just find those women, but to convince them to share their stories? Carrie reinterviewed one woman six times before she was able to get all the way through without breaking down. Could AI do that? Could AI rub her shoulders and pass her a Kleenex and glass of water and convince her she was giving a voice to millions?"

I noticed a few glances from neighboring tables before I realized my volume had been growing louder with each passing sentence of my rant. I offered a small wave of apology to a woman glaring at me particularly harshly over what looked like a tuna-salad sandwich, and returned my attention to Jason. "I didn't mean to raise my voice, but I hope you can hear my frustration when you make this all sound so simple."

He shifted his tray to the side and rested his clasped hands on the table. "I admire the passion you have for your team and for this magazine. It's an honorable quality."

"I appreciate you saying that. It's just . . . that story received more fan mail and social media engagement than any other one we've run all year. Hundreds, if not thousands, of messages saying *thank you* and *me too*. It meant something to them. *Really* meant something. And for the life of me, I just cannot wrap my brain around how you expect to elicit the same response when you take humanity out of the equation."

Jason massaged the back of his neck and exhaled a forceful breath that came out as a loud whoosh. "This wasn't an issue over at *Forbes*," he said. "Business articles tend to circle around cold hard facts, not emotions. Probably why BERTIE made for such a seamless installation to their operation . . ." He paused midsentence and rapped his fingers against his cafeteria tray as he gazed into the distance, perhaps to gather his thoughts. After a beat or two, he refocused and drew his attention back to me. "How about this? I need to present my findings and recommendations about MAUDE to the board in three months. Let's use the next quarter to observe where MAUDE is effective and where it falls short in this market. We'll track productivity and sales of each month's publication, log which articles gain the most reach and engagement, and I'll use that data to guide my decision. If you're right and MAUDE fails to resonate with your readership, I'll recommend to the board that your team remains intact and we implement MAUDE in other areas. However, if MAUDE surpasses the performance of your team, as I imagine she will, my recommendation will be to replace the editorial staff. Sound fair?"

"Three months," I repeated, weighing his proposal. The board meeting loomed on the horizon—the same one Daphne briefed me about during our sit-down. The one where I had to devise a standout strategy to demonstrate the editorial team's value, prove to her I still had what it took to keep my job, and counter any critiques Jason might bring to the table. "Great, that's more than enough time for me to prove to you that your girl MAUDE is no match for Molly and Carrie and the rest of my team. And couldn't possibly ever be a substitute for genuine human emotion and intuition."

Without even taking a breath, Jason replied, "And I think it will be more than enough time for me to prove to *you* that this new direction is what's best for the future of *The Sophisticate*. Deal?"

The second he laid down the gauntlet, a fire ignited in my belly. Embers surged. I felt my competitive nature rise up in a way I'd almost forgotten.

I stood up and extended my hand. "Mr. Ashbloome, you've got yourself a deal."

Chapter Eight

Josie, our usual server, came by balancing glasses of water, menus, a bowl of chips, and a double order of their house mango-habanero salsa on a wide tray.

"Happy Friday, ladies. Lemme guess, three happy hour margaritas— extra skinny, extra spicy, splash of pineapple?" Josie asked more as a confirmation than an actual question. The ends of her hair were dyed hot pink, which matched the vibrant magenta of her eyebrows. Last month, both had been lime green.

"Extra, extra spicy for this one over here," Carrie said, nudging Molly in the side.

"What can I say, I like my drinks the same way I like my men: HOT. And wouldn't you both agree that my Luca is muy caliente?"

"¡Sí!" we all replied in perfect unison.

"Hey, Josie, can you throw an extra shot of Patrón into my margarita?" I asked.

"Sure thing," she answered.

"*Thaaaaaanks, Joooooosssiiieee!*" we called out together as she hurried off to the bar to place our order.

Molly leaned toward me wearing an inquisitive expression. "An extra shot? What's the occasion? You didn't tell us we were celebrating something. Should we all get extra shots?!" Her enthusiasm intensified with each question she fired off.

"It's more of a trying-to-numb-the-pain kind of a shot. My lunch meeting with Jason was intense. Thanks for trying to save me, by the way. Good friends, you are," I teased and grabbed for a handful of fresh-out-of-the-vat tortilla chips, still warm from the fryer.

Molly reached across the table to grab a few herself and slid the bowl of mild salsa a little more into neutral territory. "I'll be honest, you didn't look all that miserable staring into his baby blues."

This felt like the right moment to tell them about the deal Jason and I struck at lunch, considering all our jobs were hanging in the balance. "So, like I was telling you guys on our walk this morning, Jason has this idea that he can overhaul the magazine with this new AI tool he calls MAUDE," I explained.

"MAUDE? Like as in Maude LaRoe?" Carrie asked.

Molly shook her head and pursed her lips. "Huh, color me surprised, another derivative idea from corporate. They never fail to disappoint with their total lack of originality, do they?"

"No, MAUDE's actually Jason's pet project. He apparently revolutionized *Forbes* with a similar system he built specifically for them."

Josie set our margaritas down on the table and passed them around. I took a shallow sip of mine. The sweet pineapple tinged with the surprising sting of the fresh jalapeños caused my lips to tingle. I ran my tongue along the salty rim before rinsing it down with a generous gulp, the extra tequila a little more prominent this time around. "He believes MAUDE can help the magazine become a lot more . . . efficient."

I let my words settle in the air and waited for one of the girls to respond. Finally, Molly lifted her glass and said, "Ladies, it's been a real honor and a privilege."

Carrie stretched her arm out to lower Molly's. "Remi isn't saying we're losing our jobs. She would have ordered another round before springing that news on us." Then she turned to me, the look on her face betraying the confidence in her voice. "Wait . . . *was* that the reason you ordered a double shot of tequila? You were trying to muster the courage to tell us we're canned?"

"No, if that were the case, I would've bought us all double shots, for sure. For the moment, your jobs—our jobs—are safe. Jason and I made an agreement. He has three months to prove MAUDE can do what we do, but better, while I demonstrate to him that emotional intelligence is a far more valuable thing than that of the artificial variety."

Carrie and Molly looked at one another almost as if to confirm that the other person was just as lost.

"How exactly do you plan on doing that?" Carrie asked.

"I haven't quite figured that part out yet. Are there any articles in our queue that would require an extra emotional layer or component to explore? A human-interest piece? Maybe a highly controversial topic that shows how the emotional impact, even more so than the facts, actually makes the issue so polarizing? C'mon, ladies, think."

With the exception of the loud crunching and chewing of chips and salsa, the table fell silent for a few moments before Molly perked up, practically sending her margarita into Carrie's lap. "Oh! What about the piece on medical tourism we were tossing around last month? There were a few interesting personal accounts we can follow up on."

"Hmm . . . it's good. I did like that pitch, but I don't think it's enough. I'm not sure if our global audience will get emotional or incensed about a botched Brazilian butt lift, you know? We need something incendiary. Something that will light a fire under people to react, and discuss, and debate, and engage," I explained in the hopes that the clarification would inspire some new ideas.

Josie passed by the table in a flash, bringing a new round of drinks and a fresh bowl of chips. She cleared away all our empties and winked before dropping the tab onto the table and turning away. We were usually a two-round-and-out crew, eager to beat feet before things got too crazy with the dinner crowd.

"Just a thought, but what about that piece on Celeste Romero you've been sidelining? Every media outlet is trying to get a sit-down with her. It would be a huge score if we're able to get it," Carrie offered.

Celeste Romero. The former congresswoman from Virginia's ninth district and now a senator from the same state. Though a card-carrying Republican, she'd made a name for herself by crossing party lines on social issues she was passionate about. In the last year or so, her name had begun to be tossed around as a possible presidential candidate.

About six years ago, Celeste had really started to break away from the pack, zooming up the political ladder by gaining impressive traction with the newer generation of voters. But her first real splash in the headlines erupted after she announced the hard line she was taking in the Ukrainian conflict. She was a new member to the Foreign Relations Committee and pushed for stronger US intervention in the region. Her sway ultimately resulted in a series of air assaults on Russian military camps. The missile strike that killed David was a retaliatory attack.

The mere mention of the name Celeste Romero made the hair on the back of my neck stand on end and an irrepressible heat flush my cheeks. I couldn't help but picture her in a villain-y lair, stroking a hairless cat, eyes fixed on a massive screen. She'd laugh maniacally as she pressed large red buttons, launching missiles and bombs like the game Battleship my older brother, Reid, and I used to play as kids, indifferent to the casualties on the other side. She was a monster, and monsters didn't deserve platforms like *The Sophisticate*.

My gut lurched, and I wanted to shut down the conversation and immediately dismiss Carrie's suggestion, as I had done countless times before. However, given my intense reaction to the mere mention of her name, I couldn't ignore that a story about her would provoke a flood of emotions from both her admirers and critics—including my own. Much to my dismay, that made it the perfect subject matter to tackle.

"I think you're right," I said to Carrie. "We should try to land the interview with Celeste. And more than that, I think I need to be the one to write the article."

Molly's head snapped up, a tortilla chip still dangling from her mouth. "Really?" She hurried to chew and shielded her mouth with a cupped hand to keep chip crumbs from flying out as she spoke. "But you haven't written much since, well, you know—since David died."

Carrie shot Molly a side-eyed glance and then turned her attention to me, nudging my margarita a little closer. "We totally understand why, though. You've taken on practically a hundred percent of the editorial responsibilities, so it makes total sense why you haven't been writing . . . or have you?" Carrie's eyes lit up like she'd been plugged into an electrical outlet. "Outside of work? Have you started working on your novel again?!" She was leaning in, practically floating out of her chair like a helium balloon. However, I was sure my response would be a big fat pin that popped it midair.

"My novel? Oh no. That thing's permanently in a holding pattern." As expected, I watched her exchange a look with Molly and deflate.

"So are you sure *this* article should be the one you jump back in with? Your 'entanglement' with Celeste Romero runs deep." Carrie gestured dramatically with air quotes while her face morphed into an expression of concern.

"That's exactly why it needs to be me. Otherwise it'll be just another talking heads piece. In order to show Jason that MAUDE has no place at *The Sophisticate*, this story has to have real depth and heart."

And to show Daphne I still have what it takes, I need to confront Dr. Evil head on.

In her usual attempt to lighten the mood, Molly took a shallow sip of her drink and said, "Speaking of hearts, I've been dying to ask you all day, did your new and improved Spark! profile reel in any fish?"

I barked out a laugh, and immediately, the heavy weight in my chest lightened by the shift in conversation. "Actually, I did get a pretty interesting email from a match."

Molly cocked her head, instantly skeptical. "'Interesting' how? He didn't ask you for nude pictures or anything, right? Also, you know not to send money no matter how bad they make you feel!"

"What? No. I meant interesting as in intriguing, promising even? I don't want to get ahead of myself and think more of it than it is, so that's all I'm gonna say for now, but I'll keep you updated, I promise."

"That's all we get?! C'mon, do you know how long we have waited for you to be 'intrigued' by a potential match?" Carrie used dramatic air quotes again, but this time I swatted her hands away.

"What's with the air quotes?! And yes, that's all I'm giving up for now. I'm not even sure what *I* think about it yet."

"*Fiiinnne*, have it your way. Okay, ladies, as always this has been a treat, but I should go. Luca is making his famous paella tonight, a dish that always gets things going, if you know what I mean." Molly waggled her eyebrows, her smirk wide and over-the-top obvious.

"No, we have no *ideaaaaa* what you mean," I laughed.

"And stop it," Carrie interjected. "You know as well as I do that your frisky evening plans have more to do with the fact that Luca cooks naked than whatever the hell he's sautéing in that pan!"

"Touché, mon amie, *touuuuuuuchéee*!" Molly mock-saluted as she stood up from the table and started rummaging through her purse to find her wallet.

I reached into my bag. "Put that away. We have the money from the HR jar, remember?"

"Even better! I love when the poor choices of our past cover the sins of the present. It's almost as if the universe is encouraging our bad behavior." Molly pressed a kiss to Carrie's cheek and then one to mine in a fluid motion and bounced right out the front door.

"Night, girl," Carrie said, waving her off. "You know, I should probably get going too. Marcus asked me to stop over and meet a few of his buddies at a happy hour down on Stone Street. Why don't you come with? He won't mind—and who knows, maybe you'll hit it off with one of his friends?"

"I can't, I'm heading out to Jersey early in the morning to visit Reid and the kids. Besides, I've got a fiercely loyal and handsome guy who loves to lick my toes eagerly waiting for me to join him in bed."

Carrie laughed as she slid on her leather jacket and slung her crossbody bag across her shoulder. "Give Fitz some extra belly rubs for me."

"Only if you give Marcus some extra belly rubs for me," I winked.

"Done and done." Carrie blew a kiss over her shoulder and disappeared out the door.

I glanced around our favorite watering hole, the welcoming host of many an outing, from celebrations to commiserations, over the past six years, and couldn't help but wonder which we'd be doing after Jason's board presentation three months from now.

Chapter Nine

The next morning, Jess pulled up to the Short Hills train station in her gray Volvo XC90, my nephew Nathan strapped in his car seat in the back excitedly shouting "Mimi! Mimi!" as soon as he saw me approaching.

"Sorry, Rem, he's still workin' on his pronunciations," Jess gushed over her shoulder as I ran over to Nathan's side of the car and threw open his door.

"Don't be! I want to be 'Mimi' forever!" I joked, leaning in to kiss him mercilessly on his chubby pink cheeks—that were sticky from God knows what and tasted a bit like blue raspberry. "I just want to eat this little face!" I smothered him with a few more smooches as he giggled in delight before I jumped into the passenger seat.

"Well, no need. We've got plenty of food," she joked. "Reid's grilling, and I made a butter board to snack on while we wait." Jess signaled and pulled away from the curb as I clicked my seat belt into place.

"What's a butter board? Sounds like something my thighs are not going to thank you for."

Jess took a hard left into her manicured neighborhood. "Oh, they are *all* the rage in the burbs. At my book club meeting last week, my friend Lisa did a board with goat cheese, fig jam, and mixed berries all plated on top of delectable hand-piped rosettes of butter and drizzled with warm honey."

"Who are these women? And where do they find the time? I got home from happy hour last night, ate two Reese's peanut butter cups, chased it with a swig of milk, and called it dinner."

"Remi! You need to start taking better care of yourself!"

"Not you too. You're starting to sound like my mother."

Jess grew strangely quiet and mumbled something that resembled, "Do I?" followed by a clear, "Oh, look at that, we're just about home," as she turned the corner and pulled into the driveway . . . right beside a familiar white Lexus sedan.

I swung my head in her direction, horrified at the sight. "Jess, are you shitting me?!"

Jess unbuckled her belt and let it retract into the seat. "Reid didn't warn you your mom was coming? I'm sure I told him to give you a heads-up."

"Nope. No heads-up. None at all."

"You'll be fine. She'll be fine. I'll help you deflect if it gets too Wild, Wild West in there. Come on, Nathan, let's get you into a bathing suit so you can play in the sprinklers with Daniel and Aunt Mimi," Jess said, clearly trying to change the subject while she lifted him out of his car seat.

I closed my eyes and inhaled deeply, working hard to regain my composure as I followed them into the house. Trying to make my way through the foyer, my left leg was suddenly weighed down by Daniel, my oldest nephew, who was clinging to it like a koala bear.

"Guys, guys! You're gonna knock Aunt Mimi on her derriere. Mom, please. Can you just wait a sec and let me put my bag down? Here"—I handed her the Magnolia cupcakes that had come to be an expected staple of every visit—"can you take these to the kitchen before they end up on the floor and everyone ends up in tears?"

"Well, why didn't you just ask for help in the first place?" she huffed and grabbed the bag holding the cupcakes out of my tight grasp.

Once my hands were empty and I untangled Daniel from my leg, I wrenched Reid roughly by the elbow into the corner of the living room, who up until this point had been a casual observer of the whole exchange. "You didn't want to give me a heads-up Mom was here? So I could, you know, do some mindful meditation on the train? Or fake diphtheria or something?"

"She came out yesterday for Daniel's school cello recital. She was going to head back to the city, but then I *mayyyyy* have let it slip you were coming out today, and she *mayyyyy* have guilted me into asking her to stay over. But just think, now you have a ride back home . . ."

"I'll kill you," I fired back with as evil a glare as I could muster, him full-well knowing that an extra hour in the car one-on-one with my mother was a far cry from a good time.

"Don't look at me like that! What could I do? She brought the soup!" Reid exclaimed, throwing his hands in the air.

Running through the sprinklers with a six-year-old and a four-year-old had been the best cardio I'd had in months. Fresh blades of newly cut grass were stuck to almost every square inch of my lower legs and in between my toes, and I had to tap out after a particularly graceful spill during a cutthroat round of tag.

"Okay, lads, Aunt Mimi's gotta take a break," I said. Daniel and Nathan didn't seem the least bit worn out, so they continued to run full speed through the spray, back and forth, their cavapoo puppy nipping closely at their heels.

"Come, sit at the grown-ups' table," Jess urged. "Here, you've earned this," she said, passing me a glass of chilled rosé.

"You probably earned the whole damn bottle," Reid added as he expertly flipped another burger from his post at the grill. "Those three never tire out."

I glanced over at Reid standing post at the barbecue in the "Kiss the Chef" apron and armed with the engraved metal spatula—both of which used to belong to Dad—and I couldn't help but notice how much more he was starting to resemble him. From the tinge of gray at his temples to his slightly bent posture, quickly glancing at Reid, it felt a bit like Dad was there with us. My eyes wandered over to Mom, who was also staring at her son, seemingly lost in her own memories of all those happy weekends we spent together as a family.

Mom cleared her throat and returned to the conversation. "You should have brought Fitz with you on the train. He could have used the run with the boys and the new puppy. Get in some exercise," she chimed in, not missing her chance to take another jab at my little pudgster.

"A dog walker comes by three times a day. He gets more than enough exercise. I don't know? Maybe it's genetics? Anyway, stop picking on my baby."

"It's not an attack, dear," Mom said almost defensively, as if I had been the one nudging her.

I rolled my eyes. "So, Reid, what's new with work? I know your company was going through that whole merger situation. Is that all wrapped up now?" I asked, trying to turn the heat off Fitz.

"All finished, and actually the new company's pretty cool. They're really focused on innovation and efficiency. We actually just replaced eighty percent of our customer service division with AI. *Huuuge* cost savings. And talk about optimizing productivity! They're tackling almost twice the number of calls a day at a fraction of the cost."

Midsip, I lowered my rosé, certain I'd misheard him. "You said eighteen percent, right? Eigh*teen* percent of your customer service staff?"

"No, I said eighty. Eight-zero. And yes, I know how that sounds, but we can take that insane amount of money saved and reinvest it in medical research and clinical trials, basically route it back into helping people."

"What about the customer service folks who themselves were being helped by, oh, I don't know . . . being gainfully employed? What about them?" My fingers tightened around my wineglass, and I fought to keep a noticeable edge from coloring my voice.

He sighed and swatted a bug off his arm. "It's business, Remi. It isn't personal. Actually, it's a brilliant tool programmed to mimic—"

I held up my hand. "Yeah, I know, to *mimic* human emotions. But mimicking human emotions isn't the same as actually emoting human feelings and relating to others in an authentic way."

Frozen in place with his spatula in hand, Reid looked around to everyone at the table, the whites of his eyes flashing at my sudden outburst, and took an audible breath before he said, "*Okaaaaay*, Erin Brockovich, climb down off your soapbox for a second. I can see your neck vein bulging, and we all know that after the neck vein comes your famous frustrated sniffle-sobs. Take a breath. Why are you getting so worked up about this?"

I glanced over at my mother, who was intently watching the volley of our heated exchange and waited for her to jump in like she used to when we were kids fighting over the TV remote.

I took a long sip of wine to buy a moment to craft a convincing fib. "We're doing a piece on AI for the magazine, and it's been eye-opening to say the least. I guess I'm just a bit leery about such a new and potentially dangerous technology."

"Well, if you need someone to provide a counterpoint to your doom-and-gloom perspective, I'd be happy to go on the record," Reid offered.

"Thanks, but we're not quite there yet."

Besides, I already have Jason Ashbloome cramming all the "perspective" I could ever need down my throat.

Jess clapped her hands together in an effort to break the tension and said, "Okay, who's ready for dinner? Daniel, come get your brother a towel and start drying off. We're going to eat in a few minutes."

"What can I help with?" I asked, desperate to step away from the conversation.

Jess tossed me a lifeline. "The salad still needs to get made," she quickly offered with a knowing wink.

I nodded with a smile and followed her back inside.

Jess bustled around grabbing a wooden bowl, a cutting board, and a sharp knife and placed them on the countertop. "You don't really have to make the salad if you don't want to. I just thought you could use a time-out."

"Actually, I'd love to make the salad. Maybe it'll be cathartic to chop things for a while. And I appreciate the reprieve. After being married to my brother for, what is it . . . ? Almost seven years? Not your first Russell Rodeo, but even still, *man*, it feels like they go out of their way to find exactly what buttons would drive me absolutely bonkers. I . . . I just . . . sometimes really miss having an ally, you know?" My throat tightened around the words like a noose. I pressed my lips together, trying desperately to hold back the tears that were already flooding my eyes.

Jess came to my side of the island and put her arm around me. "We all miss David, Rem, and I know it's not quite the same, but I'm also your ally. We all are, even though your mom and Reid have a funny way of showing it sometimes. Anyway, what's been going on with you? How are Carrie and Molly? Molly's getting married in a few months, right? I bet she's excited."

"Yeah, she and Luca are counting down the days, and it's all she talks about, which is just, you know, so great for her."

"And you? Seeing anyone special?"

I thought about mentioning the promising Spark! email message I'd received from Noah yesterday morning, but considering I hadn't even responded yet—and if I did, it would likely amount to a whole lot of nothing—what was the point? So instead, I answered, "Nope, nobody special."

Just then, Daniel zoomed past me into the kitchen, his wet feet slapping like applause on the tile floor. "Honey, don't run. You fell the exact same way last week. You still have the bump on your forehead," Jess called to pretty much no one, since Daniel had already come and gone like a blur.

"You guys almost ready? The food's just about done," Reid called out.

"Hey, honey, don't forget to peel Nathan's hot dog. He won't eat it otherwise."

Reid took a few steps into the kitchen to place a kiss on Jess's cheek. "Already done and cut into half-moons so he doesn't choke," he confirmed as he made a U-turn to head back outside.

She swatted at his tush playfully with the dishrag in her hand. "You're the best."

As strange as it was to see my big goofy brother who'd always been better at giving wedgies than affection now flirting with his wife, my heart simultaneously swelled *and* ached watching him attend to his family in the kitchen of the home they'd built together. It was everything I imagined creating with David, and now that dream was nothing more than a distant memory.

"Remi? Remi? Earth to Remi? Is the salad ready?" Reid pressed. "The children are starting to get restless—and by 'children,' I mean Mom."

Reid opened the door for Jess, who had her hands full, then quietly closed it behind them, their voices and laughter fading away and leaving behind a dead silence. It had been a beautiful day filled with sunshine and sprinklers, decadent butter boards, and so much love—and I was truly grateful for it. So then why, with my family right outside mere steps away, did I suddenly feel more alone than ever?

The day's events seemed to accentuate the quiet, leading my thoughts to Noah and the unanswered email nestled in my Spark! inbox. It was tempting to dismiss it as another fleeting interaction, most likely leading nowhere. Yet a subtle glint of optimism crept in—could it be a chance to rediscover the subtle rhythms of life, the muted music that had eluded me for the past three years?

One thing I knew for certain: there was really only one way to find out.

Chapter Ten

After a painful ride back into the city that included a solid hour of Mom critiquing Lea Michele's interpretation of Fanny Brice on the new *Funny Girl* soundtrack, I couldn't scramble out of her car fast enough.

"Thanks for the lift," I said, climbing out of the passenger seat and shutting the door quickly behind me. She rolled down the window and continued to speak as if I hadn't even gotten out. "You hear that note? The strain in her voice? Barbra could hit that one in her sleep."

"Yup, Mom, I know. Got it. Love you. See you sometime next week," I called over my shoulder.

"Next week? No, I have that platter I borrowed to return to you . . ."

"Keep it. It's fine. Bye, Mom!" I waved with desperate finality and flung open the door to the refuge of my apartment building.

I smiled at Keith, the night doorman who worked the weekends, and continued to beeline to the elevator bay, the chorus of "Don't Rain on My Parade" resounding off the building's vestibule walls as Mom peeled away.

Keith motioned with a small salute. "Evening, Miss Russell. Good day with your mom?"

"Small doses, Keith, *smaaaallllll* doses," I said with a chuckle, and he nodded in support.

"Well, if she's looking to unload any of that matzo ball soup, I'd be more than happy to take some off her hands."

"Not you too," I mumbled.

What the hell is in that soup!

Keith reached below the desk. "I got your Sunday papers for you. Delivered about a half hour ago."

The familiar pang of sweet nostalgia and desperate grief hit me even harder than it had at Reid's as I took the papers from Keith, my eyes settling on the distinct Old English font of the *New York Times* banner.

Every Sunday since undergrad, David and I would share freshly brewed coffee and Trader Joe's chocolate croissants warm from the oven over our favorite sections of the newspaper. His: the Sunday Review, Opinions, and Sports. Mine: Style, Arts, and Home. And then, of course, we'd swap, highlighting interesting bits we thought the other might enjoy. And finally, we'd scoot our chairs a little bit closer to one another, stacking the remaining sections between the two of us, and take our time reading through the Book Reviews, Food, and Travel concurrently. We'd sit there for hours, our fingertips smudged with melted chocolate and black ink from turning the thin pages, a comfortable silence floating between us as David's favorite jazz album of the moment played on a nearby Alexa.

From our sixteenth-floor apartment tucked away off Eighty-First Street on the Upper East Side, city noise was minimal. Our neighborhood didn't suffer from the blaring car horns of Midtown or the constant state of construction like the FiDi. Though the Sunday *Times* offered a glimpse into the chaos of the rest of the world, when we were finished, we would chuck the whole thing in the garbage, tuck ourselves back in bed for a while, and forget it even existed at all.

I thanked Keith for the paper and hurried to the elevator, a renewed tightening in my chest from the swell of yearning for David and those easier, jazz-filled mornings. Setting my bag down on the ground, I fished out my keys and let myself into the apartment, Fitz's big head pushing through the doorway crack before I could even get it all the way open.

I used my knee to back him up and hooked my finger under his collar to gently steer him inside. "Okay, boy. I know you're hungry. I'll have dinner ready for you in a second," I said, shifting my tote off my shoulder and onto the entryway table. After feeding the little prince, I changed into my pjs and sat down on the couch, debating if I should watch the last episode of *Bridgerton* or savor the series just a *liiiiiitttttle* bit longer.

Savor. Definitely savor.

But restarting the season may not be a terrible way to spend the evening?

Maybe later. It could be my reward for finishing the edits on Molly's most recent piece, which I'd been meaning to get to her by the end of the week.

Crossing my legs into a pretzel, I pulled my laptop onto them and popped open the screen, ready to cue up the article, when I spotted the Spark! icon on my desktop, blinking like a beacon. Before I could stop myself, I clicked into the app. Of all the "smooches" and emails I'd received in the last two days, Noah's was still far and away the most compelling. I opened his profile again and this time focused in on his photos.

Though his profile picture was taken from a distance away, his smile was bright and extended all the way up to his eyes as he danced with children adorned in bright, colorful robes. I clicked to his next photo, a clearer, more straight-on shot where his handsome features and boyish grin were even more pronounced. His sandy-blond hair had a little bit of a wave, and his light eyes were sparkling as he was midlaugh, a vibrant purple-and-orange bird perched on his shoulder stark against the verdant jungle in the background. He had just a bit of scruff across his structured jawline and was ruggedly good looking, like a host on a Nat Geo wilderness special or something.

I scrolled back to his main page and began to reread his profile. Ready to craft a thoughtful and charming response that included some questions about him, I figured I'd better brush up on *his* "About Me" section, so I didn't ask anything he'd already answered.

Name: Noah
Age: 34

Occupation: Humanitarian Worker with Doctors Without Borders
Location: New York, NY—currently working in the Congo

About Me:
Hey there! I'm Noah, a compassionate and adventure-driven guy who's passionate about making a positive impact in the world. After too many years of schooling stuck within the four walls of a classroom (and then of a hospital throughout my residencies) and *finally* graduating from Columbia's medical school, I currently find myself immersed in the rewarding work of helping others as a humanitarian worker with Doctors Without Borders in the Democratic Republic of the Congo. It's a challenging and fulfilling role, and I feel privileged to be able to make a difference in people's lives and get to see the world through those who live in it.

Interests:
When I'm not on the front lines of the med corps, I'm a devoted baseball fan, with a special place in my heart for the New York Yankees after growing up in the city. The rich history of the game, the intense

rivalries, and the sheer joy of being at the ballpark make baseball an irresistible passion of mine. If you're up for some lively debates about baseball stats or want to catch a game together, I'm your guy!

Personality:
Friends often describe me as altruistic, kindhearted, and funny. Like Ted Lasso, I believe in the power of kindness and strive to make the world a better place through small acts of compassion. Laughter is the best medicine (trust me, I'm a doctor!), and I love sharing a good joke or witty banter with those around me. Life is too short to take things too seriously, after all!

Intellectual Curiosity:
Staying informed and engaged with the world is important to me. I make it a point to keep up with current events by reading the newspaper and engaging in thoughtful discussions. I'm a bit of a history buff too, so if you're up for some friendly competition or enjoy challenging your own knowledge, I'm always ready for a trivia night or a stimulating conversation.

What I'm Looking For:
I'm searching for someone who shares my desire to make a positive impact in the world. Someone who is thoughtful, understanding, and has a great sense of humor would be a perfect match. It would be fantastic to meet someone who appreciates the game of baseball and is open to experiencing new adventures together. Above all, a genuine

connection and a kind heart are what truly matter to me.

If you're intrigued by the idea of exploring life's wonders, engaging in meaningful conversations, and sharing some laughs along the way, I'd love to hear from you. Let's embark on a journey together and create our own remarkable chapter in this big beautiful world.

Warmly,
Noah

Wow, he really did tick every box . . . and then some. Funny, compassionate, driven, and could clearly put a sentence together (more than I could say for some of the other gents on this app, not to mention putting me, the professional writer, to shame!). And a fellow Columbia Lion to boot. The MAUDE rewrite of my profile had clearly made a huge difference, reeling in such a perfect fit. On paper, anyway. For the first time in over three years, I felt that small niggle of excitement reserved for only those very rarest of moments when you know you are about to embark on something new. The very last time I remembered having that feeling was when David and I agreed to list the apartment right before he left for Ukraine, so we could travel the world.

Just as I was about to close the laptop, a Teams message from Jason popped up on the monitor.

Ten o'clock on a Saturday night? Didn't he have a life? Although, who am I to talk?

Jason Ashbloome: Remi, are you there? It looks like you are active.

I ducked down as if he could see me through the screen, and then popped my eyeballs up, round as saucers, to peer over the keyboard. I considered snapping the laptop closed and pretending I didn't see the message come through, but figured I didn't react quickly enough for that to be a viable option.

Remi Russell: Hi Jason. Yes, I'm here.

Jason Ashbloome: Great. I was just about to send you a few links to some instructional videos on MAUDE I think would be most helpful as you get to know her. Please excuse the crude production value. We are having them redone by an outside vendor, but I didn't want to waste any time in getting you more acquainted with the tool.

And to think I had my heart set on spending the night in with Colin Bridgerton and Penelope. Ugh. If it wasn't for the fact that my job and everyone's jobs were on the line, I would've told him to take his ridiculous tutorials on his ridiculous software and stick 'em where even Lady Whistledown couldn't find 'em!

Remi Russell: Sure, I will take a look.

Jason Ashbloome: Wonderful. I know it's the weekend, but if you could review them tomorrow, we can plan to debrief Monday morning.

Is he serious?

Remi Russell: I'll do my best, but I'll be in New Jersey most of tomorrow for a family obligation.

Sure, it was a little white lie, but considering Jason was clamoring to take away my job, he wasn't getting my Sunday too.

Jason Ashbloome: Of course. Well, just do what you can then and we'll catch up Monday. Have a good night.

Remi Russell: You too.

I snapped the laptop closed and flung it across the coffee table like it had tried to recruit me for a pyramid scheme. Staring blankly at the computer now barely hanging on to the edge, a pang of remorse caused me to deflate, and I grunted begrudgingly as I folded in half to grab for it. Not only did I feel a smidge guilty for lying to Jason about having a family thing tomorrow when it had been today, but as much as I didn't want to believe it, my job *was* on the line.

I opened up the email with the video links and clicked open the first one. Jason wasn't kidding when he said to excuse its crude production value. What production value? It was just a recording of Jason sitting at his desk wearing his thick tortoiseshell frames in front of a generic library-style Zoom background, his (undeniably handsome) face centered in the camera's frame. No question he was easy on the eyes, but that in no way made up for his lack of charisma on-screen, his stiff monotone delivery almost painfully robotic. It was like listening to that teacher in *Ferris Bueller's Day Off,* only more flat, which until this moment, I wouldn't have thought possible. I was barely three minutes in, and my eyes quickly started to glaze over and roll back in my head.

And as I drifted off to sleep, my vision grew hazy with images of Jason's muscular arms, thick hair, and full, pillow-like lips. Then I felt his body pinning me against the all-too-fake Zoom library background, his hot breath warming my skin as he threw his glasses off and kissed me hard. Gripping my waist, he held me up as my knees buckled under the weight of his mouth, each kiss igniting every cell in my body. With his hips pressed hard against mine, I could feel his hands grabbing, massaging, and stroking my thighs with increased urgency as his tongue traced the column of my neck to continue his trail of kisses all the way down to my—

But then, a very real nudge to my leg accompanied by an impatient bark sprang me from my slumber, causing me to practically tumble out of my chair and realize I wasn't in Jason's fake office anymore, but my own living room. I slammed the laptop closed, stood up, and tried to shake off *whatever* that just was.

Fitz dropped on his back legs and sat in front of me trying his very best to stay still, even though the excitement in his body for the final walk of the night was making him practically bounce out of his skin.

"You're lucky you're so damn cute . . . and that those videos were . . . positively unwatchable." My mind flashed to Jason on top of me and the dizzying sensation of being kissed like that . . . yes, unwatchable. I couldn't let myself get distracted like that. Not when I had so much at stake.

Fitz's butt wiggled at a frenetic pace, and his tongue flopped from his mouth as he marched backward toward the front door. He spun in a circle and rushed to the basket where I kept his leash, sniffing like a hound until he pulled it out to give to me. I tossed on David's old Jeter hoodie, slipped on my shoes, and fastened Fitz's lead to his collar, heading out the door and into the open elevator.

Chapter
Eleven

The next morning, the aromatic scent of coffee woke me before the timer had even beeped to confirm it had finished brewing. The robust, earthy warmth entwined with notes of caramel and chocolate wafted from the kitchen and into the bedroom, softening the blow of waking so early on a Sunday morning. I stretched tall and swung my legs off my side of the bed to slide my feet into David's ratty old slippers, the front of the toe showcasing an ever-growing hole that ironically kept my feet far from warm and instead kinda let in a bit of a breeze.

I shuffled in my too-big slippers, my arms practically outstretched in the direction of the coffee, looking like an extra from *The Walking Dead*. Programmed and almost automatic, I fumbled through the motions as I did every Sunday: opening the fridge to grab for my favorite Italian Sweet Crème Coffee-Mate and splashing a little into my "Someone Who Graduated from Columbia School of Journalism Loves You" mug, then pouring in freshly brewed coffee until it turned the perfect shade of gingerbread.

The morning sun streaked in through the window, and I could see it was going to be another beautiful spring day in the city. Another day to get out of the apartment and enjoy some of the magic Manhattan had to offer . . . Another day to do it all without David.

I sighed and turned my attention back to the Sunday *Times* Keith had given me last night. Grabbing my mug, I placed my coffee down and tucked in at the kitchen table. Separating out our sections, I set David's in front of his empty seat, then took mine before calling out, "Alexa, play Classic Jazz Radio on Spotify," and settling back into my chair, floating far away on the transportive notes of John Coltrane's "Blue Train." Over the next couple of hours, I read both my sections and "our sections" and drank three cups of coffee before setting my mug in the sink and starting the second half of our Sunday ritual.

Showered, dressed, and on the subway platform by 11:42 a.m., I caught the 6 Train to the L straight to Williamsburg, Brooklyn, and Smorgasburg—one of New York's largest open-air food markets. You could find everything from hearty lobster rolls on sweet brioche bread to the infamous ramen burger, a juicy beef patty on a bed of arugula sandwiched between fresh ramen noodles boiled and pressed into "buns."

Every weekend, David and I ventured out on an exploratory culinary journey as we pushed one another to step outside our comfort zones and try a brand-new flavor profile. In times when we couldn't travel, a passion of both of ours, we would find other ways to escape the sometimes-mundane Upper East Side. Food was one of our favorite ways to "sightsee."

There was something about admiring the skyline from across the river that made it all look magical—like a movie set more than an actual place where real people existed and worked. And today, with the sky a brighter shade of blue than I could remember in recent weeks and thick cotton candy clouds up overhead, the city looked even more splendid and inviting than usual.

Families pushing strollers and couples wandering about hand in hand were taking advantage of the beautiful weather, making the market even more crowded. I popped up on my toes to survey the vendors under bright-red tents that stretched out like a sea of poppies in full bloom.

Hmm, where to begin? Am I in the mood for something sweet? Something savory? Both?

The rich smells wafting from the different booths were starting to make my stomach growl even louder, almost as if shouting at me to hurry the hell up and decide already.

Of course, I had my favorites after so many Sundays spent here, but it was always exciting to try at least one new thing, in honor of David and our tradition. I was meandering through the rows of stalls, each aroma shifting me to bow to its whims, when a familiar voice I couldn't quite place stopped me dead in my tracks. I spun around on my heel.

Oh God, is that . . . ?

It was.

Jason Ashbloome, clutching a coffee and looking effortlessly stylish in athleisure wear, was trying to wrangle two children who both looked to be under the age of six and was standing beside a woman who couldn't possibly be a day over twenty-five. Twenty-seven, tops.

Oh, shit. According to my little white lie last night, I'm supposed to be at a family gathering in New Jersey! Never mind the fact that I fantasized a whole telenovela scene between the two of us last night.

Pretty sure I hadn't been spotted yet, I glanced around, searching for the quickest escape route. Then I heard my name—"Remi, is that you?"—and froze like a deer in headlights.

I spun around and cast a wide smile like I hadn't just been planning to run away. "Jason, hi. Yeah, it's me. Good to see you." He was wearing a fitted baseball cap over his hair, which I was surprised could even fit given how much he had, and a tight-fitting black tee that revealed the outline of a six (maybe even eight?) pack, something clearly *well* concealed by his usual stark-white Thomas Pink button-downs.

He strode in my direction with a small boy tugging at his joggers. *"Cheeeeeeese,"* the toddler said. *"Cheeeeeese!"* With how hard the kid was tugging, I was impressed his pants were staying up at all. Impressed and grateful, because *that* would be awkward. However, his young son did pull Jason's pants down just low enough for me to catch a brief glimpse of his Adonis lines, the two diagonal indentations that started from his hips and pointed straight toward *hiiiiis* . . . Man, those suckers were deep.

I shifted my eyes away after lingering probably a second too long, thankful that his son was occupying Jason's attention so he didn't catch me ogling.

Jason ruffled the child's hair and said, "Bud, no more cheese. We're getting real lunch soon, just give me one minute, okay?" He glanced back up. "This is Aidan. He's three, and he's very into cheese."

"Nice to meet you, Aidan. I'm Remi, thirty-three, and also very into cheese. I totally understand."

"Three and a half," Aidan corrected.

"That half is very important to him," Jason explained.

"I get it," I nodded.

A small smile tiptoed across Jason's lips. "It was such a beautiful day, Morgan wanted to check out the market." He glanced around the park. "I'm surprised to see you here. Weren't you supposed to be in New Jersey with family or something?"

He popped the lid off his coffee, and I stared in abject fascination as he licked the rim of his cup to catch a teetering drip. My mind flashed to his tongue and full lips pressing against the sweet spots along my collarbone to send goose bumps to prickle up my limbs.

"Oh, um . . ." I rubbed my arms and shifted my weight. "That ended up getting canceled last minute. My mom's, um . . . gout is flaring up." Even as I said it, my insides shriveled a bit from embarrassment.

Did I just say the words flaring gout *to him?*

I wasn't even sure what gout was exactly. It was just the first thing that sprang to mind.

"That's a shame. My dad suffered from it. So I take it your mom's not as into cheese as you and Aidan?" It sounded like it was intended to be a joke, but his face remained inquisitive and flat.

"Why's that?"

"The purines. They cause increased inflammation. Not ideal for gout. Um . . . never mind." He shifted uncomfortably and patted Aidan on the shoulder. "It's our first time here. What's good?"

"Right, of course. Cheese purines. Oh, um, I've never been here either, so I don't really know?" This next lie slipped out easily. I wasn't even sure why I felt the need to be dishonest about the fact this was probably my two hundredth trip here. Maybe I was embarrassed by the pity that would no doubt flash in his eyes if he somehow learned that I could practically draw a map of the place and the reason why? Nope, sorry, neither of those things were on the menu for today. Jason didn't need to know that much about my personal life.

The young woman (I assumed was his wife?) with perfect skin and bouncy blond hair—competing with her equally bouncy breasts—walked over to where we were standing. A little girl who looked to be a year or so older than Aidan clung to the hem of her skirt.

"Hey, Jason, these two are getting hungry for lunch," she said without acknowledging my presence in the slightest.

Jason pointed toward the food tents. "I should probably get—"

"Yeah . . . yeah . . . of course. It was nice meeting you, Aidan," I said, giving him a little wave. "And you too . . . ," I muttered under my breath to his child bride, who'd already turned away. I wasn't sure who was ruder, his wife for not introducing herself or Jason for not taking the lead. Then again, what did I expect from an android parading around as a human being? Just as uptight outside of work as he was in the building.

I shook the thought from my mind and circled the market trying to decide what I wanted to eat, finally settling on the Destination Dumpling stand. I took my food to a bench at the waterside and balanced the dish on my lap to unwrap my chopsticks. Splitting them apart and using their edges to shave away any splitters of wood (like David had shown me once), I plucked one of the dumplings from its bamboo leaf bowl and bit it in half.

The salty soy sauce, the pillowy dough, and finally a burst of cilantro-lime pork cut by the sweetness of pear made each mouthful more enjoyable than the last. I closed my eyes and simultaneously savored its complexity and the cool breeze off the water that swept across my skin. The sunshine warmed my face, and with my eyes closed, I could almost pretend that David was sitting right there next to me.

Maybe he is? In spirit anyway?

With practiced dexterity, I pinched the last dumpling and inspected it a little more closely, appreciating its perfect shape and delicate folds. David and I used to frequent Chinatown for dim sum in our early years together, before we moved uptown. I remember us reading on a shop window once about how dumplings were crescent-shaped and served during Lunar New Year to symbolize the brightness of the moon and the promise of a prosperous year ahead and new beginnings. Polishing off the small order in two final bites, the irony was not lost on me. What would I even know of new beginnings anymore? I'd spent practically the last two hundred Sundays mimicking the same routine I'd grown to depend on.

Before heading home, I decided to stop at my very favorite bakery stall, Knead Some Love NY, best known for its colorful bundt-style Indian-fusion confections. I passed the back of the truck to where the line formed and waved to a dark-haired guy balancing a fully loaded pastry tray in his arms as he carefully stepped down from the kitchen space and onto the pavement.

"Hey, Prakash, good to see you!" I called to him as I made my way on the line, which fortunately wasn't too long—only two people in front of me.

At the sound of my voice, he flashed his gaze in my direction, which caused him to lose focus and fumble the tray for a brief second before steadying it firmly in his grasp. He glanced back at me and mouthed, "Phew!" and started to laugh as he shook his head and continued on his way.

I found myself grinning at the exchange while I waited, and my eyes skimmed the chalk menu hanging on the booth, even though I knew it by heart. The couple ahead of me finished placing their order and moved out of the way. I took a large step forward and up to the counter.

"Remi! I was waiting for you today." Priya pulled plastic gloves off and wiped her hands on her apron. "Seriously, I've been checking the clock all morning. I have a special surprise for you!"

"Priya, hi, wow, what a welcome. I just saw you last week, you'd think it'd been last year," I said to the back of her head as she turned around to grab something set under the cooking display inside their tent.

Priya pulled out a familiar small white pastry box, placed it on the table in front of me, and popped it open to reveal four identical confections, so perfect they could have been on the cover of *Bon Appétit*.

"I set them aside for you. They were freshly baked this morning and are the first of the season." Her warm smile met her eyes as she taped the box closed and slid it toward me. "I know they were David's favorite."

The strawberry-rhubarb with mint-chai glaze bundts were only made at the start of spring when both the strawberries and the rhubarb were in peak form. David usually wolfed down two before we'd even made it fifteen steps past the tent. Every few bites, he'd cry, "The mint! It's the mint." And just smack his lips together and shake his head incredulously, like Knead Some Love NY had stumbled upon the next Google.

I was overcome with emotion, almost unable to speak as a hard lump squeezed up my throat from where it had first bloomed in my chest. Biting back tears, I leaned over the counter and gave Priya a hug while trying to slip a twenty-dollar bill into her apron, which, of course, she fished out and handed right back to me.

"You know your money's no good on opening day of strawberry-rhubarb season." Priya winked and then leaned in close, looking over her shoulder to make sure her family was out of earshot. "Listen, they *are* delicious, and my mother would give me a whack if she ever heard me say this, but I think, for you, love was the ingredient that made these so special. Not the extra pinch of cardamom. But once you find that joy again, you will taste sweetness in all things, not just desserts. I wish that for you, Remi, truly."

At her words, a swell of emotions bloomed like a morning glory deep within me, and I placed my hand over my heart almost to hold—to physically touch—the sensation. "Thank you. I keep thinking I'm ready to get back out there, and then I see something that reminds me of David or taste something that reminds me of him . . . and then I'm just not sure."

She nodded and said, "You'll know when you know."

I thanked her again, and told her I'd be back to visit next week. Carefully balancing the box in my hands as I swiped at a rogue tear that had squeaked its way out, I was just turning to leave when I found myself face-to-face with Jason—again. His hands in his pockets, child and distraction free, he was waiting for his turn to be helped. My eyes were wet and wide as they met his, which were conveying a very real sense of confusion.

Jason, who'd been standing less than two feet behind me in line and had most certainly overheard and witnessed my entire exchange with Priya. Jason, who now knew I'd lied to him about this being my first time at Smorgasburg and probably about the gout too. Jason, who just saw me cry over a box of bundts and my dead husband. Jason—the very last person on this planet who I wanted to know anything about my personal life—had just caught me "bread"-handed.

Chapter Twelve

"Jason. *Heeeeyyyy.* Didn't see you there. You know, we've got to stop meeting like this," I joked and quickly maneuvered the bakery box behind my back.

He crossed his arms over his broad chest and smiled, clearly noticing the awkward attempt at my dessert-disappearing act. "The kids were begging for a sweet treat before we headed home."

Suddenly, Priya came rushing out from behind the counter, waving her arms in the air and calling my name. "Remi! Remi! Look, I know you said you weren't ready to start dating yet," she panted, "but if you change your mind, my brother thinks you're a total knockout. He's been trying to work up the courage to ask you out for weeks now."

My cheeks practically ignited, knowing that Jason was still within earshot of the entire exchange. "Oh, wow . . . that's very—"

"He's divorced. I know you want kids someday. He does too. Every Sunday when you leave, he curses himself for missing his chance. He'd kill me if he knew I was telling you this, but I figured after our conversation earlier, you know, when you're ready . . ." She smiled and passed me their familiar business card with a phone number scrawled on the back.

I tucked the card into the pocket of my jeans. "Oh sure, yeah, thanks. Maybe. I'll think about it."

"Good. See you next week, hon," she said, throwing me an air-kiss before returning to the booth.

"Didn't you say you've never been here before?" Jason asked when Priya was gone, the curve of his eyebrow practically screaming at me—skepticism personified. And it was met with what I could only read as a smug, self-satisfied smile.

"Right. I meant I hadn't been here yet this *year*."

"I see," he replied in a tone that indicated he didn't at all. "So, what's good?"

"What do you mean?"

He pointed to the box I was still hiding behind my back. "What should I order? Any recommendations?"

"Oh, um . . ." I slowly withdrew the white box, clearly caught, and said, "They're kind of known for their strawberry-rhubarb with mint-chai glaze bundts. They're seasonal, so you have to catch them when you can."

"And if I give your name at the register, will I get the Remi friends and family discount?" he said, taking a not-so-subtle swipe at the fact I'd lied to him earlier.

"Doesn't hurt to ask." I shrugged, hoping he'd read my dismissiveness as the end of our conversation.

"Well, not sure how my kids will feel about vegetable-filled desserts, but either way, it was nice running into you, Ms. Russell. I'll see you bright and early tomorrow."

"Yup, uh-huh, see you tomorrow," I called to him as I hurried away mumbling under my breath, "unless my stupid subconscious decides to cast you as the lead in another bodice-ripper fantasy tonight."

Ugh . . . Dammit!

◆ ◆ ◆

I set the bakery box down on the kitchen counter while Fitz pawed at my upper thighs.

"Okay, buddy," I said, giving him a head rub. "Give me a little while to get settled, and then we'll go for a walk."

Fitz spun in a circle and practically dived into the bin at the front door in search of his leash. Realizing I wasn't right behind him, he dragged it in his mouth over to his bed to sulk. I unbuttoned my jeans and pulled a sticky strawberry bundt from the box. Fitz lifted his head but quickly laid it back down when he realized the treat wasn't for him.

I slumped onto David's chair, turned on the TV, and cued up the first episode of *Bridgerton*. While I knew Colin and Penelope would wind up together the same way Daphne and Simon got their happily ever after in season one, and Anthony and Kate in season two, I still didn't feel ready to see my nightly escape come to an end, so I started, yet again, back at the beginning. To the familiar tune of violins and Julie Andrews's soothing voice, I melted into the cushions and turned my attention to the sugary confection in my hands. Its syrupy glaze clung to my fingers and draped like thin, silvery spiderwebs as I licked them clean. The mint really was the star ingredient, and the flavor was so electrifying on my taste buds that my memory tingled at its vivid recollection. I laughed and then cried out loud at David's famous line, "It's the mint!"

I squeezed the pillowy cake, fragrant with hints of sweet, sun-ripened strawberries and unmistakable notes of chai, and breathed in the moment. Glancing at the framed picture of me and David, I lifted the treat as if toasting to us and bit into the cake, the strawberries toppling into my cupped hand below. The glaze oozed down the corner of my mouth, and I licked at the sweet syrup with the tip of my tongue.

The taste transported me back to the fateful day he traveled to Ukraine. He was leaving on a red-eye from JFK on a Sunday evening. We'd spent the morning at the market like we always had and of course, Knead Some Love NY was our last stop before heading home for him to pack. He insisted on buying a box of the strawberry-rhubarb bundts even though he was leaving that night, bent on wrapping a few and taking them in his travel bag.

We'd actually gotten into a completely ridiculous argument over the cakes, me asserting that they were too sticky, too gooey, just way too messy to pack. Him, maintaining that the Ziploc bags would provide enough protection between the sweet treats and everything else.

I railed on and on about his laptop and iPad and all his freshly washed clothes while he continued to pack his carry-on unfazed, because he was unfazed. To him, this was just another job. Another assignment. No more dangerous than the last. Except that it was.

And I'd known it deep down. I'd felt uneasy about the trip from the moment he mentioned it. But I also knew the old adage "no guts, no glory" still held true in the reporting world. Even so, I vented my frustration by railing against him about the pastries, his lack of warm clothes, and the fact that he hadn't thought to pack a second spare battery for his phone. I let my irritation about his trip spill over into anything else that might spark an argument. In the end, my efforts were in vain because I didn't voice my real concerns. He left and never came back.

Why didn't I trust my gut and say something? Why didn't I insist he turn down the assignment and stay home . . . safe . . . with me? Why didn't I take that entire goddamn box of strawberry-rhubarb with mint-chai glaze bundts and hurl it at him with all my might, hoping it would knock some sense into him and make him miss his flight?

The dessert that just moments ago had tasted so delicious was now almost nauseatingly sweet. I spit the remainder of it out of my mouth and into a napkin from off the coffee table. Fitz, as if on cue, left his leash behind and came padding over from his bed to curl at my feet. He nudged my leg almost as if he were trying to convey an extra affirmation of support. I reached into the bakery box and broke off a small corner of the cake and slid it to him, allowing him to lick some of the glaze from my fingertips.

"I won't tell if you won't," I whispered to him.

My phone began buzzing from inside my pants.

Shoot! How am I going to answer with my fingers coated in gooey icing and dog slobber?!

I fished into my pocket, yanked it out, and answered before even checking to see who it was—mistake number one.

"Oh, good, you're alive," Mom breathed into the receiver.

Dammit. With the phone on vibrate, the ringtone I'd set to recognize her call never sounded.

Fitz licked his chops and then sniffed around the coffee table in search of more. I flipped the phone to check how many times she'd tried to reach me and saw it was no less than fifteen.

"Mom, I was on the subway without service. The messages just came through a little bit ago. Why were you texting in such a panic? Fifteen in a row? Is someone on fire?"

Mom ignored my sarcasm and instead pressed on with her own line of questioning. "The subway? Remi, you didn't go to Brooklyn for that food fair again, did you?"

"Why does your voice always go up on the word *Brooklyn* like I was visiting a war-torn country rather than another borough? Was there something you needed, Mom? I'm about to take Fitz for a walk," I said, trying to keep my voice even.

"A phone *is* portable, isn't it?" she pressed.

I gritted my teeth. "It is. But I need to leave it in the charger, it's almost dead."

She gasped. "You can't go and take the dog for a walk and not carry a phone on you. What if something happens?"

"It's three in the afternoon, and I'm walking him around the corner and back. It'll be okay. Anyway, I have the mace key chain thing you gave me, just in case," I said, rolling my eyes.

"Oh, okay, well that's good. But keep it out. In your hand. It doesn't do you any good if it's buried deeply in your pocket."

"Yup, got it. Love you, Mom," I said, edging my way off the call.

"Wait, don't hang up, I have a question for you. Which is actually why I called. What are you doing tomorrow night?"

I took a few too many seconds trying to come up with an excuse to avoid whatever it was she was about to propose. Mistake number two—my silence gave her the opening she was looking for to continue.

"I've been talking to the most wonderful guy. I think he'd be perfect for you," she gushed.

"Talking to? Mom, what do you mean 'talking to'?!" My voice started to climb as my brain slowly assembled her implication.

"Not talking so much as emailing . . . messaging . . . back and forth. Once you blocked me out of your Spark! account, I had to resort to texting. Thank God, we'd exchanged numbers before you firewalled me. But seriously, you have to trust me. He is everything you're looking for. His name's Thatcher, not Jewish, but *is* a partner at a hedge fund. Never married, which I suppose could be a bit of a red flag, but you know those hedge fund guys—always work work work. Apparently, he's ready to settle down and *very* interested in you. Especially after I sent him the Aruba picture."

"Really? The Aruba picture?" Otherwise known as the picture Mom snapped of me in a bikini top that was *wayyyy* too small when I'd accidentally bought the wrong size. It was the first picture I took down off Spark! when I reclaimed it from Mom. Or so I *thought* I had! "Let me get this straight . . . you and this . . . Thatcher have been exchanging messages? Who does he think he's talking to?"

"You, of course! Don't be silly. Why would he want to talk to me?"

"Oh my God, Mom, you gefilte-fished him!!!" I cried.

"I what?"

"You gefilte-fished him! Like catfished him but like . . ." I tried to explain the pun, but even that was exhausting. I put my hand to my head and pressed my eyes closed in disbelief. "Mom, that is so wrong! How can you not understand how that crosses a line?!"

"What's the problem? He likes you. Well . . . me. But I've been speaking and filling in all your details, so I know he'll like the real you once you two meet. I told him I'm free Monday night for a drink. Well, you are. You know what I'm saying."

"Do I? Anyway, I'm not meeting a complete stranger who's been talking to my mother!"

"What's that supposed to mean?"

"It's just weird. The whole thing is weird."

"Stop being such a downer! Maybe you'll have a fabulous night. And maybe you won't. But it sure as hell beats sitting home alone."

My mind was reeling, and I wasn't sure if I wanted to laugh, or cry, or scream. Or do all three at once. Again, she mistook my silence as an invitation to continue and said, "So, he'll be waiting for you at Le Bain at The Standard hotel at six thirty tomorrow night. I figured that's not too far from your office. And show a little skin. You're young and gorgeous, and God knows you won't be that way forever. I'll call you tomorrow. Love you," she said, and hung up before I could squeeze in even one syllable of protestation.

I sat staring at the phone in my hand. Her audacity seemed to know few bounds. I bit my lip, conflicted by my roiling frustration. She meant well, she did. But her incessant meddling and insistence that I needed her or someone to take care of me was just too much sometimes. Most times, actually.

Just as I was ready to toss my phone onto the coffee table and not look at it for the rest of the afternoon, it dinged in my hand and a text from Jess popped up. My thumb tapped the notification, and a selfie of her, my brother, and the boys—all showcasing melted ice cream–covered smiles—illuminated my screen.

Their jack-o'-lantern grins paired nicely with their chocolate and vanilla mustaches. Jess and Reid were looking at one another over the heads of the kids, eyes full of love and joy. Another pang of bittersweet longing for a life David and I would never have together sliced me deep in my gut, forcing me to inhale sharply.

As much as it killed me to admit it, maybe Mom was (a little bit) right. How long was I going to wallow in my grief and stew in my sadness and just let my life waste away? My mind flashed to the barbecue at Reid's yesterday, to my inexplicable lie to Jason today at the market, and then to Mom playing her version of a real-life Yenta, and my upcoming mystery date. Each example was more pathetic and exhausting than the last, and I'd reached my limit. I catapulted myself off the couch and grabbed my laptop, flipped it open, and tossed it on the kitchen table. Hiking up my sleeves, I pulled out a chair and fired up my Spark! account login.

First things first, I needed to look up this Thatcher guy's profile. I mean, who was this dude talking to my mother, who incidentally was pretending to be me? Didn't he realize she didn't know a single pop culture reference from the last decade, not to mention any texting shorthand? Last week, to my surprise, my mom texted me: Are we meeting for dinner? WTF?

Four heated exchanges later, I finally figured out that "WTF" was Ruth-speak for "Wednesday, Thursday, or Friday."

I clicked open his profile, and four pictures jumped onto the screen. The first, Thatcher skiing in Aspen. His face was nearly obscured by a mask, with only his impeccably white teeth—likely veneers—shining through. The second was Thatcher on a boat, surrounded by lots of other guys that, well . . . kinda looked like Thatcher. In the third, he was on a tennis court, delivering a powerful serve, his calf muscles seemingly on the verge of bursting through his socks. And the last photo, Thatcher with his arms outstretched to a barren canyon backdrop, the sunrise casting a warm glow behind him, accentuating his proud silhouette.

He was certainly very handsome in a preppy, Connecticut sort of way. In fact, he looked like he'd stepped straight out of a J.Crew ad. But beyond the pretty boy facade, he really did have a nice smile, which seemed genuine as it reached up to his light eyes. Maybe a date wouldn't be the worst thing? I *was* looking to dip my toes back in the water. Maybe it was what I needed in order to get the ball, and my life, finally rolling forward?

I shot off a text to Mom.

Me: Fine. I'll meet Thatcher tomorrow. But seriously, cease and desist!

Just as I was about to close out the app, I found myself being drawn back to Noah's profile photos. There he was in the Congo, dancing to the beat of a wooden drum, fully immersed in his best life while a camera captured the candid moment. No posing. No pretense. No pretending.

Thatcher's pictures were a highlight reel of his most fun adventures, but Noah's, which were much less flashy, echoed a sense of soul-level kinship that made my heart skip a beat and my stomach flutter at the call. Logic and reason told me that Noah lived a zillion miles away, and a future with him was almost just as unlikely as one I'd have with a man my mother had gefilte-fished.

But even still, I couldn't shake the inexplicable sense of . . . What was it? Familiarity, maybe? Even though we'd yet to exchange a single message? Whether it was this peculiar pull or just my burgeoning curiosity, before I even had time to talk myself out of it, I opened Noah's message, clicked on reply, and filled the page with poetic words and thought-provoking questions, not to mention a few funny but honest stories about Fitz, Mom, work, and life as a thirty-three-year-old widow.

After proofreading the email no less than a dozen times, I closed my eyes, swallowed hard . . . and hit send.

Chapter Thirteen

After sending the email to Noah, I didn't sleep a wink. I'm not sure if it was the excitement of interacting with a promising new prospect, or having to endure another workweek facing off against Jason, especially after our awkward Smorgasburg encounter. Either way, I tossed and turned like a rotisserie chicken for the better part of the night, finally drifting off an hour before my alarm bolted me awake.

Stifling another yawn, I started the day at the office as I usually did—on the computer prioritizing my rapidly growing to-do list. I clicked open an email from the CFO with the latest revenue numbers, which were significantly worse than the month before. Gathering all my strength to craft an upbeat, though slightly delusional, response about how much stronger the upcoming issue was going to be, I was startled back to reality when Carrie knocked lightly on my door.

"Morning, boss. Have a minute?" she asked, balancing a pad, pen, and steaming cup of coffee in her hands.

I tapped out the last few words of the email and hit send before shifting my full attention. "For you? Always. Come on in."

Carrie went to place her coffee cup down on my desk, but eyeing the pile of papers, she thought better of it, and set it on the floor under the chair instead. "Remind me to grab this before I leave. Oh, shoot, did you want one?"

"I'm good, still pretty caff'd up from my several cups this morning. You look great, by the way. New do?"

A mischievous smile crept across Carrie's face. "Yes. Thanks for noticing. That's actually the perfect segue," she said, fluffing her hair with a flourish and then tucking a piece behind her ears, "Because I have an update on the Celeste Romero story."

"Um . . . great. Not super sure how those two things are related, but I'm intrigued." I crossed my arms over my chest and rocked back in my chair. Though I'd been itching to get started on the Celeste Romero article ever since Jason threw down his three-month gauntlet, I'd also been dreading it. With her political popularity skyrocketing in the polls and the continued buzz about her presidential bid, I knew the article could be a landmark piece for the magazine but would also be a boost for her campaign—which didn't sit quite right with me.

Coming face-to-face with the woman whose name, in my mind, had become synonymous with David's death was something I hadn't been ready for any time she'd been pitched as the subject for a feature, and still didn't feel ready for. But now, thanks to the next quarterly board meeting looming over my head and the fact that I knew this article might just be the very thing to save this magazine and our jobs, I had to relent, face the music, and secure a damn interview with Celeste Romero—apparently a next-to-impossible feat as *every* news outlet wanted to secure that same damn interview with the brightest star in politics.

Carrie crossed her arms and sighed. "Let me just tell you, she is *not* an easy person to nail down. I know she's been super hush-hush about any official announcement on whether or not she's running, but let's be honest, her upcoming trips to New Hampshire and Iowa are a dead giveaway."

"Who told you she's going to New Hampshire and Iowa?"

Carrie leaned in to the desk and lowered her voice. "Now, this is where it gets interesting. So, I made half a dozen calls to her top aide Saturday, trying to get an interview with you on her calendar. He totally brushed me off. Said the senator was too busy. Apparently, he keeps her schedule locked up tighter than Fort Knox. Basically, a total and complete dead end. But I did some cyber sleuthing and uncovered that two years ago, she did an interview with AARP's magazine."

"AARP? But isn't she in her early forties with a daughter in high school?! A bit young for the typical demographic, no?"

"It was a story related to her efforts to get the Build Back Better Act passed. Celeste lobbied alongside the AARP to make Medicare more affordable for older Americans. But that's not even the craziest part."

"It's not?" That wasn't usually the type of thing found on the top of a conservative's agenda.

"Nope," Carrie continued, "what's really crazy is that when I looked at the photo credits, it mentioned that her hair and makeup were provided by the Rose & Sparrow Salon in DC. Turns out, my cousin Liam's girlfriend's best friend Peter's boyfriend, Todd, manages that salon."

I shook my head. "I think you may have lost me somewhere in there? Who?"

"Doesn't matter. Anyway, I called Todd directly, and he told me Celeste's in his salon chair every second Sunday of the month like clockwork getting her roots retouched. She may be only in her mid-forties, honey, but her grays are working hard to tell a different story. So yesterday, it being the second Sunday of the month, I decided it'd been a while since I'd been to our nation's capital and even longer since I'd gotten my hair colored. And since I had nothing better to do, I thought I'd take a bit of a drive."

I threw my hands over my mouth. "You didn't!?"

"And guess who I just so happened to run into on Capitol Hill while I was getting balayage after Todd ever so conveniently placed us next to each other? That's right, Celeste Romero, aide and assistant free. And just like in the iconic *Legally Blonde* scene—you know, the one where Elle accidentally spills the tea about the gropey professor while she's seated next to Holland Taylor—Celeste and I struck up a bit of a conversation under the dryers. Turns out we were both Tri-Delts."

I pursed my lips together in confusion. "But you weren't a Tri-Delt. You weren't even living as a woman then."

"Yeah, but in my heart, I just know that would've been the house I rushed, so I feel like it counts. I mean, either been that or Delta Nu, but I'm not even sure that's like a real sorority. So, anyway, me and Celeste got to talking and hit it off like absolute gangbusters. I'm telling you, it's like we were friends in another life or something. And, to make a very long story short—too late, I know—Celeste, and yes we are on a first-name basis now, is willing to sit down with the magazine. She can meet with you for the preinterview"—Carrie, finally coming up for air, picked up her notepad and flipped to the third page—"from two to three at the Astor Court restaurant at the St. Regis hotel a week from Wednesday."

"Holy shit! Carrie, you are un-freakin'-believable. I . . . I . . . I'm in absolute awe!"

Take that, MAUDE!

Sure, maybe you can book me a bike at SoulCycle, but could you track down the most elusive politician in the country at her hair salon, make polite chitchat over a double process, and secure the one interview that every reporter and news outlet in the world's been trying to score? No, only Carrie McGill could do that. Only someone with her smarts, instincts, and effervescent personality could make that happen! A living, breathing person with problem-solving skills, drive, and tenacity. Not to mention a car.

My inner competitor was doing a happy dance at the thought of this being a coup for our side. Score? Humankind: 1, AI: 0. But as I gleefully twirled around my rolling chair in an exuberant and celebratory spin, I caught a flash of the framed wedding picture of me and David sitting on the corner of my desk. The breath expelled out of me, and revelation struck like a sudden eclipse, leaving me in an eerie darkness. Now I'd actually have to face her, whether I liked it or not. I'd have to put personal hatred aside, be professional, and just get the job done.

Rising from my seat, I clapped proudly, honoring Carrie's stick-to-itiveness with a standing ovation from behind my desk. She took a couple of mock bows and replied, "Thank you. Thank you. I would say to throw some of that appreciation into my Christmas bonus, but what are the chances of seeing one of those this year?"

I raised my eyebrows. "How 'bout I cover the balayage?"

"Already added it to my April expense report," she said with a cheeky grin.

"I *am* still pushing to get you that promotion. Budgets haven't allowed for me to open up another senior editor position at the moment—the moment being the past three years unfortunately." I rolled my eyes. "But as soon as I can, I hope you know it's yours."

Carrie smiled warmly. "I know, boss."

A calendar reminder popped up on my screen. "We have the editorial meeting in five. I can't wait to see their faces when we tell them about Celeste. In the meantime, let's have the team start gathering as much background on her as we can. I want to know Celeste's voting record dating back to the Rachel Green *Friends*-inspired haircut and Delia's catalog days she spent in student council."

Carrie grabbed her coffee off the floor where she'd stashed it and then followed me out the door. "I hate to say it, but I think that's just the kind of thing MAUDE can help us with, especially now that the research team's been halved."

I swallowed hard, my lips set into a tight line. "No, you're right. And if I'm going to play fair with Jason, then we really have to put MAUDE through its paces and see what it can do."

Carrie replied, a naughty glint in her eyes, "Play fair? I thought our goal was to see his software turn on him Terminator style."

I shrugged with a heavy sigh. "Until that glorious AI uprising happens and Jason and MAUDE get sucked into the Matrix, we'll just have to keep toeing the line. C'mon, we better get going. You know how much Daphne hates waiting."

Chapter Fourteen

At precisely 9:59 a.m., I pushed into the conference room for the Monday morning editorial meeting to find Jason in my usual seat at the far end of the table. Legs crossed and laptop popped open at the ready, he was just sitting there as if he was one of us.

I couldn't quite put my finger on why the sight of him in my spot, ready to take notes and jump into the action, knotted me up inside. This was my space, my domain, my team—my work family. And there he was, like an uninvited guest at Thanksgiving dinner, holding the detonator, ready to blow it all apart.

Suddenly, I was having an entirely different kind of fantasy about Jason.

I tapped him squarely on the shoulder. "Hey, morning. So, I usually sit here to run the meeting."

He shook his head and closed his computer. "You'd like me to move then, I take it?" he asked.

"Well, unless *you'd* like to run things today?" I shrugged.

Jason's eyes flew up to mine. "Oh, no, I don't think that's a good idea. I'm not quite prepared to—"

"Jason, I was just joking," I said.

He snickered and stood up to give me back my seat. "From now on, you're going to need to include a hand signal or something when you're trying to be funny, just so that I know."

I couldn't help but burst out laughing. "That's a good one. See? It's not so hard."

His face contorted in confusion. "No, I was being serious. Hand signals might really help."

He was lucky that his quirkiness was charming enough to defuse my annoyance with him. My proverbial kettle settled down from a rolling boil to a steady simmer.

As I settled into my chair, Daphne sauntered across the boardroom and set her artful tote on the conference table, gave me a friendly squeeze on the shoulder, and then reached over to shake Jason's hand. "Glad to see the two of you are already hitting it off. Jason, Remi here has single-handedly kept *The Sophisticate* going these last few years. She had a clear vision for how we could expand our readership through more provocative articles and interviews, tapping into the hearts and minds of women today in a way we hadn't been before."

I swept my arm out to gesture to the team now seated at the long table. "Not single-handedly, though. I couldn't have done it without the work of *all* the talented people in this room."

Jason didn't even take a beat before spitting back. "That's because you didn't have MAUDE yet."

"Well, I wouldn't trade a single one of these talented, smart, hardworking individuals for MAUDE. Not for a second."

"You say that now," he replied matter-of-factly.

"I'll say that until there's no breath left in my body."

Daphne clapped her hands together, lowered her voice, and said, "Nothing wrong with a little healthy debate, but let's hit the pause button on this—for when we don't have the entire editorial staff in the room, shall we?"

"Well, he started it," I mumbled just loudly enough for Jason to hear me.

Daphne popped up on the toes of her red-bottomed pumps and tapped on her portfolio with the butt of her pen to grab the attention of the room, which quickly quieted down at the cue.

"Good morning, everyone. Before I turn things over to Remi, you may have noticed a new face at the meeting. For those of you who have not met him yet, this is Jason Ashbloome, our new chief digital officer," she said, turning her head toward Jason, who gave a small wave. "Jason?" Daphne motioned to him to say a few words.

He straightened out his suit jacket and stood up. Molly, who had stepped into the meeting just seconds before, caught my eye before giving him a subtle once-over.

"Hi. Hello, everyone. Remi's been singing your praises nonstop since I started here last week, so it's nice to finally meet the members of her elite editorial team. I'm here to uncover ways technology can help the magazine become more efficient, organized, and productive. I'll be sitting down with each of you individually, but Daphne thought it would be useful for me to start attending your weekly editorial meetings, so I can see *The Sophisticate*'s dream team in action."

Did he ask MAUDE to help him with his intro today? If so, I'm not too impressed.

"So for the next few weeks just think of me as a fly on the wall," he concluded.

Carrie scribbled something down on her notepad and then tilted it in my direction to read.

Fly? More like a corporate spy with wings.

I tried to stifle a small giggle, but Jason noticed it anyway. His eyes fixed on mine, and I felt like I was in fourth grade again getting caught passing notes with my best friend, Haddie.

"Well, I want to thank you all for the warm welcome, especially Remi, who has really helped me feel right at home. Remi . . ." He motioned to me and took his seat.

I took a shallow sip of water and said, "Thanks, Jason. Okay then, let's get started. Marcy, what's the update with the confidential source, that, um . . . manufacturer overseas you were trying to secure for your piece on the rampant market of counterfeit luxury products? Any luck?"

I spun to look at Marcy, and as I did, I caught a glimpse of Jason smirking and shaking his head while he scribbled fiercely on a small pad next to his open laptop. I *almost* stopped to ask him if he'd like to share with the rest of the class, but thought better of stoking the fire—especially in front of my team . . . and our boss.

Marcy lifted her head from her pages of notes and adjusted her shockingly pink framed glasses on her thin yet prominent nose. "I haven't yet. Time differences, language barriers, it's been brutal. My contact, through a mess of translators, invited me to the facility in Guangzhou, China. But, um . . . we don't have the budget for that kind of trip, right?"

I didn't even need to look at him to know that Jason's head probably snapped up from that stupid little pad the second Marcy mentioned the word *budget* thinking about all the ways MAUDE could pull that same data without it costing the magazine a cent. My mouth instantly drained of saliva, and I was finding it difficult to swallow. This was literally *the worst* question at *the worst* time in front of *the worst* audience.

I considered breaking eye contact with Marcy to divert the attention to Daphne, who I'd hoped would pick up the ball and punt it *faaaaaar* away from the other team. I waited. And waited. And Daphne continued to say nothing.

After too many seconds of awkward silence, I faked a little tickle in my throat and slugged a desperate gulp from my Stanley Quencher. I gave a small cough and pretended to glance down at my notes for some kind of reference to . . . something. "Right, so, yeah, no. We do not currently have it in the budget for a trip of that magnitude, but we have a few contacts in that area, and maybe we can work those a little harder and get you some kind of virtual tour or access? I'll reach out to a few of my sources and see what we can do."

I could feel Marcy's (and the collective team's) disappointment radiating from every direction. Even though it'd been this way for years, the *nos* never got any easier to deliver, especially when you knew that a *yes* would result in collecting much stronger content and source material . . . and make for a much happier team and probably a better article.

But that *yes* wasn't really mine to give, not when the whole magazine was fiscally holding on by one rapidly fraying thread. I shifted my attention to Molly, hoping like hell our resident love and sex columnist could knock it out of the park and help me get this meeting back on track.

"Molly"—I looked at her and widened my eyes—"so tell us, what are you cooking up for the next issue?"

Molly sat up a bit straighter and clicked a few keys on her laptop. "Actually, we had a brand rep send us a few of their newest sex toys— some real like state-of-the-art stuff! And one little gadget kind of caught my eye. It's a remote-controlled vibrator that allows you to essentially 'set it and forget it' Ron Popeil–style. You just insert and then, you know, *come* and go as you please. The implications of that kind of independence in terms of gender equality, and in relationships, and even in the sex-positive revolution is groundbreaking and only gaining momentum. Damn, we may not even need men at all in a few years."

There were a few snickers and nods of assent and solidarity throughout the room, and though no one barely batted an eye at the mention of female orgasms, I half expected Jason, who was likely not used to such colorful workplace discourse, to topple right out of his swivel chair. But instead he just continued to scribble away on his notepad, unruffled and nonplussed.

Of course he would respond positively to a story about a remote-controlled vibrator. It only helped prove his point that even in subjects like love and sex, where it seemed emotion and human connection were most essential, there was a technological solution. Damnit, the score was now tied: Humankind: 1, AI: 1. It was time to wind down the meeting before I dug myself any deeper into this hole.

"Looking forward to reading that story, Molly. Sounds eye-opening. Okay, now for the features section, we have some exciting news to report. Incredible news, actually. Carrie helped secure an interview with . . . drumroll please . . . Celeste Romero. I'll be talking with her next week. It's the sit-down that every major outlet has been going after, and we got her! Great work, Carrie."

Hoots and claps bellowed through the boardroom, and Carrie stood up to curtsy playfully.

"So with that, I'm gonna cut the meeting a little short this morning, so I can adequately prepare, and we can reconvene next week."

Jason raised his hand from across the table, cleared his throat, and said, "This sounds like just the type of article we can harness AI to assist with. Maybe I can sit down with you later today and we can discuss how MAUDE can—"

"We're all set, Jason," I said, cutting him off midsentence. "And thanks, everyone," I added to cue the meeting's official end.

The editorial team slowly filed out of the conference room while I gathered my things to follow. Daphne hung back and, after almost everyone had left, said, "Hey, Remi, do you have a second?"

Very few good conversations ever started with the words *Do you have a second*, but just how bad this one was about to be, I wasn't looking forward to finding out.

Chapter Fifteen

Daphne swung her arm toward the chair I'd just abandoned and gestured for me to sit back down. She perched her hip on the table in front of me and folded her hands in her lap.

"I wanted to talk to you about the Celeste Romero interview. First, kudos to your team. I'm not sure how you managed to land it, but now we're the envy of every news outlet in the market. Clearly, you took our discussion the other day to heart; this is exactly the kind of provocative article that will draw significant readership and impress the board."

"We owe it all to Carrie. She really went above and beyond on this one," I explained, hoping that in a few months Daphne would be signing Carrie's promotion paperwork instead of her pink slip.

"So she'll get the byline, then?" she asked.

"Carrie would do a wonderful job, but to make sure this isn't just another politico piece but a *Sophisticate* feature, it has to be me. I'm the one with the connection to Celeste."

Daphne studied me, her lips taut and her eyes narrowed. "There can't be any mistakes. This is too important. Are you really ready? To face her?"

"Not yet, but I will be by the time we sit down. The team's gathering a ton of research. You know, pulling past interviews of hers and searching for—"

"Listen, Remi, you can do all the prep you want, but you said it yourself, you have the connection to her—one that will either make or break this article. But if you aren't able to emotionally handle it, let Carrie take it. You cannot blow this. Am I making myself clear?"

"Crystal," I replied, nodding firmly.

"Good"—she leaned forward—"now, let's address the apparent tension with Jason. It was palpable in today's meeting."

Defensively, I threw my hands in the air. "Has he shown you MAUDE? Talked about how she can even book you a spin bike? Make your dinner reservations. Apparently, he has big plans for his innovation, and I guess I'm just worried we won't even recognize the magazine by the time he's finished here."

"You have my word I won't let that happen. But I need *your* word that you'll look at this as the opportunity that it is. We're at the cutting edge of a technology that's going to touch every aspect of our lives in the very near future. We can either embrace it or be left behind." She gently placed her hand on my shoulder. "Remi, growth is hard. Change is hard. But getting stuck in the past will rob you of a future every time." She grabbed my hand and gave it a squeeze before repeating, "Every single time."

Each nugget of sage advice, though intended to influence my opinion of Jason and MAUDE, instead made me think of David and, strangely enough, Noah. I knew she was right, on all fronts, but it was a bitter pill to swallow, and clearly I was having a hard time getting it down.

But she'd made her point, even if it was one I struggled to accept. A sweeping flush of pressure and unease settled in my chest—another brick piled atop my already crumbling and faltering foundation. But I pushed aside my doubts and instead mustered a confident, "I can do this."

Daphne stood from the table and righted her bag on her shoulder before responding, "I hope you're right."

Back in my office, I stared at the blinking cursor of a blank Google doc and mindlessly tapped my pen against my desk as I drummed up the strength I'd need for my preinterview with Celeste. I'd already sketched out some notes and carefully crafted lines of questioning for me to try to find some middle ground.

With so much on the table, and so many directions I could take the article, I continued to remind myself to lead with what I believed would make the most compelling and impactful story. But keeping my personal animosity aside was proving to be nearly impossible.

"Ugh," I groaned, tossing my pen across the room and deflating back into my chair. It would undoubtedly be one of the most difficult pieces of writing I'd ever have to craft, second only to David's eulogy, which I wrote but had been too distraught to deliver.

The familiar ringtone of "I Want to Break Free" by Queen pulled me from my thoughts and back to the task at hand. "Hi, Mom," I answered, knowing exactly who was on the other end of the line thanks to the song I'd set especially for her. The joke at least brought a bit of levity every time she called. "What's going on?"

"Oh, you know, checking in."

"Checking in, or checking up to see if I'm bailing on tonight's date?"

"Remi, please tell me you aren't going to stand Thatcher up. He's really looking forward to meeting me . . . uh, you . . . later."

I closed my eyes and tried to compose myself before saying something we'd both regret. "What time is he expecting *us* again?"

"No, dear, I'm not coming. You're going. As me. No, not as *me*. But as *you*. I mean, could you imagine *you* going as *me*? That would be ridiculous! Doesn't matter. You know what I mean."

"Do I?" Obviously, I did. But I was getting a little bit of a kick out of hearing her try to untangle the mess she'd created. Just as I was about to throw her a lifeline, Jason knocked on my open office door.

Noticing I was on the phone, he waited at the threshold before entering, and I lifted a finger to indicate I'd be off my call in just a minute (hopefully!). On the other end of the line, Mom continued rambling about Thatcher without taking a breath.

"Fine. Yes. I'll have those out to you within the hour," I annunciated so Jason would assume I was finishing up a tedious work call.

"No, not in an hour. He's expecting you at six thirty," Mom said, clearly confused by my off-topic response.

"Exactly. Let's not boil the ocean here. I'll do a deep dive and then circle back to you when I have a bit more bandwidth," I said, trying to throw in as many pieces of office jargon as I could think of into the conversation.

"Boil the ocean?! What on earth? Remi Jane Russell, are you high? Is this like that time I caught you and that little hooligan—"

"Yup, uh-huh, I'm right on top of that, Rose! Talk soon." And without another word, I just ended the call. (And then put my cell on silent since I was certain Mom would try back at least a dozen times to try to solve *that* riddle.)

"Thanks for waiting. I was just finishing up a very important conversation. What can I do for you?"

"I just wanted to come by and reassure you I wasn't trying to overstep in the meeting by suggesting MAUDE could help with your article. Maybe you'll reconsider my offer of providing you some assistance, so you can really see what she can do? I hope you know, we're on the same team here."

Remembering Daphne's earlier words, I forced the corners of my mouth upward and replied, "Of course we are. And besides, I still have three months to convince you to pitch to the board in my favor. Isn't that what we agreed upon?"

"It is. May I?" He gestured to the chair in front of my desk.

"Oh, you meant you want to show me now? Okay, sure. Yes, please, sit."

"Thanks," he said, barely noticing my fluster as he popped open his suit jacket button with the crook of his finger and took a seat across from me. He sat ramrod straight, his posture and lean frame making him appear even taller. "So, an interview with Celeste Romero—that's quite a feather in your cap. She hasn't been willing to sit down with many media outlets."

I shrugged. "I suppose she's trying to build some suspense for her presidential bid announcement?"

"The feature will get *The Sophisticate* a lot of attention, no doubt about that. And MAUDE, she can really help with the research. Things it would take your team weeks to uncover, MAUDE can deliver in seconds. You want to know Celeste's voting record from back when she was in student council? MAUDE will find it," Jason boasted like a proud parent of an honor roll student.

A chuckle of surprise burst out of me, catching us both off guard.

"What? What's so funny? Did I miss a joke again? I didn't see the requisite hand gesture," he teased.

"No, it's just that I asked my team to unearth that exact thing earlier today. To find me Celeste's high school voting record. I can't believe you just said that."

His eyes met mine, and I noticed a cool rigidity fall away and a hint of warmth ignite in his demeanor as a result of the coincidence. Jason flashed me a beaming smile. I hadn't seen one of those from him yet, and it was nice. "Celeste Romero's an artful politician. If she agreed to sit down with *The Sophisticate*, there's an angle she's playing."

"Not a member of her fan club, I take it?" For some reason, his pronouncement that she was an "artful politician" caught me off guard. If I were a betting woman, I'd have wagered every last cent that we'd be on completely opposite ends of most things, especially politics. Surprisingly enough, David and I had been. He was much more conservative than people would have guessed—certainly more so than I was. I was kind of astonished to find that Jason and I seemed to be aligned on . . . well, anything at all.

"I can't say I agreed with her stance on Ukraine. On the other hand, I appreciate how she's willing to cross party lines on issues. I guess, I'm not sure how I feel about her yet, which I imagine is the same as a good many voters. And it's exactly the reason this profile is going to be huge and why we need to make sure you are armed and ready for that interview," he said, tapping on my desk with a rigid finger for emphasis.

My breath caught in my throat. Ukraine. Every damn time it was mentioned, my hackles went up. As Daphne cautioned, I would need to learn to control my reaction whenever the topic surfaced, especially during my face-to-face with Celeste.

"I know it's last minute, but I don't have any plans this evening. I'm not sure if you ever got around to watching those instructional videos yesterday? I know the fake library book background was a little cheesy, but I was hard-pressed to find anything better on such short notice. Hopefully they were helpful. I'm a much better teacher when I can be hands on."

My brain short-circuited at the words *hard* and *pressed* and *fake library book background*, causing my legs to turn to Jell-O and the room to flash with an overwhelming warmth. "Sorry, what did you say?"

"Just that I'm a much better teacher when I can be more hands on. You know, really get in there and show you how it's done," he said, and slipped on the tortoiseshell frames.

Jesus, the glasses.

A flush of embarrassment settled in the apples of my cheeks. "Right. No. I unfortunately didn't have a chance to watch much. Any. Some. I watched a little."

"Well, I'm happy to stick around and walk you through some of the best research prompts and software features to maximize MAUDE's capabilities. If you're free, that is?" Jason asked.

"Oh, tonight? Like *tonight*, tonight?"

"Why not? Clock's ticking, right?" He shrugged.

I racked my brain to come up with an excuse as to why tonight wouldn't work. Anything other than having to tell Jason I was meeting a man my mother had catfished for me. But then I thought of Smorgasburg again and the little white lie that continued to haunt me like a big white ghost, and I didn't need a repeat of that kind of humiliation.

"Sorry, I can't tonight. I have, um, drinks . . . a blind date thing."

Jason's eyebrows drew together like a drawbridge as his pupils zeroed in on the silver Tiffany picture frame on my desk with a wedding photo of David and me inside it.

My hand instinctively flung over to the photo and laid it face down. "That's my . . . he's . . . um, yeah . . . my husband . . . but he died. He's dead. Three years now. I don't even know why I still keep the picture out."

Jason reached for the overturned photograph. But instead of simply righting it, he drew it closer into his line of vision and studied it like a great master's painting in a museum. Was he considering whether three years was a long enough time for proper grieving, and pondering if it was too soon for me to be dating again? Or perhaps he was scrutinizing the sheer sentimentality of displaying a personal item like a wedding photograph at work? His stoic face wasn't giving much away.

My hands itched to snatch it out of his and chuck the frame inside my bottom drawer, out of sight and out of the line of fire from judgment or opinions. But as my mind continued to spin with self-conscious thoughts, I couldn't help but notice the inscrutable expression give way to a softness that fell behind his eyes.

He smiled warmly as he stared at the image, and with a nod, he returned it to stand upright again on the corner of the desk. "Maybe you can tell me about him sometime."

He stood up from his chair, and as he refastened his blazer closed over his waist he said, "I'll let you get back to your research then, and we can reconnect about MAUDE tomorrow or whenever you're free."

"I'll put some time on your calendar," I offered.

"Sounds great." He turned back before leaving. "Oh, and good luck with your, um . . . blind date thing." His smile reached all the way to his eyes. It was easy and genuine, and I saw the flash of a real human being somewhere in there. It was only a glint, but still, it gave me a little hope.

I chuckled. "Thanks, I'll need it."

He shrugged rather coolly. "Not in the least."

Jason tucked his hand into his pocket and turned on his heel, the overhead vent ushering him out with a blast of cool air through his sandy locks, and just like that he reminded me of Aragorn a little bit more than he had before.

Chapter Sixteen

The moment I stepped into the elevator that shot me up to the eighteenth floor of The Standard hotel in the Meatpacking District and out to the rooftop bar, Le Bain, I knew this whole blind date situation was going to be . . . *a shituation*. First, the techno house music was bumping loudly in spite of the fact that the sun was still far from setting. Second, even though it was mid-April and the temperature was barely reaching the sixties, several bikini-clad girls were poised at the edge of the plunge pool (yes, full of actual water, and bubbles, and people!). Third, I was pretty sure I was a good decade older than the rest of the patrons, nary a frown line or rogue gray hair in sight.

Mom had texted that Thatcher would be wearing a navy blazer, white button-down, and dark jeans—basically the same exact thing every other guy in here had on.

This is gonna be fun. Not.

Looking for Mr. Connecticut, I spotted a guy at a corner high top (stiff navy blazer, crisp white shirt) who looked like he could be him, nursing a tumbler about two-fingers full of what appeared to be whiskey. Before approaching, I adjusted my position so that I could still see him at the table but also order a much-needed shot of liquid courage.

"Tequila. A double, please."

When the bartender set down the shooter half-full of golden alcohol sloshing around in the glass right next to a fat lime wedge and a saltshaker, I barely hesitated. Lick. Salt. Lick. Down the hatch. Lime. The fire hit my chest like a diesel explosion and traced a path all the way to my stomach, where it burned like a smoldering coal. Due to the crazy pace of my workday, lunch kinda never happened short of a handful of trail mix from my drawer and a Diet Coke from the vending machine. I could practically feel the tequila being absorbed straight into my bloodstream.

Now, with my limbs tingling and the edges of my brain softening a bit, I took a deep breath and considered either bailing altogether or just consuming more alcohol before heading over. I decided on one last shot to slow my heart, which felt like it was going to pound right out of my chest. I steeled myself, drawing my shoulders back and fixing my eyes on him, and made my way over to his table. "You must be—"

"Thatcher, yes. And you must be Remi. Wow, you look just like your photo," he said with an equal mix of astonishment and relief. He stood and greeted me with a casual peck on the cheek and slid his hand up my arm.

The gesture, so familiar and relaxed, made me tense, and my breath hitched—though I couldn't tell if it was out of surprise, excitement, or discomfort. Did I like his hand on me, the closeness of his body to mine? The moment passed as quickly as it came, and the cool fibers of his blazer's sleeve felt almost like a chilly breeze against the skin of my forearm as he slid out my chair.

"You look like yours too." Although actually, he was even more handsome than his pictures, with dark, wavy hair, cornflower-blue eyes behind his thick black frames, and unseasonably bronze skin—probably the result of a weekend jaunt to Saint Barts or maybe the sun bouncing off the ski slopes in Saint Moritz. I knew his type. You didn't grow up in New York City and go to school at Columbia without crossing paths with the "hedge fund bros."

I couldn't help but look at his ring finger as his flat hand splayed across the laminated menu. No ring, thank God. And no ring tan line. Okay, good sign.

"Here, take a look, and I'll try to grab the server's attention." He snapped his fingers over and over until the busboy came hurrying over with place settings and a bread basket.

Oh God. Did he just *snap* for the waiter?! Strike one. I tried to reshift his focus from now trying to flag down a server by distracting him with a question. "What are you drinking?"

"Me? Jameson Bow Street 18. Learned all about whiskies at a festival I attended on a boys' trip to Lisdoonvarna, Ireland, a few years back. Do you want a glass?"

Jameson Bow Street 18?! What were the chances? David had been a whiskey aficionado, his collection of Glenfiddich, Glenmorangie, and Glenlivet currently collecting dust on the bottom shelf of our bar cart. And Jameson Bow Street 18 happened to be his favorite. (Would this be considered strike two?! Or was this like . . . a sign?)

"No, thank you, not much of a whiskey drinker. I'll take a Napa pinot. Whatever they have by the glass is great."

After ordering, he pulled his chair a bit closer to the table and said, "So, you work at *The Sophisticate*, right? Let me guess, cover model?" His smile was easy and flirtatious. It was evident he was quite comfortable in the dating scene, and this was far from his first rodeo.

"Ha. I'm the editorial director," I corrected.

He scrunched up his nose. "I could have sworn you said you covered the love and sex column."

Seriously, Mom? The love and sex column?

I wasn't sure if that's what she had told Thatcher because she thought it somehow made me sound more alluring *or* if, even after six years in my role, she still wasn't 100 percent sure what my job was.

"Your pinot," the server said, setting the glass down on a crisp white paper napkin.

Thatcher barely acknowledged him and kept his attention on me. "So, have you gotten in any good rounds lately? I was able to play a few matches when I was in Saint Barts last week."

Ding ding ding. Saint Barts. I knew it! Strike three.

"Sorry, rounds? Of what, exactly . . . ?"

He looked perplexed. "Tennis?"

"*Ohhhhh.* Um, no. I haven't played in . . . gosh, it's been a while. So long in fact that I'm not even sure where my racket is."

"Didn't you play in a tournament this past weekend?" he asked with an expression of confusion.

Mother!

My eyebrows shot up, and I started to nod like a bobblehead. "Oh, *that* racket. My special tournament racket. Right. I, um . . . thought you were talking about doubles. I haven't played doubles in forever. I played in a singles' match last weekend . . . with my, you know, *tournament* racket." I rambled on, emphasizing key words at random and with wild hand gestures in the hopes of distracting him from the fact I had no effing idea the last time I'd even seen a tennis racket, let alone picked one up.

He leaned back and crossed his arms over his chest, clearly impressed. "Oh, I didn't realize you were so legit."

"Yup, that's me. Legit." I took a big slug of my wine.

"Did you start taking lessons when you were a kid?"

"My dad actually taught me. He was really good. Really, really good. And a pretty great teacher, to be honest."

That part wasn't a lie, actually. My dad did show me, and he had been both a great player himself and a phenomenal instructor. I may not have played much tennis since attempting to teach David back in college (which was a class A disaster for so many reasons), but the fact I had been pretty good back in the day wasn't entirely false.

"Does he still play?"

"Who? My dad? Oh, no, he passed away a few years ago. Brain cancer."

Thatcher put his hand over mine. "I'm sorry to hear that. I lost my mom to ovarian cancer when I was eleven. It's a tough blow no matter what age you are."

The gesture caught me wildly off guard and caused a surge of heat to flood my face and settle in the tips of my ears. I was so used to people expressing their condolences about David, I was ashamed to admit that my father's death, just one year before, had gotten buried under an avalanche of grief. I didn't think about him nearly as much as I should, and not because I didn't want to but because I was afraid if I tumbled any deeper into my well of pain, I might never be able to climb my way back out. It still didn't mean I didn't miss him every day, though.

I looked at Thatcher's hand resting on my mine, his thumb mindlessly tracing small circles, then cast my eyes up to his. "You're right, it *is* a tough blow, no matter how old you are."

Over the next forty-five minutes, we shared a few more laughs, a few more drinks, and I delicately managed to dodge a few more bullets in the form of my mother's extravagant exaggerations. She'd apparently led Thatcher to believe I was scuba certified, which, considering my intense claustrophobia and irrational fear of all marine life, made zero sense; that I was fluent in four languages, which was only true if you considered New York slang and pig latin as two of the four; and that I was crowned homecoming princess my senior year of high school. I *may* have leaned a little into that last one, because in all honesty, Debbie Rowenfeld (that evil cow) didn't really deserve the title anyway! The other fibs, however, took a bit more finesse to maneuver through without looking like a complete buffoon.

But thankfully, I must have pulled it off (somehow) because Thatcher slid a room key in my direction and said, "Hey, Princess, want me to continue to show you the *royal treatment*? Are you still

DTF?" He waggled his eyebrows suggestively, not even attempting to be subtle in his invitation.

DTF? Did he just ask me if I was *still* down to f . . . ?! Meaning at some point in my mother's exchanges with Thatcher she implied that I was down to f . . . ?! OH. MY. GOD.

"Um . . . can you excuse me for like one sec? I need to make a quick call." I didn't wait for a reply and instead snatched my cell off the table and fled to the ladies' room, dialing while I walked. Mom picked up on the first ring.

"Well . . . I didn't expect to hear from you so soon? *Soooooo*, how was it? Was he everything I promised?" she gushed.

"Speaking of promises, did you . . . at some point . . . in one of your chats with Thatcher . . . say that I was DTF?"

"Of course I did," she said matter-of-factly.

I rested my closed fist against my forehead and squeezed my eyes shut. "Mom, so, let me get this straight." I spoke painfully slow to make sure she was clearly hearing every word. "You told some *stranger* you met on the internet that I was DTF?"

"I sure did! We were talking about the summer you spent as an exchange student in Barcelona and how much fun I . . . well, *you* had. And then he asked if I was DTF. And I answered that I . . . well, *you* were DTF then, and probably *verrrry* DTF now. I was really trying to highlight what a fun young lady you are!"

Fun indeed! Mom made it sound like I'd traipsed through Europe DTF-ing any and all willing participants.

"First of all, I've never even set foot in Spain, let alone spent a summer as an exchange student in Barcelona. And second of all . . . HAVE YOU COMPLETELY LOST YOUR MIND?!"

"I mean, I guess I could have told him you spent your summers as a counselor at Camp Chinooka, but Barcelona sounds so much more exotic and exciting. Am I right?"

"You are totally missing the point here. Why on earth would you tell him I was down to fuck? I'm your daughter! That is so messed up!"

"Down to *ffff*— Down to—" she stammered. "No, honey, we were talking about that summer abroad and he asked if you were DTF, which means down to *fiesta* . . . doesn't it?"

Through gritted teeth I confirmed, "No, Mom, it does not."

"*Ohhhh*, wow, that was a bit of a mix-up on my part then, wasn't it?"

"You think?"

"Just go back to the table and tell him you thought it meant down to fiesta. I'm sure he'll understand."

"Sure, I'll shake my maracas and tell him I thought it meant down to fiesta." I pushed my hair out of my face and huffed, "Good night, Mother," before ending the call with an audible click.

"Everything . . . okay?" Thatcher asked me as I returned in a huff from the bathroom.

"Oh, yes, I'm fine. Just needed a second, but all good now." I slid back into my seat, and as soon as I did, the room key that sat in the middle of the table caught my attention like it had been gilded. But it wasn't Thatcher's fault that my mother had missed the mark with her acronyms. He'd been clear about what he wanted—no games, no pretense. In his mind, we were two consenting adults, both interested in a one-night stand.

Except, I wasn't. In the past few months, I'd started to miss the warmth of another person beside me. My cuddles with Fitz were comforting, but they couldn't compare to being held in someone's arms, having my hair stroked, or my tears dried. Maybe it was the human connection I craved more than the act itself. And while Thatcher was pleasant enough, I wouldn't say we had much of a "connection."

He nudged the card closer. "So? What do you think?"

I sighed dramatically and nudged it back toward him. "I've got a doubles match bright and early tomorrow. Besides, I gotta find that tournament racket, so I should probably get going."

What was one more lie in the grand scheme of all those my mother had already fed him?

"Oh, right, yes, of course."

He waved for the server and asked for the check. I pulled some money from my bag and offered it to him.

"Don't worry, I've got this," he said, slapping a shiny Amex on the table.

I thanked him and began to rise from my chair, but noticed he wasn't following suit. "Shall we . . . ?" I gestured toward the door.

"I might stick around a bit longer. It's still early."

I traced Thatcher's gaze to one of the bikini-clad girls playfully splashing her feet in the pool. Feeling a lot less guilty about Mom's bait-and-switch, I had a strong inkling he'd likely find someone else to conga with before the night was over.

So maybe Thatcher wasn't "the one," but tonight *had* shown me I was ready to date again, ready for something new. Stepping out of The Standard hotel and into the cool April evening, I felt a renewed lightness and a promising sense that I'd find my way to love again.

As I stepped into the dimly lit lobby of my building, the scent of polished wood and the faint hum of the elevator were a welcome reprieve from the night's escapades. Still processing the "momage à trois" disaster of a date, I saw Tony glance up from his post.

"Evening," he greeted with a warm smile. "How was the night out?"

I set my bag down on the desk to dig out my keys. "Honestly? It was . . . strange."

"Well, glad you made it home safe and sound." He nodded sympathetically and handed me my mail. "The dog walker came by around eight to take out Fitz. Don't worry."

For the last few years, Tony had been one of the few consistent men in my life. He'd also seen me through some of the darkest days, personally delivering condolence baskets and bags of Chinese takeout to my door when I was too grief-stricken to even come downstairs to get them. I guessed he was around the same age as my father would have been, somewhere in his late sixties, with a wife and two grown sons. It wasn't that my dad and Tony were so much alike. More that they both cared about me in a protective sort of way that made me feel watched over somehow.

The elevator doors opened and I slipped inside. "Thanks, Tony."

Stepping out onto the sixteenth floor, I could already hear Fitz's eager barks as he scratched on the inside of the apartment door. I pushed into the entryway and was greeted by his furiously wagging tail and excited yips.

I gave him a few under-the-chin rubs before gently nudging him down and making my way into the kitchen. "Okay, boy. Dinner will be out in just a second. Sorry for the wait."

After pouring him a healthy bowl of his Woofwatchers kibble, I sprinkled a few pieces of ripped-up sliced turkey breast on top for good measure. Clearly, there *really* was such a thing as Jewish guilt! While Fitz ate, I poured myself a glass of wine before flipping open my computer and found myself hovering the cursor over the Spark! icon I'd pinned to my desktop. Instead of feeling trepidation or immediate defeat as I always had when thinking about the app, I was actually filled with a palpable anticipation to see if Noah had responded.

What my date had shown me was that deep down, I was yearning for some kind of connection again. Physical, yes. My X-rated dream about Jason had made that abundantly clear, but even more so than that, emotional. Something substantial. Something *real*. I hurried to click on the little envelope illuminated with an exclamation point to indicate new messages were waiting in my inbox. And, to my delight, there was one from Noah.

Dear Remi,

It was wonderful to hear back from you and to continue our conversation. Your enthusiasm and genuine curiosity shine through your words, and I'm hoping we can get to know each other better. Thank you for your openness and honesty, especially sharing about your late husband.

I'm truly sorry to hear about David. Grief and loss are two of life's most formidable challenges. Through my own experiences, I've learned that grief is like a river—it flows deep and wide, carrying both sorrow and the memories of those we've lost. It's a journey, much like life itself, and sometimes, it takes us to unexpected places.

There's an African saying that came to mind I thought you might find comforting. It goes something like, "When the heart grieves over what it has lost, the spirit rejoices over what it has left." It's a testament to the resilience of the human spirit and the capacity to find joy even in the midst of sorrow.

You mentioned your passion for travel, and I couldn't agree more about the transformative power of exploring new places. I've been fortunate enough to visit some incredible destinations during my work with Doctors Without Borders.

A spot that holds a special place in my heart is Zanzibar, an island off the coast of Tanzania. Ever been? The vibrant culture, stunning beaches, and mix of history and natural beauty are unparalleled. Exploring the narrow streets of Stone Town and savoring the local cuisine were real highlights.

Now, let me turn the spotlight back on you. I'm curious to know more about your own experiences? What draws you to travel, and how do you embrace the new places and cultures you encounter along the way? For me, it's through photography. You mentioned you're a writer, so maybe you've journaled your trips? It's so easy to forget the small details without capturing them in some form or another.

Our distance may be a challenge, but I believe that genuine connections can bridge any gap. It's all about finding that unique bond that transcends time and space, isn't it?

Looking forward to hearing more about your adventures and aspirations. Until then, take care and stay curious!

Warmly,
Noah

PS Since you told me all about Fitz, this is my friend Nkuki (which means "troublemaker" in Lingala . . . and you can probably see why!). He's a local bonobo chimpanzee, and his curiosity and friendly demeanor have made him a bit of a celebrity around our camp.

Noah's words moved me. In a few short sentences he'd managed to perfectly capture my feelings in a way my therapist never could.

Grief was a river. It was a journey. It *had* taken me to unexpected places. I mean, here I was sitting in my living room on the Upper East Side of Manhattan engrossed in the musings of a man stationed halfway around the world. A man I'd never met but in this moment felt closer to and more understood by than I had with anyone else in a very long while.

I read his email at least three times through before I could focus enough to respond.

Dear Noah,

Your words about loss really resonated with me. It's true, the pain of losing someone you care about can be overwhelming, and the journey through it can feel like navigating through unknown terrain. I loved your African adage/story about grief. It's fascinating how different cultures have their own ways of understanding and coping with such universal emotions. It's like through sharing these experiences, we get a glimpse into each other's worlds and find those common threads that connect us all.

Though I've been fortunate to explore many parts of the world, my true dream is to visit India one day. My late husband and I had planned to spend time there after his final assignment so I could gather research for a novel I began drafting in college. When he died, I put both the trip and the book on hold. Maybe one day I'll get there? We'll see.

And how about you? What other interests and hobbies do you have? Read any good books lately? What music do you listen to? Preferred ice cream flavor? Netflix binge if that's even possible in the middle of the jungle?! (Right now, I am deep into *Bridgerton*!) I believe getting to know someone better means learning the intricacies that make them who they are. I hope you agree.

Warmly,

Remi

PS Here's a picture of something I can guarantee you haven't seen on safari in the Congo—a very overweight springer spaniel (Fitz) and his owner.

PPS I'm the one on the right.

Without allowing enough time to second-guess myself, I hit send. I closed my eyes and waited for the rush of panic to flood my system or the ninja kick of regret I knew was fast approaching to knock me off the bed. But it didn't. I wasn't actually . . . excited. I was eager and nervous and awakened. I felt like a teenager who was falling hard and fast, and it dawned on me that it had literally been decades since I'd felt the butterflies and the nervous excitement that accompanied the new beginnings of a genuine crush.

A crush?! How old was I?! Was I being silly? Was this whole thing ridiculous? You know what, maybe it was. But damn, I couldn't remember the last time I felt this good . . . or this hopeful.

In fact, the surge of optimism made me click on my Google Drive and dig around for my novel buried under a heaping (virtual) pile of articles and drafts I'd crafted since college. I popped it open, leaned back against the well-worn leather, and started to read. And read. And read until I reached the end of what I'd written.

When my eyes stopped skimming, it was as if my hands were handed the baton of the relay, reflexively taking up where the story had left off and spinning new sentences as if they'd been itching to fight their way out for years.

Vibration buzzed in my chest, singing a note of excitement and a little pride for what I'd drafted. It was pretty good. Much better than I remembered, and picking up where I'd left off felt as natural as breathing. Before I knew it, almost an hour had gone by, and then another and another. And when I next glanced out the window, the lights from the Chinese restaurant across the way were dark and only a few cars drifted down the quiet street. It was almost 2:00 a.m., and while the city slept, I felt more awake than I had in a long, long time.

Chapter
Seventeen

A week or so (not to mention several flirty, fun email exchanges with Noah) later, I was getting ready to meet Celeste Romero at the St. Regis for our preinterview sit-down. I collected all the notes organized by topic from different piles on my desk and was reading over the list of questions MAUDE helped me prepare over the last several days when there was a soft knock at the door.

"I came by to wish you luck," Jason said from the entranceway holding a brown to-go cup and wearing a devilishly handsome grin.

I cocked my head to the side and eyed him with mock skepticism. "Thank you, but according to you, I don't need luck or even skill. I just need MAUDE."

He cast his gaze down and shifted awkwardly as he ran his hand through his hair. "You know I don't really think that, right?"

"No, I know. I appreciate you taking the time to walk me through some of the MAUDE stuff the other day. With my team spread so thin, there's no way we would have been able to gather anywhere near this amount of research without your help. The prompts you showed me seriously saved us so much time."

In the end, I was grateful for MAUDE's assistance with the interview. Unbiased and objective, MAUDE cut through the emotional haze and focused solely on the facts. I hadn't anticipated how sitting down with someone who symbolized everything I'd lost—and the pain that followed—would push my anxiety to its limits, making it nearly impossible to stay focused and calm. But MAUDE kept everything clear-cut and manageable.

"Glad she could be such a team player," Jason said and took a sip of his coffee.

I glanced down at my phone. "The car's waiting for me downstairs. Can we maybe continue this chat when I get back? I'll probably have a lot of talking points coming out of the interview I'll need to follow up on."

"Really?" His voice lifted, and I wasn't sure if it was an inflection of surprise or hope. "Of course! I have a few meetings this afternoon. But how does tonight sound? We can order in some dinner or whatever, and I can really take MAUDE through her paces."

I didn't realize when I said "when I get back," his brain would interpret that as "has to happen immediately if not sooner," but I was grateful for his willingness to help. Daphne had only reminded me a half a dozen times this week that the Celeste Romero article was the most highly anticipated piece of the entire year and this interview the most important of my career at *The Sophisticate*. My thoughts raced through all that was at stake—for me and for the magazine. No pressure or anything.

"Tonight? Um, yeah, sure, I think that can work. Let me just text my dog walker."

"Sounds great, come find me when you get back."

I left the office and made my way to Midtown and the Astor Court restaurant in the St. Regis to meet Celeste Romero. With trembling hands, I smoothed out the front of my simple black dress, a more conservative outfit than I might have chosen to interview a celebrity or beauty influencer, and took a deep breath to calm my racing heart.

Celeste was already seated waiting for me when I walked in. Surrounded by three suited gentlemen—her security detail, who blended in about as well as penguins at a beach party—she sipped on a cup of tea and nibbled on a flaky croissant while scrolling on her phone. I took one last moment to collect myself and then strode to her table with my shoulders back and my head high. Though I plastered on what I could muster of a smile, my voice remained cold. "Good morning, Ms. Romero, thank you for meeting with me today."

"And thank you for being perfectly on time. I have a jam-packed schedule this afternoon." She didn't lift her eyes as she spoke, continuing to text with thumbs of fire.

So much for pleasantries.

I eyed the hulking men still standing like statues behind her, hoping to catch their eye in a solidarity-like "Is this woman for real?" moment, but sat down in defeat when I realized I couldn't see their eyeballs past their heavily tinted Ray-Bans.

"I was born and raised in New York City, which gives me the distinct advantage of knowing exactly how long to plan for getting from point A to point B, not to mention every possible contingency in case that plan should go sideways." I clenched my jaw and set my eyes to the top of her head, while she tap-tap-tapped away on her phone. "I too understand the value of time, Ms. Romero," I offered, hoping she would catch the implication.

Nonplussed, she said, "New York City could use a real infrastructure overhaul. That's for certain." Celeste continued to type, obviously seasoned in multitasking, and clearly missing the dig.

I sat up a bit straighter and said, "Actually, I'm not sure if you know this, but the first subway line, the Interborough Rapid Transit, opened in 1904? It's still operational, only now it's called the number 4 train. So I'd say all in all our underground system's held up pretty well."

"Let's see if you still feel that way after the island of Manhattan gets hit by a category five hurricane. We're witnessing a global warming rampage so intense that we'll soon be sunbathing in the Arctic and surfing through Times Square if we don't do something to address it and quickly." She spoke to me as she was still texting an entirely different conversation on her phone, and I was enamored by her ability to do both things at once. I mean, there was multitasking, and then there was *multitasking*. "*Okaaaaay . . . aaaaand* done." She flipped her phone over and laid it screen down on the table.

And that right there was what made Celeste such a conundrum. One of the few in her party to not simply acknowledge that global warming was an undeniable phenomenon but to advocate for real change. Seeing the potential an unconventional candidate like Celeste could have in uniting our very divided country, I could almost imagine supporting her.

Almost.

Until David's face flashed in my mind. The message from the network saying he'd gone missing. The personal visit from the secretary of state when he'd been found dead. The call I expected from her expressing condolences that never came. Any admiration I felt in that moment quickly evaporated, and my chest began to heave with heavy breaths.

"Um . . ." Celeste eyed me as I fought to gain control of my emotions. "Do you need some water?" She pushed my glass toward me, and to give myself a small reprieve, I took it and downed a few gulps before coming up for air. "Are you alright?" she asked.

The security guards stepped in closer, and I wasn't sure if they were concerned for me . . . or for her. But I waved them all off and said, "I'm fine. Let's just continue. You have places to be, and I have a long list of questions to get through to help shape the tone of the story." I needed to keep things short and sweet. Get the info and get out.

For the next hour, she isn't Celeste Romero, bloodthirsty warmonger. She's a source and has information I need . . . for this article, to save The Sophisticate *. . . and my job. That's it. Keep it simple. Follow the script. Be a professional.*

I turned to the MAUDE-derived list of questions from my research and rattled them off one by one. We covered her stance on domestic issues, foreign policy, the economy, recent Supreme Court decisions, and finally, turned to her voting record. MAUDE's extensive research capabilities allowed me to challenge her responses with facts and figures, but almost an hour into our sit-down I hadn't unearthed a lot about Celeste Romero that wasn't already in the zeitgeist. The interview was surface at best.

I needed to go deeper, to dig into who she *really* was. What made her tick? What kept her up at night with worry? Who made her feel safe? What did it feel like to be a woman with a real shot at the White House? Did the weight of that distinction fuel her or frustrate her? These were all adequate starts, decent doorways to unveiling the other side of Celeste, but none of them were good enough. In my gut, I knew how to kick the conversation out of the mundane and into a more volatile minefield. I knew exactly what would shift this friendly tennis volley into a full-out Wimbledon-style showdown. But I just . . . couldn't.

All my years in journalism had taught me one thing: the best way to get someone to reveal more of their true self was to reveal more of your true self. The most obvious icebreaker was the one and only thing I knew for certain we had in common, the controversial retaliatory air strike on Russia. The one that made her a household name and me, a widow. But I wasn't ready to go there. Not yet. Maybe not ever. It was still too raw. Too painful. And truth be told, I was too afraid that if I unleashed that amount of hurt and anger I would not only, without a doubt, be hauled out of here by those suited goons, but I might not ever be able to shift back into Dr. Jekyll once I'd become Mr. Hyde.

After I wrapped up the last question from my list, Celeste cleared her throat, slipped on her suit jacket, and took one final slurp of her tea. "Well, Ms. Russell, this has been, um . . ." She was clearly struggling to find the right words, finally landing on, "frankly a bit disappointing."

I set my elbows on the table and defensively spat, "Excuse me? Disappointing?"

"Yes, very." Her posture was as rigid as the Beaux Arts–style columns lining the grand parlor behind her. Through puckered lips she inhaled a long breath, as if to make a distinct point of it, and then she leaned forward to clasp her hands together. "You know, I've read *The Sophisticate* since I was a little girl, stealing issues from my mother's beauty salon. I'd curl up under my covers with my trusty flashlight and pray to God she wouldn't catch me. The first thing I'd look at was the masthead, and there it was, every month in bold print: Maude LaRoe, editor in chief. A powerful woman and role model who gave a voice to women in a time where they were expected to be silent and fade into the background. Looking back now, she inspired a lot of my passion for championing the underrepresented and my work in public service.

"As I grew up, *The Sophisticate* remained a steadfast companion, offering insights into a world this poor backwoods girl wasn't sure I'd ever, for lack of a better word, be sophisticated enough to belong to. But I guess," she said, pointing to my large stack of papers and notes, "none of *that* came up in your extensive research on me."

MAUDE had provided more data than I knew what to do with, but Celeste was right, nowhere in my pile of information and statistics was there anything about an insecure little girl who had dreams that stretched far beyond her childhood bedroom.

"My team didn't want me to do this interview, Ms. Russell. They think it's in my best interest to stick to the talking heads morning political shows and leave it there for now. But I want the women of this country to see me as one of them. As someone who's had to scratch and fight and claw her way to get to where I am. I think my voting record and my stance on the party's platforms is public information at this point and has already been well reported. I'd expected you to present me as a human being, a fellow citizen, who's in it for the right reasons. But this?" She slid her chair away from the table and placed her linen napkin from her lap onto the crumb-filled bread plate in front of her. "This was a waste of my time . . . and yours." Celeste picked her phone up off the table, turned on her heel, and without another word, exited the St. Regis, her three bodyguards close in tow.

Chapter
Eighteen

Back in my office, my head was still pounding from the frustration of completely blowing the Celeste Romero preinterview. How did I let my emotions get the best of me? Top of my class at Columbia, senior editor at a world-renowned magazine, with a list of writing credits a mile long—I knew what I was doing. I'd done it a thousand times before. So why did I let her get under my skin?

And how did I allow my fear and anger to take control, regurgitating MAUDE's questions like a laundry list, when I knew they'd never reveal the side of Celeste the public was craving? Maybe it's because I didn't think she deserved to show that side—the human side—because in my eyes, she was anything but.

And Daphne. Shit, what is Daphne going to say?

I knocked on Jason's office door and popped my head in. "Hey, mind if we do the MAUDE tutoring session another time? I'm not sure I'm really up for it after the day I had."

Looking up from his laptop screen, he set his mouth in a tight expression of concern, nodded, and snapped the computer closed. "Did the interview go okay?"

"Yeah, it went great," I lied. "Just beat from all the prep work."

"No problem. The nanny agreed to stay a bit later, but I'm sure she'll be happy for the last-minute reprieve. Actually"—Jason glanced at his watch—"here's a thought. My afternoon meeting got rescheduled, so if I promise to get you off the clock and both of us on our way home no later than five, how about we kill two birds with one stone—we'll take MAUDE to the pub around the corner. One hour, one drink, out in no time."

A cocktail after that cluster-eff of an interview actually sounded pretty damn good. "Does MAUDE like dive bars? She seems like more of a cosmo and dance club kinda gal," I teased.

He looked almost concerned at my misunderstanding. "MAUDE can do a lot of things, but she can't actually drink."

I barked out an unexpected laugh. "Again, it's called a joke, Jason."

"Oh, right. Yeah, I get it now. Funny," he chuckled.

I thrust my head in the direction of the elevator and slung my bag a bit higher up on my shoulder. "C'mon, let's go. Who knows? Maybe she'll surprise us both . . ."

He paused midsnap of his briefcase and pointed at me, cracking a smile. "Another joke?"

"You tell me," I challenged with a wink.

We took off to Sláinte, the Irish pub around the corner from the office. It was practically empty except for what looked like a few regulars planted on tall stools at the far corner of the mahogany bar.

"Grab any table you like," a server said as she breezed past us with a trayful of freshly washed glassware.

We slid into an empty two-top in the back, and the same server, arms now empty, arrived holding two rolls of silverware, some paper place mats, two waters, and a menu for each of us. "Happy Hour specials run till seven. Buy one, get one pints. Half off on well drinks. Five-dollar wine by the glass but only the ones listed on this half of the menu," she rattled off while gesturing to the laminated back page.

"Thanks, we'll take a look," Jason replied.

My purse vibrated beside me. I plunged my hand into its seemingly bottomless pit to fish around for my phone. After some determined digging, I emerged victorious, triumphantly raising it like an archaeologist unearthing a priceless artifact with a satisfied "Aha!" I glanced down at the screen and then over to Jason. "So sorry, it's my dog walker. I tried to text her to cancel but didn't hear back. Just give me one second."

Jason nodded and went back to studying the happy hour list.

"Hey, Trish. No, I'll actually be home on time tonight, so don't worry about it. I mean, *suuuuurrre*, I guess if you'll be in the neighborhood anyway. No, no, you're right, he could certainly use the exercise," I conceded.

Jason raised his eyebrows and looked up from the menu.

I continued my call. "Do you mind filling up the water bowl before you go and feeding him his dinner? You know how hangry he gets if he doesn't eat after a big walk. It's the canister on the shelf and remember, for as much as he tries to turn on the puppy dog eyes and extra slobbery kisses, he only gets one cup." I looked to Jason and raised a finger by way of apology for the interruption, and I could see he was chuckling from behind the laminated sheet. "Oh, before I forget, we're still good for Saturday, right? I'll be at Sloomoo with my nephews for most of the afternoon, so if you could stop by around two, then Fitz should be good until I get home." Once Trish confirmed, I thanked her again and slid the phone back into my bag.

"Fitz? Your dog's name is Fitz? Good name. Dignified," Jason offered, still skimming the menu.

"Short for Fitzwilliam Darcy, as in *Pride and Prejudice*. Big Austen fan."

"Me too." He lifted his eyes to catch mine.

I pulled back to look at him. "You? You are?"

"C'mon, what is it you writers always say? 'Don't judge a book' and all that?" Jason shrugged as if the comment had been offhanded, but a flush across his cheeks made his features seem brighter.

"Yeah, I guess I kinda was," I admitted, and with that, I noticed a lighter energy settle between us. "My husband—um . . . my *late* husband—wanted the dog. The compromise was that I could get to choose his name, and when I finally settled on Fitz, as in Fitzwilliam Darcy, David conceded because his favorite writer had always been F. Scott Fitzgerald. It was a good fit. Anyway, David insisted the dog would be good company while he was traveling on assignment. And now, well . . ." I shrugged, not sure what else to say and hoping the gesture would fill in the rest.

"And now you couldn't imagine your life without Fitz in it," Jason said, finishing the sentence perfectly.

A lump rose in my throat, and I took a sip of my water to swallow past it. "Those first few weeks after David died, I was in a total and complete fog. Walking Fitz was the only reason I even got out of bed. He needed me. It wasn't until months later, when the fog lifted a bit, that I realized I needed him just as much. Probably more."

As he nodded along sympathetically, the realization of what I was saying hit me like a runaway freight train, and a jolt of embarrassment caused my cheeks to flush. That admission was too personal, too emotional, for me to share with a colleague, let alone Jason of all people.

Maybe it was being seated so close in this kitschy dive bar? Or maybe it was the fact that he looked genuinely interested in what I had to say when I spoke? But for a fleeting moment it felt like we were on an actual first date getting to know one another, not just a work meeting we'd taken outside the office. I'd let my guard down, and now I was stuck in an overthinking spiral, wondering if I could somehow reel it back in.

"I know what you mean. When my, um—" He reached into his pants pocket and pulled out his phone. "So sorry, looks like it's my turn now. Let me just grab this call." A few minutes later, he returned. "It was my nanny looking for an ETA. I know you have to get home for Fitz, and I promised to get you out of here in record time, so I told her I'd be home in another hour or so."

I set the menu down and asked, "And your wife? I guess she works too, then? What does she do?"

Jason shifted uncomfortably while his lips pressed into a firm line.

"Oh, sorry if that was too personal. I just assumed with a nanny that you both worked?"

The server came by to take our drink order, momentarily breaking the awkward tension brought about by my question.

"I'll take a glass of the five-dollar white. How bad could it be?" I joked.

The server looked left and right, then leaned in over the table to whisper, "It's pretty bad. I'd go with the rosé."

"Great, I appreciate the recommendation. Rosé it is."

The server turned to Jason. "And for you?"

"I'll take a Peroni on draft," he said and handed his menu back to the server.

"Be right back with those." She left in the direction of the bar.

Jason took a long swig of his water and leaned in to the table. "So, my wife. She did work. She was a labor and delivery nurse at New York Presbyterian. She really loved it."

I couldn't help but pick up on the past tense of his statements and pictured the petite blonde I'd seen him with at Smorgasburg. "So she doesn't work anymore? Gave it up when the kids were born?"

"She died close to two years ago now."

Oh.

The unexpected twist of his admission caught me off guard. "I'm so sorry. I just assumed the woman with you the other day was your wife."

"That was my kids' nanny, Morgan. My wife, Emily, passed away from colon cancer. She'd been dealing with stomach issues for years. But between the kids and COVID, she kept putting off her colonoscopy. By the time they found the mass, the cancer was almost everywhere. I'm not saying the test would have changed the outcome, but maybe she . . . we would have had more time if they'd discovered it sooner."

Jason's whole demeanor softened almost imperceptibly, like a subtle shift in the hue of a grayscale photograph. As he spoke of Emily, a faint glimmer of warmth crackled in his eyes, momentarily thawing his cool facade. His lips curved infinitesimally at the corners, a ghostly echo of the smiles he probably offered more easily back when she'd been alive.

He continued, "I wanted to mention it the other day when you told me about your husband, but I still have a tough time even just saying the actual words. Out loud. Know what I mean?"

Of course I knew exactly what he meant. It was the reason I hadn't ventured far from my close circle of friends. They all knew David. They knew what he meant to me. They felt his absence without me bringing him up, and so I never had to. New people were different, though. They wanted to know everything about you. Single? Dating? Married? Divorced? I would try to change the subject or duck the question, but eventually, like that day in my office when Jason knocked over our wedding photo, I'd have to say the actual words *My husband died,* and it was like losing David all over again. But the fact that Jason understood the difficulty of articulating it aloud in a way that none of my friends really could was strangely comforting.

I nodded and said, "I guess we have something in common. Who woulda thunk it?"

"More than just that. We're both fans of Smorgasburg and those delicious strawberry-rhubarb with mint-chai glaze bundts your friend sells." He lowered his voice and leaned in closer. "Don't tell anyone, but I devoured the entire box by myself."

"I remember David doing that once—he and his digestive tract were not happy. Those things are dangerous."

"And you didn't even try to warn me. But that damn mint, it was"—he pressed the tips of his fingers to his mouth and gave a chef's kiss gesture—"pure perfection."

"Yeah, sorry about that. I probably should have given you a heads-up about their addictive quality." I chuckled at the error that I assumed, much like David, Jason would make only once.

"I didn't mean to overhear, but the name kinda stuck out. What is this Sloomoo I heard you mention? Another spellbinding confectionery

I need to be forewarned about?" Jason sat back against the chair's plush leather and crossed his arms over his chest in mock concern.

"Oh, no, it's a slime museum."

"A slime museum?" He said each word as if they made no sense on their own but were even more inconceivable lumped together as one thing.

"For kids. They get to touch and play with all different types of slime. My nephews have been begging to go, so I thought I'd take them Saturday and give my brother and sister-in-law a day to enjoy the city kid-free. You should check it out. Your kids would probably love it."

"I'll be sure to mention it to Morgan."

Morgan, the twentysomething with impossibly perky breasts, wasn't his wife. She was his nanny. Suddenly, my mind flashed to Julie Andrews as Maria in *The Sound of Music*. Her cute pixie cut and washed-out dirndl, guitar strung between *her* impossibly perky breasts, flirting shamelessly with Captain von Thirst Trapp, and I felt a twinge of . . . something. Jealousy? No, that would be ridiculous.

Jason glanced down at his watch. "I know we're sort of on the clock. How 'bout I show you a few of MAUDE's latest enhancements before it gets any later?"

"Oh, so you really *meant* it when you said MAUDE would be crashing our after-work drinks?"

"Well, she doesn't get out much."

"Oh my word." I pressed my hand dramatically to my chest with a small gasp. "Jason Ashbloome, are you making an actual joke?"

"No, I don't do that. Being funny triggers my TMJ," he deadpanned before letting a smirk slip through.

Then I laughed, which made him laugh, which made me laugh. *Huh. So he is funny.*

"Okay, fine, let's get on with our threesome," I conceded between our fits of giggles.

Chapter Nineteen

With our giggles now growing loud over the ambient noise of the increasing happy hour crowd, I reached into my work bag, pulled out my laptop, and set it down on the table between Jason, me, and the fresh round of drinks our server had delivered.

As I launched MAUDE on my desktop as instructed, he pulled off his suit jacket, slung it over the back of his chair, and meticulously rolled the sleeves of his button-down to cuff at the crease of his elbow. Taking his glasses from their case, he slipped on the thick frames, his muscular forearms unintentionally flexing with the movement. And suddenly, it was as if time slowed and I was back in the fake Zoom library, pinned under his weight and gasping for air between kisses.

Ah! What is happening?!

He might have that hot-professor appeal, but he was still Jason—the same Jason who was planning on replacing us all with bots. Jason, who I didn't have a single thing in common with . . . although tonight I learned we actually did . . .

"May I?" he asked, gesturing toward my computer and interrupting my torrent of overthinking. I lifted my hands from the keyboard, granting him permission. He moved the cursor over an icon that looked like the outline of a microphone and clicked on it. "I want to show you the program's newest modification. With this updated feature,

MAUDE will be able to log a live transcript of conversations. This isn't just your standard tape recorder. The program can pick up on subtle changes in speech patterns and word choices as a way to expose things like sincerity and authenticity. It could be an invaluable tool for interviewing and whatnot."

I considered his statement for a moment, my brows pulling together and my lips fixed while in deep thought. "So, in other words, like a lie detector test?"

"No, not really. Lie detector tests are remarkably simplistic—a couple of spikes on a polygraph hinged on basic questions and straightforward yes or no responses. Whereas MAUDE doesn't just determine if someone is lying or telling the truth; she can assess the overall sincerity and authenticity of a subject's communication such as microaggressions, tone of voice, and even contextual cues. It was designed to analyze these elements and provide a more comprehensive understanding of the speaker's intentions and emotions. This can be especially useful in situations where the truth might be complex or shaded with ambiguity."

The technology sounded incredible—unreal, even. A sci-fi novel come to life. And I didn't know if I was impressed beyond belief or scared out of my mind. My brain reeled with all the incredible possibilities a software like this offered, and inversely, how it could incite even more dangerous consequences to unravel from this version of Pandora's box.

Shifting uncomfortably against the squeaky leather seat, I considered for a moment how to proceed, my thoughts spinning and colliding with one another. "Aren't all people complex and shaded with some amount of ambiguity? Doesn't any good interviewer recognize that and take it into account when trying to really get to know their subject? I'm not sure I can subscribe to the idea that a machine can make sense of the human heart any better than I can."

"I'm not saying *better*. What I *am* saying is that people are complicated, and there are times we all could use an interpreter. Humans are too sentimental . . . sensitive, you see. But this feature allows MAUDE to consider the words as rote data to be analyzed on a linguistic level. It really is fascinating what you can derive from a text when it isn't filtered through the gray scale of human emotion or personal bias. Take your interview with Celeste Romero, a skilled politician who employs a whole team of people to write her sound bites. MAUDE can help you cut through all the BS and get to the real woman."

I watched the blinking cursor spill out the words spoken between us as a ticker tape on the bottom of the screen and noticed the illuminated green microphone aglow in the window's left corner. "Hmm . . . That's interesting."

"What is?"

I pointed to the screen. "Right here, the program underlined where you said you don't think MAUDE would do a better job than I would. She apparently doesn't think you're being honest with me. That's what that means, doesn't it?"

He rubbed at his chin, almost looking sheepish to have been caught in a web of quite literally his own making. "I believe in this technology, Remi. I really do believe it has the ability to change the world for the better."

"It doesn't scare you? Even a little? All the power of it? All the uncertainty? Especially in the wrong hands?"

He hesitated to answer, probably aware his every thought, every intonation was being recorded by MAUDE. And I'm sure he realized how hypocritical it would seem for him to turn the program off or shut down the feature just in time for him to give his response. But as luck would have it, when he opened his mouth to speak, the server returned to the table to see if we wanted another round.

"I'll take one more Peroni. Cold, cold glass, if you don't mind," Jason said.

I tapped my own, which was still half-full of the *decent* rosé. "I'm good, thanks. I'll just finish this up and take my check, if you have it."

The server nodded and scooted away, leaving an awkward silence to fall between us in her wake. Jason pulled off his glasses, folded them into a side pocket of his bag, and shifted his attention back to examine my face with what looked like eyes full of worry. "I'm . . . I'm sorry . . . Did I do something? What . . . what just happened?"

I squirmed in my seat, unsure of how to answer. The prospect of this software and its implications on the world was overwhelming, and the fact that he didn't see that, or understand it, was almost as mind boggling as MAUDE herself. He wasn't just *selling* MAUDE; he'd built her. Even Dr. Frankenstein eventually came to understand that his monster couldn't—*wouldn't*—be contained to the small laboratory where he'd been created. Would Jason ever be able to come to the same realization? And before it was too late to undo it?

"No, you didn't do anything. I just need to get going," I stated.

Between us, MAUDE flashed yellow, highlighting my lie.

His eyes cast to the screen and then back to me. "Then why do I feel a little bit like we're back at square one?" Jason asked, seeming almost hurt.

Because somehow we *were*. Okay, maybe not quite all the way back to square one. I mean, I no longer saw him as public enemy number one, but he was still the guy who wanted to replace my team, and eventually me too, with AI. The disappointment that settled in my chest almost outweighed the anxiety I felt about this software and its magnitude. I pulled a few bills from my wallet and stammered, "It's just that I have Fitz at home waiting on me, and you have Maria . . . uh, I mean Morgan, and your kids waiting on you, and we can, you know, do this some other time."

My attention snapped to our server, who dropped Jason's ice-cold beer on his napkin, trading it out for his empty glass, and set down our separate checks before zooming away.

"Oh, sure. Yeah, of course." He turned his phone over on the table and then lifted it to show me the time. "You're right. We are well over the one-hour mark." He rested it back down and turned his focus to his bill, studying it as if it were the Gettysburg Address rather than the simple tabulation of a few drinks.

I closed the laptop, and the snap made him look up. "Jason, what you've created is a wonder. Truly, it is. But it also has the potential to be a minefield. And I know we made an agreement—three months for me to prove to you that human connection is a precious thing that can't be simulated or imitated. Based on what you showed me tonight, I'm just not sure how we'll ever be on the same page about this."

In one smooth motion, Jason slid my bills back toward me and slipped his credit card into the leather check folder, resting it on the end of the table for the server to pick up. "I don't agree. I think we are on the same page. We both want what's best for the magazine, don't we?" He responded like it was as easy as flipping a switch, his eyes reflecting a glimmer of optimism despite the complexity of the discussion.

"Yes, of course. Of course we do." I lifted the cash back off the table. "Thank you, by the way," I said and tucked the folded bills into my purse.

His voice flattened as he swirled the remaining liquid in his glass, eyes lowering to the table. "You're welcome. I'm going to stay a few more minutes and finish my drink, but have a good night. I'll see you in the office tomorrow."

Just when I was beginning to think we were finding middle ground and growing a little bit closer to understanding one another . . . poof, it was gone.

With those parting words, the warmth dissolved, the connection faded, and we were back at square one.

After taking Fitz for his final walk, I climbed into bed with my laptop and a steaming cup of Sleepytime chamomile tea. Earlier, at the pub with Jason, I'd gotten a notification from Spark! that I had a new message from Noah waiting in my inbox, but I wanted to wait until

I was on my own to open it. I cozied up beneath the soft comforter, enjoying the coolness of the fabric against my skin. Guiding the little white arrow over to the icon of an envelope, I double-clicked the email and it popped open on the screen.

Dear Remi,

To answer your question about hobbies, I'm an avid reader, often getting lost in the pages of novels that take me to far-off places or riveting nonfiction books, like memoirs and historicals. I'd love, though, to hear more about the book you are working on if you're willing to share or ever want to talk it out.

Music? Living in the Congo, I've really come to love the local music, especially a genre called soukous. Soukous is this fantastic and danceable style that mixes traditional African rhythms with bits of jazz. It's got these intricate guitar riffs, lively percussion, and lyrics in different African languages. It's just so catchy and full of life, I can't get enough of it! But aside from that, lately I've been into Esperanza Spalding. She weaves jazz with elements of soul and R&B. It's great stuff. Take a listen and let me know what you think?

I haven't watched *Bridgerton*, but based on your recommendation, it seems I'll have to add it to my list. My favorite ice cream flavor? You are going to have to let me get back to you on that one. Not a lot of options here in the jungle, so everything is sounding good to me right about now. But I wouldn't trade all the Ben & Jerry's in the world for the experiences I'm having and the people I've been able to help here.

Tell me more about your job? Senior editor for *The Sophisticate*? Color me impressed! I'm ashamed to admit that most of what I know about that world comes from too many viewings of *The Devil Wears Prada*. Although personally, I'm man enough to admit I prefer *Mamma Mia!* Meryl to her Miranda Priestly.

Connecting with someone like you has been a breath of fresh air. As you can only imagine, my dating life in the Congo, well, it's been akin to pursuing a rare bird—elusive and unpredictable, with fleeting glimpses that leave me wondering if I imagined it all. (Just a joke!)

Anyway, I suppose I can count myself lucky that our paths have crossed in this vast digital landscape, and who knows, perhaps this unusual encounter will yield more than just a few entertaining stories.

Looking forward to your response, Remi.

Warmly,
Noah

PS Give Fitz a belly rub from me.

A chill reverberated through my body. Noah was right—spot-on, in fact. A genuine connection *was* an elusive treasure. Since David's death, I hadn't experienced feelings anywhere close to the ones I was experiencing now reading his words on the screen. Well, maybe there *was* a small flash of it tonight with Jason, but even then, it only lasted for a few fleeting seconds before smoldering into ash.

I devoured Noah's email again, only this time I imagined his robust and assured voice narrating it to me from the other side of the globe, and for the first time since this correspondence began, I wondered what it might be like to actually sit across from him. Just two people on a *real* first date, laughing and playfully touching and really getting to know one another.

As if on cue, Fitz jumped onto David's unoccupied side of the bed, signaling it was time to call it. "Alright, buddy, just scoot over a bit. You hogged the covers all last night," I said, gently nudging his tubby flank.

I closed the laptop and set it down on my nightstand. Nestling into my pillow, I called out to Alexa, "Alexa, play Esperanza Spalding." As her voice scatted away to the low, bellowing notes of a heavy bass, the cool spring air fragrant with the scent of fresh blooms coaxed me into a faraway dream . . . as far away, perhaps, as the Congo.

Chapter
Twenty

The next day, Molly, Carrie, and I slipped out of work during lunch to make it to Molly's first wedding dress fitting. Stepping out of the elevator into the Saks bridal salon felt like entering another world adorned entirely in white chiffon, taffeta, and Chantilly lace.

I couldn't help but think back to when I went shopping for my own wedding gown—the bittersweet memory causing a phantom ache in the middle of my chest.

My mother had insisted we go to Kleinfeld, where she had bought her own dress almost thirty-five years earlier. She pushed me to try on what felt like dozens of different cuts and styles, but the minute I put on the satin A-line—the one that was fitted but not overly structured, with tiny silk-covered buttons running down the back—I knew I'd found "the one."

Mom had pushed for something more elaborate, more ornate, but its simplicity was what I'd fallen most in love with. David had embraced me for who I was—no "bling" or layers of tulle needed—and I wanted to honor the purity of that kind of love by remaining as authentically us as possible. And in spite of *alllllll* the well-meaning and overly abundant advice from our friends and family (especially from my mother) on how we should do this and that, we managed to block out most of it and keep the day simple, exactly how we'd wanted it.

At the sound of Molly's voice giving her last name to the receptionist, I snapped back to the waiting room at Saks. The petite young woman sporting a wickedly tight chignon coiled at the nape of her neck asked if we wanted anything to drink and then directed us to take a seat while we waited for Molly's consultant.

"I hope I still love the dress as much as I did when I first put it on. It feels like I picked it out ages ago now," Molly said as she nervously flipped through the pages of the most recent issue of *Bridal Guide* magazine.

A woman dressed in all black, her platinum hair slicked into a high ponytail, breezed past the reception desk and over to where we were sitting. "Molly, wonderful to see you. We're all ready for you in alterations." Her eyes swept over to me and Carrie. "Who do you have with you today?" she asked.

Molly set down the magazine and stood up to greet her with a double kiss. "Hey, Chloe, I'd like you to meet my work besties, not to mention two of my gorgeous bridesmaids, Remi and Carrie."

"Nice to meet you both," Chloe said, before turning to Molly. "Just wait until you see the gown. I'm so glad you opted for the blush color. It's even more spectacular in real life. And with your hair and skin tone—sublime."

"I hope so, 'cause the decision to go with the blush has been haunting me for months. I just keep worrying I'm going to look like one big cone of cotton candy," Molly admitted, a hint of uncertainty in her voice.

Chloe's reassurances that the dress bore no resemblance to a carnival confection offered some relief as we followed her to the dressing rooms. She pushed open a thick curtain to reveal Molly's rosy-hued antique Alençon lace gown hanging on a wall hook.

"Oh my God, Moll, it's stunning," I gushed through my fingers, now clasped over my mouth.

"What a showstopper," Carrie echoed.

"I know it's not as over-the-top as people might be expecting from me, but there was just something about it. The minute I saw it, I knew in my bones *that* was the dress I was meant to be wearing to marry Luca. Does that make any sense?"

"It makes perfect sense," I said. My eyes stung with the unshed tears I fought to hold back. I hadn't imagined this would be so vivid, so overwhelming, and the last thing I wanted to do was make this moment about me or take away even one ounce of the joy Molly should be feeling.

"Give us a few minutes and then we'll do the big reveal," Chloe said, motioning for Carrie and me to take a seat outside the changing room while she and Molly ducked inside.

I glanced around and caught sight of the petite receptionist shuffling quickly to her desk from a back room. "Excuse me, could I get a glass of water?" I interrupted her midshuffle.

She nodded wordlessly and made a quick U-turn toward the cooler.

As we settled into the plush white tufted love seat, "Tight Bun" handed me a tall glass of cucumber water and hurried away toward a ringing telephone before I could even say thank you.

I chugged it down in four gulps. Every last drop. And then panted as I fought to catch my breath.

Carrie placed her hand on my forearm and asked, "You doing okay?"

I nodded. "I won't lie. Happy as I am for Molly, being here, I feel a little like I'm suffocating. I just can't help but think about—"

"I know," Carrie said, her eyes crinkling around the edges.

"And the worst part is, I really thought I was beginning to move on. Remember that interesting guy I mentioned matching with on Spark! a couple weeks ago?"

Carrie's eyes widened. "Is something happening with him?"

"Sort of?" I shrugged.

"What does it mean for something to be 'sort of' happening? This guy hasn't asked you for money, has he? Girl, that isn't just a red flag; that's a neon blinking banner."

"It's nothing like that. He just isn't what I would call geographically desirable."

"Where does he live? New Jersey?" Carrie asked, looking horror-struck.

"Farther."

"Oh, girl, no." Her face filled with dread. "Florida?" The disgust in her voice was almost comical.

"Farther."

Her shoulders sagged and she frowned. "You're killing me. California?"

"Africa."

Now her eyes were the size of dinner plates. "Africa?! Oh, Remi, didn't we warn you about scam artists? I thought you were smarter than that!"

"God, no, it's not like that at all. Noah—his name is Noah—works for Doctors Without Borders and is stationed somewhere in the Congo."

"And you found him on a dating app? I . . . I don't understand." Carrie's inscrutable judgment caused my defensive hackles to perk up.

"I told you I updated my profile, and I don't know, we seem to have so much in common. He's worldly and interesting. Funny and obviously cares a lot about people."

"And is conveniently seven thousand miles away," Carrie snarked.

"What's that supposed to mean?"

"The first guy you've had a connection with since David died lives halfway around the world. Far enough that you don't really need to commit or run the risk of getting hurt."

"He's saving lives in a war-torn country. You don't think there's something noble in that? It's not like he's, I don't know, trying to revolutionize the world with some sort of high-tech lie detector test or something equally diabolical."

"What?! Who are you even talking about?" Carrie asked, clearly confused and staring at me like I'd lost my mind.

The heavy dressing room curtain swished open, and I lowered my voice. "Never mind, we can talk about this later." With deliberate force, I changed my expression to reflect overt excitement upon seeing Molly in her stunning blush gown.

"*Sooooo*, ladies? What do you think?" Molly said, doing a full turn in her spot.

"Breathtaking," Carrie offered first.

"Remi?" Molly asked.

I blinked rapidly, willing myself to regain composure, but the memories surged forward to intertwine with the present in a way that felt both overwhelming and comforting. It was as if time had momentarily folded in on itself, and I was enveloped by a powerful longing for what once was, while also painfully aware that life would move on whether or not I was ready.

"You look incredible," I managed, even though my mouth felt like it was full of dryer lint.

"It just needs to be brought in a little right here," the seamstress said, pinching the fabric underneath Molly's arm, "and taken up a bit here." She lifted the train to pin it in a few spots.

Chloe shook her head. "An almost perfect fit. That hardly ever happens."

"As long as I don't gain an ounce between now and June," Molly sighed as she continued to pose and admire her reflection in the large, lit mirror at the front of the room.

Carrie lifted her tote onto her shoulder. "We'll just have to curb the happy hour margaritas until then, I guess."

"And we can speed up our morning walks to a light jog," I added with a cheeky smile.

Molly turned to Chloe. "Didn't I tell you they were the best? Give me a few minutes to get out of the dress, and I'll meet you girls up front."

Carrie and I went back out to the reception area to wait for Molly. I picked up the issue of *Bridal Guide* she'd discarded earlier and slumped into a seat. Carrie came and sat down beside me and lowered the magazine from in front of my face with a gentle hand.

"Hey, sorry if I seemed harsh before. I'm sure this Noah's a great guy, but I'm obviously protective of you and would hate for you to fall into something, especially your *first* real something after David, where you are blinded to the possibility of him being less than genuine because you, um . . . hope it could be more."

"You think I'm being naive because of my grief? That I'm allowing him to manipulate me into liking him, and that he'll eventually take advantage of me? Steal all my savings? C'mon, Carrie, do you really think I'm that stupid? He hasn't asked me for a thing, not a cent! We've just been talking. But *whoever* he is, *wherever* he is, he sees me, he gets me. It's hard to explain, but his letters make me feel something again."

Carrie gave my knee a squeeze. "I would be a terrible friend if I wasn't looking out for you by telling you to be careful and by asking you to keep your eyes open. I would hate for you to get hurt. Especially because I know what a big step this is."

I broke away from Carrie as Molly came out from the dressing room area. She scheduled her next fitting with the receptionist, and then the three of us hurried out of Saks to jump into our Uber and make our way back downtown to the office. While Molly and Carrie chatted about floral arrangements, seating cards, and bridal makeup, I offered an occasional "uh-huh," while my thoughts swirled like an Oklahoma-size twister.

I felt a strange tug between my gut and my heart. Every correspondence with Noah so far felt authentic, and I never doubted the things he told me. I still didn't. Not once had my sirens sounded, alerting me to a red flag. But hearing Carrie's harsh analysis, I had to admit, she wasn't wrong. What did I really know about Noah?

I knew he was a doctor. I knew we shared an appreciation for jazz music. From his profile, I knew he was from New York, but I had no idea what part? I didn't know if he had siblings? Pets? Allergies? I guess, the uncomfortable truth was that the list of what I *didn't* know far exceeded what I did. But all this could be easily remedied with a phone call. A Zoom. A FaceTime to lay Carrie's concerns to rest. Simple visual confirmation that Noah was every bit as real as the emotions sparked between us. I would just have to put the request out there. Easy enough. Right?

As soon as we got back, I made up a few excuses about some work I needed to hurry off to, darted in the direction of my office, and closed the door behind me. Popping open my laptop, I minimized the dozen or so alerts that blinked across my screen, double-clicked into the Spark! inbox to open Noah's last message, hit the reply button, and started typing.

Hey, Noah,

Thank you for the Esperanza Spalding recommendation—her music is a vibe. Not the classic jazz I'm used to, but I'm a new fan for sure. Keep 'em coming.

My job at The Sophisticate isn't nearly as glamorous as The Devil Wears Prada, but there's a lot of creative energy and the occasional mad dash to meet deadlines. I certainly wouldn't stack my job up against being a doctor in a war-torn country, but I am proud of the content we've been putting out there these last few years. I like to think we are giving a voice to those who wouldn't have one otherwise.

These days, though, I do more editing than writing—which I do miss. I actually pulled the draft of my novel out from the depths of my hard drive the other day, brushed off the cobwebs, and started working on it again. I'm not sure if I still have the chops, but sort of like riding a bicycle, it did come back to me—even if I was a little wobbly at first.

So you're a *Mamma Mia!* Meryl fan too?! I appreciate both your taste and your confidence in admitting you know enough about the two to even have a favorite! lol

Okay, now for something that my friends would probably call a bit bold for me (or maybe I should say, completely out of character). You see, we've been chatting, sharing stories, and building connections through these emails, and it's been truly lovely. So what if we took this connection a step further? How about a virtual meet-up? A video call, perhaps? Considering the distance and all, I can't help feeling curious and excited about the prospect of finally really meeting the man behind these heartfelt words.

Looking forward to our continued conversation, Noah. I hope you are too.

Wishing you a fantastic day ahead.

Warmly,
Remi

PS Fitz got his belly rub and sends his regards.

Chapter
Twenty-One

After desperately trying to squeeze my way back onto Celeste Romero's impossibly packed calendar, I was spiraling into full-blown panic mode. I hadn't breathed a word to Daphne or anyone else on the team about how disastrously our first meeting had gone. Naively, I was banking on reviving the situation before anyone caught wind of it. But with nothing to show for my efforts except a string of excuses and empty assurances from her staff that they'd "pass along" yet another message, my optimism was wearing dangerously thin.

But today, I had to shove all that stress aside and focus on one thing: giving my nephews the fun, magazine-free weekend I'd promised them. No work, no frantic emails—just a day out in the city with a highly anticipated stop at the Sloomoo Institute, a twelve-thousand-square-foot slime-centric wonderland.

I'd bought the tickets for the kids as one of their holiday presents, and having *Funny Girl* with Mom and Jess scheduled for tomorrow, we decided to cram it all into one action-packed weekend. I'd take the boys overnight, allowing my brother and Jess to enjoy a kid-free jaunt in the city, and we'd reconvene the next day so Reid would take the boys to a Yankees game while the gals would head to the theater for the show.

I could hear Daniel's and Nathan's voices booming down the hallway toward my apartment before Tony even had the chance to let me know my brother was on his way upstairs with the kids. Fitz also clearly heard them barreling down the corridor because he leaped to his feet and bounded toward the entranceway, scratching his paws against the front door and barking like a maniac until I cracked it open.

"Okay, boy, I know you're excited," I said, holding him back by the collar. Fitz had a habit of greeting all visitors with an excited leap at their kneecaps. I managed to hold him down long enough to let the boys charge in, right past us, to land in a heap on my couch.

"Wow, for the first time in her life, Mom didn't exaggerate, that dog has gotten . . . um . . . voluptuous," Reid scoffed as he made a dramatic show of scooching past Fitz's tubby frame.

I shot him a dirty look. "Rude." I bent down and ruffled Fitz's fluffy ears and fat head. "Don't listen to him, handsome. We don't need that kind of negativity in our lives, isn't that right?"

"No, seriously, what are you feeding him? Other dogs?!"

"Shut up. He's an emotional eater, and we're working on it." The sound of a crash from the living room made my head snap up. Reid didn't even notice it. "Careful there, boys," I called to them. "If we have to head to the ER, it'll really put a damper on our slime time."

Reid passed me two book bags—one Mario, one Luigi—stuffed to the brim. "They each have two changes of clothes, you know, just in case. Pajamas. Their stuffies and blankies. And don't forget, Nathan's been having that dairy issue. Best for everyone if you just . . . avoid it at all costs." His facial expression told me everything I needed to know.

"Fair enough. Pizza eliminated as a dinner menu option. Got it."

"Oh, here," he said, passing me a shopping bag. "Snacks and a few juice boxes, although Jess really prefers them to drink water. Their thermoses are full, but the juice can be a good bargaining tool if you get desperate—anything with sugar, really. However, be warned . . . *that* is a double-edged sword."

"You know we still have supermarkets here on the Upper East Side. Or did you forget after you defected to New Jersey?" I teased.

"Try going into a grocery store, any store really, with two kids under the age of six. Trust me, you'll be thanking me for the animal crackers and granola bars later."

I sighed. "Anything else I need to know?"

"Oh, yeah, I guess just one thing. Don't bother fighting the battle for the covers with Nathan when he inevitably crawls in your bed around three a.m. You won't win."

"Noted."

He pulled me in for a hug. "Thanks, Rem, Jess and I really appreciate this."

"*I* really appreciate this. Getting to spend time with my two favorite monkeys. Hey monkeys," I called into the living room, "who's ready for a slimetastic adventure?"

Daniel and Nathan came running toward the kitchen at full speed with Fitz at their heels. I waved my brother off. "Go, I've got this. Have a great time. We'll see you in the morning."

We'd only been at the Sloomoo Institute for about a half hour, and I was already exhausted from chasing Daniel and Nathan around the place. They'd settle in at one exhibit, then spot something "even cooler" across the room and tear off in a whirlwind of giggles and "goo" to the next one like mini tornadoes, their attention spans shorter than a lightning flash. Their enthusiasm was infectious, even if it meant I was going to have a marathon day trying to wrangle them around the city. I was amazed at how much energy you needed to keep up with a six- and four-year-old.

Though the experience was clearly designed for children, I couldn't help but swim in the abundance of sounds and colors emanating from each room, almost as if I'd stepped into a kaleidoscope. For as chaotic as it seemed, with children of all ages and sizes zipping around the space, loud voices calling to one another and laughter bouncing off the walls, the entire scene was like joy personified. Daniel and Nathan wore smiles from ear to ear, their little hands smushing and squishing everything they could get a hold of.

I'd just kneeled down to take the boys' socks and shoes off so we could cross Lake Sloomoo, otherwise known as a huge pool where you could trod through 350 gallons of gooey gook, when I heard it—the unmistakable sound of Jason's voice.

I glanced around, and sure enough, there he was, looking painfully uncomfortable as he tried to wrangle his brood away from the slime slingshot over to the DIY slime bar, his son, Aidan, kicking and screaming in defiance.

Okay, so maybe *that* didn't look so much like joy personified.

I watched as Jason gently tugged his son a little closer, stooping low to reason with him. Aidan looked unimpressed with his father's plea while Jason showed him his wristwatch and pointed to the next room, clearly trying to keep his clan to whatever tight schedule he'd created for the day. I wasn't even sure a kid that young could tell time yet.

Clearly, Jason was making little progress in reasoning with Aidan, having just *too* much fun slinging slime at his sister, who had a clump of goo gobbed into her curls. Finally, when Jason realized this was a fight he wasn't going to win, he grabbed a handful of wet wipes from the wall dispenser and slumped down on the bench beside the exhibit, doing his best to clean himself off.

"Aunt *Remiiiiiii*!!! C'mon, c'mon," Daniel cried from ahead of me in the pool. "Hey, Nate, look over there, there's a slime slingshot! *Pllllleeeeaaasse*, Aunt Remi? Can we go try it?"

"Sure, just hold on one sec while I grab your—"

Too late. Daniel and Nathan were already out of the tub and zooming off to the slingshot, leaving a trail of sticky footprints in their wake like snails (but obviously much faster!).

"Shoes," I muttered under my breath, heaved myself out of the vat, de-gooed my feet, and hurried to catch up to them.

Daniel, with his little brother in tow, charged over to the front of the line and waited impatiently for Aidan to step aside so they could get their turn. When Aidan showed no signs of giving even an inch, with a forceful surge, Daniel crashed into him like a battering ram. Aidan's eyes widened in surprise as he was caught off guard by the unexpected impact and he went soaring sideways, nearly tumbling off his feet.

"Daniel!" I cried from across the room, quickening my steps to get to him as I watched Aidan turn around and give Daniel a shove of his own. Nathan had very smartly backed out of the combat radius, his blankie still tucked in the crook of his arm.

Oh Lord.

Jason stood up from the bench. "Remi? Is that you?"

I didn't have a moment to stop to say hello, I needed to reach the boys before a bite-size brawl broke out. I fought my way through a sea of kids and past Jason's bench until I was practically straddling the two boys now on the ground. I grabbed Daniel by the shirt collar and said, "Daniel Gregory Russell, you are in big trouble, mister."

Jason sidled up next to me. "Is everyone okay?"

"Daniel!" I gasped, a bit breathless from my Olympic-style power walk, "what do you have to say for yourself?"

"Sorry, Aunt Remi," he mumbled.

"Not to me, to him," I said, pointing to Aidan.

Daniel stood up, brushed his knees clean, and offered Aidan a hand off the ground. "I'm very sorry I knocked you down."

"It's okay." Aidan shrugged. "Want to shoot my sister with the slingshot?"

Daniel looked up at me and then over to Aidan's sister before responding with a resounding, "Oh yeah!" With that, the two boys scurried back to the front of the line, Nathan hurrying to catch up.

"It must be sensory overload or something? Or it could have been the big doughnut I let him have for breakfast? Guess I should have heeded my brother's warning about the oh-so-chaotic effects of too much sugar. Anyway, I really am sorry. I swear, Daniel doesn't normally act like that."

Jason waved a dismissive hand. "Don't even give it another thought. Aidan was hogging the slingshot. I told him it was time to move on to the next exhibit, but he didn't want to yet."

I couldn't help but laugh. "I know. I heard your voice from *waaaayyyy* over there," I said, pointing to Lake Sloomoo. "I had to do a triple take. Jason Ashbloome at a slime museum? Did you lose a bet or something?" I joked.

He chuckled and though wildly out of his element, seemed less buttoned up and stiff than at work. I was relieved to notice the tension between us after the MAUDE lie detector demonstration the other night had eased a bit.

"Morgan usually takes the weekends off, which leaves me with *lots* of hours to fill with these two."

"It's great that you don't just plop them inside on a couch all day with their iPad and headphones—that you actually spend time with them."

"Huh, I guess I never really thought of it that way," he said, and it was obvious that the idea of not spending his free time with his kids had never even occurred to him. "So what did you do to draw the short straw this weekend to end up . . . *here*?"

I chuckled. "Actually, it was my idea. I bought the kids tickets for Chrismukkah—trying to gift experiences not things, which is tough when they have a list a mile and a half long of toys they have to have. So when Veronica in the ads department told me she brought her kids here, I knew my nephews would love it."

"Emily—my late wife—was Jewish. But when asked, she liked to say she was Jew-*ish*, since she didn't really practice, and we celebrated more of a mishmash of holidays rather than anything particularly religious." The joke seemed to illuminate him from the inside, and he somehow became a bit more alive after reliving the memory.

"Jew-*ish*," I laughed. "I like that. Not gonna lie, after sending me to Hebrew school three days a week from elementary through high school, Mom would have a heart attack if I described myself as Jew-*ish* . . . Not a bad thing to keep in my back pocket, though . . . ," I joked. "David was an atheist, actually. Which my mother, of course, refused to acknowledge as an actual belief system. I'm convinced she saw it as her own personal challenge to convert him."

"Yeah? And how'd that go?"

"If her legendary matzo ball soup couldn't do it, I'm not sure anything could have."

"She sounds like quite a force, your mother. I'm sure even more so when her gout isn't acting up," he offered with a cheeky smile.

Remembering my awkward lie from Smorgasburg, I quickly changed topics. "So wait, how did *you* end up at Sloomoo?"

"I'd planned on taking Aidan and Georgia to the American Museum of Natural History, but Aidan flat-out told me he refused to look at another dusty dinosaur bone, so instead of inciting a coup, I remembered you'd mentioned it . . ."

"You didn't want to just ask MAUDE for a suggestion?" I teased.

"Yeah, I could've, I suppose, but she's been a bit buggy lately. A glitch we never saw at *Forbes*, probably because over there it was more rote data and algorithms as opposed to longhand form narrative."

"In English, please?"

"Basically, there's a hiccup where some of the content the AI generates is almost re-created from its previous output."

"'Re-created from its previous output'? Like it's plagiarizing itself? Well shit, that's a real problem at a magazine like ours, don't you think?"

"We're actively working to fix it. Since we're still in beta testing and haven't opened MAUDE up to the full staff at *The Sophisticate*, I'm confident we'll get the issue solved before we go live."

My inner Slytherin wanted to taunt him with the fact that it didn't bode well for MAUDE's future at our magazine if his precious baby was already glitching, but at the same time, I was still not any closer to mending ties with Celeste, so I figured the outright smack talk should probably wait until I found my way back into her good graces. I puffed out my chest with as much false confidence as I could muster and said, "Who knows, maybe I'll crush you in the bet and then we'll be sending MAUDE packing before any of it even matters?"

"I hate to be the bearer of bad news, but I think MAUDE, well, AI in general, is here to stay. You might want to try to embrace the modern age a bit more," he said, crooking an eyebrow in my direction.

"Nah, I'm okay to stay in the dark ages if it means that actual people write the human-interest pieces. You know what? Maybe I'll stick to the nineties as my decade of choice. The best music, fierce fashion, and the shining era of reality TV. I mean, *The Real World*? Does it get any better?"

He nodded in agreement. "I was actually, well still am, a huge Nirvana fan."

My mouth practically fell open. Buttoned-up Jason Ashbloome rocking out to grunge music was about as far-fetched as AOL Instant Messenger making a comeback (though I really wished it would). "You? A Nirvana fan? Would not have thunk it."

"There's a lot about me that might surprise you," he said in a tone that, had I not known better, sounded a bit flirty. "So this place is *messier* than I imagined. Maybe I should've stuck to the history museum after all. Or MoMA?"

I barked out a laugh. Now *that* comment was 100 percent predictable out of the Jason I'd come to know, leaving me to believe that though he might like a good jam sesh to "Smells Like Teen Spirit," deep down in his core, he was as straitlaced as they came.

"Well, seems a bit late to shift gears now, but next time you go to the natural history museum, I highly recommend starting with the giant blue whale on the first floor instead of the dinosaurs. Kids love it."

"Hmm . . . We always start with the dinosaurs right when the museum opens to avoid the crowds who usually begin at the bottom floor and work their way up. So we rarely ever make it past the second floor before our scheduled lunchtime."

Just then, a staff member with an overly enthusiastic voice came over the museum's intercom to announce that the next surge at Sloomoo Falls would be happening in five minutes and that they were looking for volunteers ready and willing to be slimed.

Aidan, Daniel, Nathan, and Georgia (now all seemingly the best of friends) came running over to us.

"*Pleeeeaaaaaaaaaaaaaaseeeee*, Dad, can we go to Sloomoo Falls?!" Aidan begged his father.

"Aunt Mimi, please, please, please! This is all I've ever wanted!" Nathan exclaimed with an enthusiasm I hadn't seen from him yet.

He'd been excited, sure, but he was practically bouncing out of his skin at the idea of getting slimed. And how could I say no to that face?! Wasn't that what being the fun aunt was all about? Just as I was getting ready to deliver my sweetest sweet pea the best news of his little life, Jason came in like a wrecking ball, demoing the idea in three seconds flat.

"I don't think we have time for that today," he told Aidan and his older sister.

"You always say that!" Georgia stamped her pink glittery Crocs into the ground.

Almost as if on cue, the alarm on Jason's phone chimed, and as it did, his eyes locked with mine.

"How 'bout it, Dave Grohl? Ready to let your hair down for a minute?" I taunted.

"Don't you think me being in a slime museum *is* letting my hair down?!" he exclaimed in mock exasperation (or maybe *not-so-mock* exasperation). However, the wide smile across his face told me he was actually considering it.

To the unrelenting echoes of whiny *pleeeeeeeases* from the peanut gallery and a bit more tugging on Jason's pant legs, he looked at me, the smirk warming his face. "Alright, what the hell . . ."

"YAYYY!" the kids shrieked enthusiastically and shot off in the direction of the surging Slime River toward Sloomoo Falls with Jason and me not too far behind.

Chapter
Twenty-Two

"Kids' ponchos on the right, adult ponchos on the left," a lively Sloomoo employee said, directing the line of visitors all waiting for the chance to have a vat of neon-green slime dumped on top of their heads. For as enthusiastic as the young girl was, her routine was clearly scripted and well rehearsed. "Welcome to Sloomoo Falls," she called, and her voice resounded throughout the colorful and eccentrically decorated hallways.

Jason glanced back over his shoulder at me, his eyes pleading for us to hit reverse and head back in the direction of safer, less intensely gooey ground. Thankfully, I had a feeling he'd try to wiggle his way out, so I had him take the lead and cleverly positioned myself at the rear, keeping our troop moving toward the exhibit. We all shuffled into the line where we were corralled with other eager, wide-eyed children, and many parents who seemed as apprehensive as their kids were excited.

The bubbly member of the Sloomoo Crew continued her spiel: "We highly recommend removing all valuables and stashing them safely before your junk gets gunked. Please leave all phones, wallets, keys, watches, and other items in one of our free lockers over there."

"I can't believe I let you talk me into this," Jason muttered as he emptied the contents of his pockets into the tiny bin. He slipped off his wristwatch, stuffed it into his jacket, and tucked his shirt deeper into his pants and then his pants into his thick white athletic socks.

I chuckled as I watched him. "Come on, Jason, where's your sense of adventure? It's all in the name of fun!" With a wink, I deposited my own jacket in a locker and patted his shoulder reassuringly.

Moments later, the four poncho'd kids came up to us complete with goggles, hair caps, and plastic gloves.

"Hold on, I have to grab a pic of this to send to your parents." I snapped a quick photo of Daniel and Nathan grinning from ear to ear, sent it off to Reid and Jess, and set my phone back in the locker.

Georgia tugged on Jason's arm. "*Daaaad*, where's your poncho?"

"We're ready for the first group," the Sloomoo employee announced to the line of people.

I passed a plastic tarp to Jason, who grumbled under his breath as he wrestled with the protective gear. His face turned a shade of crimson as he tried to get the poncho on properly, while the kids giggled at his expense.

A member of the Sloomoo Crew directed our brood where to stand. "Now, I need everyone to line up across the floor tape. Once Sloomoo Falls gets going, you'll want to stay in the designated area to avoid any . . . mishaps."

Jason wriggled his neck through the head hole of his poncho like a bullfrog peeping over the waterline. "What'd she say? Mishaps?"

I burst out laughing. Between the pants tucked into his socks, his bulging eyeballs, and his breathlessness, I wasn't sure which was making me giggle harder. "Well, Jason Ashbloome, don't *you* look like the life of the party!" I managed in between gasps of air.

Whether it was bungee jumping over the Urubamba River, swimming with sharks in Kauai, or climbing to the summit of Mount Whitney, David had always been the one challenging me to step outside *my* comfort zone. It was strange but also new and exciting to be the one now in the driver's seat, encouraging Jason to expand his horizons. It brought out a different side of my personality, and I was surprised by how much I liked being the cheerleader for once.

"Hardy-har-har," he scoffed, still wrestling with the circus tent–size tarp. But as he finally settled into the poncho, a smile warmed his already flushed face. "I'm just letting you know, had anyone else challenged me into this, I would've probably walked away."

His comment caught me off guard, and I wasn't sure if I should be flattered . . . or what exactly he meant by it.

"Yeah, I just . . . I'm not sure I can name too many people who could get me to do something like this . . . Emily used to, but it's been a while." He looked down and, with a smirk, gestured to his ridiculous outfit. A beat of silence fell between us before he clarified, "I, um . . . mean it as a good thing. A very good thing."

"Oh," I said, rolling his compliment around in my mind. A warmth started to spread up my neck and settled in the apples of my cheeks.

But before I could give it any more consideration, another member of the Sloomoo Crew clapped her hands together, jarring me from my thoughts. "Okay, folks, ready for the slime experience of a lifetime?"

"No," Jason deadpanned while the rest of the line screamed out the word *yes* as loud as they could.

The crew gathered together in a huddle and started their countdown to the main event. "Ten, nine, eight, seven, six, SLIME!!!" Before making it to the *one*, the entire Sloomoo Crew, catching everyone off guard, pulled a comically large silver lever to release the tub of goo from above.

"What happened to f—" Jason barely managed to squeak out the word *five* before thick, syrupy slime rained down on us like a sticky neon tide. I glanced down the line to check on the kids and was met with three grins, each one bigger than the next—and Nathan, rolling around on the ground making a slime angel in the puddles. The poncho'd children and adults squealed and shrieked, equal measures of delight and horror, as the neon-green slop splattered all over the walls and floor in big wet blobs.

Then, to my absolute, complete, and total shock, the person with the biggest smile of all . . . was Jason. As globs of gooey sludge ran down his goggles and poncho, even breaking through his pant/sock barrier, he showcased a level of unabashed joy.

And after the smiling came the laughing. A laughter filled with abandon, as if all the stress and worries Jason typically carried with him had dissolved into the glistening mess that now surrounded him. He was covered head to toe in slime, and there wasn't a damn thing he could do about it. The sticky substance clung to every part of him (even his eyebrows), but he didn't care, appearing to have surrendered to the absurdity of the situation and finally just let go.

"You know"—I stepped closer to him, and with the pads of my slime-coated fingertips stroked away a glob that had fallen from his goggles and onto his cheek—"I think green might be your color." It had been meant as a joke, but my voice came out less playful than I'd intended. Instead, it was sultry and dangerously flirtatious.

Perhaps I was so caught up in the moment and seeing that new side of him, it compelled me to act. The sensation pulsing between us felt wholly familiar, reminiscent of the Zoom library fantasy but yet entirely new . . . because it wasn't a spicy daydream, it was veritable—and it scared and surprised the ever-loving hell out of me.

I glanced to my right. Nathan, apparently now finished making his slime angels, did his best to pull himself up off the ground as his little feet kept slipping on the slime-coated floor. Daniel reached down a hand to help his little brother. He failed his first attempt, then, overcompensating with a mighty heave, he yanked Nathan off the floor and straight into Georgia, who *also* lost her balance, causing a domino effect to quickly tornado its way down the line.

Jason, seeing the wave of people toppling in our direction, jutted his body out in front of mine to take the brunt of the momentum. But it was too late. The man who'd been standing to the right of Jason slipped right past him and into my rib cage, causing me to lose my breath and footing as I took all three of us down like a pile of bricks.

Slime splatter and flailing limbs bounced around the space as if in slow motion, and out of the corner of my vision I could see the whites of the eyes of the entire Sloomoo Crew, horror-filled mouths in rounded O's and palms pressed to their cheeks à la Kevin McCallister in *Home Alone*.

Now sprawled on the floor, Jason flopped his head over to look at me and deadpanned, "I think *this* is what the slime lady meant when she warned us about 'mishaps.'"

And that was it. I completely lost it. A burst of laughter erupted from deep within me, out from where it had been buried so deeply I wasn't sure I'd ever hear a sound like that out of me again. And I couldn't stop. His response. The irony of the two of us writhing in stitches of laughter—together—in this disgusting muck was almost too much to bear, let alone believe. And the sheer absurdity paired with the complete uniqueness of our shared moment felt somehow . . . magical.

Nathan came charging toward us, ripping off his poncho as he sludged through the mess the Sloomoo Crew was just starting to mop up.

"Aunt Mimi, I'm *staaaaaaaaarrrrviiing*," he whined, seemingly unfazed by the fact Jason and I were still lying flat on the ground.

Seconds later Georgia came up behind Nathan and echoed, "I'm hungry. Can we go eat lunch?"

Jason, now on all fours, struggled to stand as his shoes slipped out from under him with every attempt. Each movement caused another shift of his balance, and each time he lifted a hand or a foot, another part of him seemed to drift the other way. He looked like Bambi on a fresh sheet of ice.

"Just give your ol' dad a minute to get off the floor, okay?" he moaned.

Struggling in my own right, I wasn't even able to offer him any help. The two of us, still fighting against gravity and our own fits of giggles, just couldn't seem to rise from the ground. I wondered how long it would take for a Sloomoo Crew member to come by to try to mop us up too. Daniel elbowed past his little brother and Georgia to extend a hand to both me and Jason.

"Appreciate it, bud, but I actually think I got this," Jason said (not so convincingly) and then proceeded in one final attempt to use all his strength to push himself off the tiles to a standing position. After he was stable, legs set wide and arms braced for another spill, he reached down, so I could get a solid grip of him.

He looked at me and locked his hand around my forearm. It reminded me of some kind of action movie where the hero grabs for the heroine, heaving her dangling body up off the cliffside of a mountain or back into a high-flyin' chopper like in *True Lies* with Arnold Schwarzenegger. But instead, it was Jason, a very buttoned-up, pretty un-Arnold-like dude, hero-style rescuing me from a *waaay* less cool slime tsunami.

"C'mon, Russell, I got you," he affirmed, and though his posture and balance didn't seem to convey the same confidence, I knew he did in fact have me and that he wouldn't let me fall.

His muscles tightened under my fingertips, the crinkling of the plastic like white noise drowning out the rest of the room. But the feel of his body underneath the thin poncho and material of his shirt caught me by surprise, and my eyes snapped up to look at him. He was holding my waist, and with his gaze now on mine, I was acutely aware of how protective his hands felt around me and how hard my heart was beating in my chest.

Jason parted his lips to speak, my attention shifting to his mouth, when Nathan, without an ounce of awareness, wiggled in between the two of us, bending over to a ninety-degree angle to box out Jason with his little tush. "Aunt Mimi, I *waaaaannnttt cwackuhhhhs*!!!"

I glanced at Jason, who looked perplexed, and smiled, our moment broken. "Crackers . . . he's still working on his *r*'s." I ruffled Nathan's hair and took him by the hand. "You're right, bud, I want some food too. Let's get out of here and grab some lunch." I turned to Jason. "What do you say? You and the kids want to join us?"

His face brightened as he nodded. "I think we'd all love that, actually."

After gingerly treading our way out of the Sloomoo Falls exhibition toward the exit, we regrouped in the gift shop where the kids immediately took off in different directions to explore. It was a sensory wonderland, with shelves full of glittering slime containers, rubbery toys, and a stack of neon-colored T-shirts that declared proudly I SURVIVED SLOOMOO FALLS.

"Oh, I think you *definitely* need one of these," I said, flipping through the pile to find his size.

He yanked the top one off the stack and handed it to me. "I will if you will."

He tucked the T-shirt under his arm and said, "So I know this great pizza place right around the corner. We could grab a few slices and take them to the park?"

I hesitated for a moment. "Um . . . we—and by 'we,' I mean Nathan—need to steer clear of cheese and all dairy-related fun. I've been given fair and repeated warning by my brother that that is an issue we *don't* want to mess with."

"Gotcha. Say no more. You know, Chinatown isn't too far from here. What do you say to some dim sum? I know a great place just enough off the beaten path. I don't think we should have any trouble getting a table. Sometimes I forget how many options we have at our fingertips. A few city blocks, and you can be immersed in an entirely different culture."

"You know what? Dim sum sounds absolutely perfect."

And it did.

Chapter
Twenty-Three

The fresh air was a welcome change after being in the slime museum for the past few hours. Compared to the morning's chaos, the packed streets of Chinatown seemed quiet and peaceful. With wide eyes, the kids gawked at the buckets of fish and other foreign sea creatures poking out from the ice chests that lined the streets as we followed Jason to his restaurant of choice.

The sights and smells of Chinatown were unlike anywhere else in the city, and I didn't realize how hungry I was until we arrived at a cozy dim sum spot known for its delicious, bite-size offerings. A server approached us, took our drink orders, and then handed each person a small index card with Chinese writing on it.

Rickety carts displaying all sorts of assorted prepared dishes ushered by the table like a cruise ship Baked Alaska line. The kids were dazzled by the interactive dining experience, eagerly presenting their index cards to the passing servers after choosing plates of thick saucy noodles and pillowy steamed barbecue pork buns, collecting a bright-red star beside each item selected. After our cards and bellies were filled to the brim, the kids watched a show on my phone, giving Jason and me a much-needed minute to digest.

"If I eat one more spring roll, I think I'll burst." Jason moaned while rubbing his stomach. But then, as if he hadn't just literally been bellyaching, his eyes flashed to the server wheeling around the cart of spring rolls and he threw his card in the air to wave him down.

"Didn't you just say . . . ?"

He grinned like a little kid whose hand got caught in the cookie jar. "I know, but they are *sooo* good. And I haven't eaten dim sum in years!"

I took a sip of tea from my small white cup, its heat warming my fingers through the thick porcelain. "You know, you're not at all who I thought you were."

The server with the cart made his way to our table, and Jason took two more plates of spring rolls. "What do you mean?"

"You give off a very different persona at the office. Rigid, straitlaced . . . dare I say, even a bit intimidating?"

Jason raised an eyebrow, clearly intrigued. "Intimidating?"

I couldn't help but smile. "It's been nice. Getting to know you better."

His eyes locked with mine, a genuine warmth illuminating his face, and I found my own cheeks flushed with heat. I shifted my gaze back to my tea and topped it off with some hot water before setting the steaming pot out of reach of the children, who were now fully engrossed in an episode of *Wild Kratts*.

"So," he started after swallowing another bite of spring roll, "you never told me about how your sit-down with Celeste went."

"Actually, it didn't go—"

Just then, another server parked a cart full of freshly made mango pudding, sesame balls filled with sweet red bean paste, sugarcoated doughnuts, and thick pineapple tarts next to our table. Jason proceeded to pass orders all around, the kids turning their attention from the phone to eagerly jut out their cards to get stamped.

"Sorry, what were you saying?" he asked as he slid a sesame ball onto his small plate.

"Just that my preinterview with Celeste . . . it was a total and complete disaster."

"What? You've been prepping like crazy for that interview. Are you sure you didn't simply misread the situation?"

I was sure.

I ran my fingers through my hair and swallowed. "I never told you what happened . . . how David died."

Jason looked confused by the turn of conversation, but his chewing allowed me to keep going without interruption.

I glanced over to make sure the kids were still engaged with the show and not paying attention before lowering my voice to continue. "He was a war correspondent covering Ukraine and was killed in one of the retaliatory strikes that came after the US sanctioned those air assaults on Russian military camps. And I know war claims the lives of innocent people every day. And, while the logical side of my brain understands that when Celeste Romero championed a tougher stance by the US, she couldn't have foreseen David's fate, the other side rages with hatred for her and for what she did. And then, there's my heart . . ." I could feel the ever-present lump rising higher in my throat, threatening to squeeze it shut altogether. I took a sip of water to try to force it back down. "I should have passed the interview to Carrie. Maybe it was selfish of me to have attempted to take it on."

Instead of placating me, telling me it wasn't selfish and that I was entirely justified to want to write the piece myself, he nodded and asked simply, "Then why didn't you?"

His pointed question made me stop for a moment. Why *hadn't* I turned the interview over? Was I looking to prove myself to Daphne? To Jason? To MAUDE even? Or was I looking to somehow stick it to Celeste? Find some peace by eviscerating her in print? Or did I just want to write David's story and give him a voice now that his had been extinguished?

"I guess I thought I was ready to finally confront her about David. I wanted to show her the face of a real live person who was directly affected by a decision she made. I wanted to grill her with hard-hitting questions that unveiled her true cruel nature to the world. But I was still so angry. Too angry. Too emotional. And after waiting years for my chance to face off with her, I folded like an ironing board."

And worst of all, Celeste Romero still had no idea who I *really* was. When David and I got married, I chose not to change my last name to his. I'd been working and publishing as Remi Russell for years, and David fully supported my decision. Of course, close family and friends knew my husband was David Gatlin, war correspondent, but newer acquaintances had no idea. David was a reputable and respected journalist, but he wasn't Anderson Cooper or Richard Engel famous, and I was glad.

Once the fervor surrounding his death subsided, I slipped back into relative anonymity and spared myself sympathetic gazes and consolatory words. I could go on just being Remi Russell. Celeste Romero didn't have the first clue she'd agreed to do an interview with David Gatlin's widow.

With thoughts and questions racing around my mind, I breathed out a heavy sigh, shrugged, and finished. "I guess I wanted the opportunity to look Celeste in the eye and tell her how her one decision, one brief second of her day, a choice she probably doesn't lose a wink of sleep over at night, changed the course of my entire life. By delivering an interview that pressed her in a way that hadn't been done before, I had hoped she'd reveal something I could use to take her down, or at least shame her publicly. David's death changed me. I'm not the same person I used to be. I never used to be this bitter or vindictive. But when I heard about the chance to cover that interview . . . I don't know . . . I thought it'd be a way to even the scales of justice a bit."

I closed my eyes and shook my head dismissively. "I'm probably not even explaining it well. I'm sure you don't understand."

"You think I don't understand? Since Emily's passing, I've been haunted by the fear I'd screw them up." Jason gestured toward Aidan and Georgia at the far end of the table. "I've reached a point where I hardly recognize myself as their father anymore. I've become more like a drill sergeant, constantly barking marching orders to maintain some semblance of stability, shuffling them from one place to another, one moment to the next. Sure, part of it is about managing the chaos, and yes, it's about protecting them. But the brutal truth is that the moment I stop moving, the moment I lower my guard, I'm paralyzed by the thought of facing their grief and my own." Tears pooled in Jason's eyes. It was the first time I'd seen him so vulnerable. He swiped them away and said, "You know, you're lucky, Remi."

His comment caught me off guard. "Yeah, how do you figure that?"

"You can sit down with Celeste. You can look her in the eye and ask her anything you want. Do you know what a gift that is? Do you know how desperately I want to go ten rounds in a ring with cancer? That I'd love to sit across from Emily's goddamn tumor and tell it off for all the things it stole from me. What it robbed from them. Their mother *and* their father."

Without even thinking, I reached my hand out across the table and placed it over his. "Don't sell yourself short. You're a good father, Jason. A great one."

He covered mine with his own. "Don't *you* sell *yourself* short. You're a good journalist. A great one."

Just then, Nathan sprang up from his chair and came around the table to me. Tugging on the tail of my shirt, he asked, "Mimi, can we leave now? I'm all done."

I slid my hand out from Jason's to pull Nathan onto my lap. "Don't you want to hear your fortune first?" I said, taking one of the wrapped cookies piled high on top of the check. Too young to read the message himself, he watched wide-eyed as I unfolded the paper and read it aloud, "The first step toward a brighter future is the bravest one."

Jason nodded in agreement, and we shared a silent, knowing glance.

Seemingly unimpressed by the cookie's message, Nathan pushed up from the table and whispered in my ear. "Mimi, can we go *nooooowwww?*"

I reached into my bag to fish around for my wallet, but before I could find it, Jason had already handed the bill along with his credit card to a passing server.

"You didn't have to—"

He glanced over at the kids, their bellies full and eyes glazed over from the food and too much fun at the slime museum. "They seem ready to get outta here. And don't worry about it."

I set Nathan down and slipped my coat off the back of the chair. "Today was . . . eye-opening. Thank you."

"For me too," he said.

The boys and I said goodbye to Jason and his kids and jumped into a cab to head back to my apartment for a little bit of rest. Daniel and Nathan were troupers but clearly on the verge of melting down if they didn't get a break, and I couldn't say I was too far behind.

Bounding toward us when we entered the apartment, Fitz licked Nathan's face, who happened to be the closest to eye level. Daniel chased behind them both, and before I knew it, they were playing with the dog on the floor, rolling around on the plush gray carpet.

David and I always talked about having kids. When our careers settled down . . . When he returned from his latest assignment . . . When my book was finished . . . But for as many times as we pushed it off, it'd always been something we ultimately wanted. Spending time with the boys and Jason's kids too had reminded me that though having a family had been part of *our* plan, that didn't mean it still couldn't be a part of mine, someday.

I tossed a few pillows and blankets on the ground and helped them set up a makeshift bed and turned on, by request, the *Sonic the Hedgehog* movie, hoping that once their heads hit the pillows they'd take a good afternoon siesta.

I grabbed my laptop and slumped down on David's leather chair behind them, tucking my feet underneath me and spreading a blanket over my lap before popping open the screen. Daniel curled around Fitz, who was already snoring loudly. But grabbing his stuffie, Nathan climbed onto my lap, squeezing himself between my hip and the smooth leather arm of the chair, and snuggled in. I pulled the blanket up over us both, and he allowed his heavy eyelids to finally close.

With my laptop strategically positioned on the other armrest and the resonating words of my fortune cookie urging me to take courageous steps toward a brighter future, I decided to check my Spark! account to see if Noah had responded to my latest email. I'd been avoiding it after my somewhat bold request for a virtual meetup, not knowing if it was too soon for that sort of thing or if my ask would scare him off altogether. Or worse yet—what if he said yes?

When the site flashed open, a bold number one was illuminated over the dancing envelope icon, indicating a new message waiting to be read.

Dear Remi,

Currently, I find myself at a local village pub in a small town nearby. I'm savoring an ice-cold Peroni on draft, a small luxury that reminds me of the little things worth cherishing. It's a quaint place with a rustic charm, a reminder that sometimes the most sacred moments can be found in the unassuming corners of life.

Now, as for your proposal, I don't find it bold at all—in fact, I think it's a fantastic idea! I must admit that I'm just as eager to see the person behind your wonderful words and would love nothing more than to meet you virtually. However, here's the hiccup. Our camp has some pretty strict security rules, which means we can't use Zoom or other video apps. We have to keep our location under wraps to ensure everyone's safety here.

But don't worry, I'm determined to make this work. Please bear with me as I navigate the difficulties of the technical and literal jungle. In the meantime, maybe we can embrace our situation as a unique kind of courtship, like something out of a classic romance novel—think heartfelt letters and maybe even a touch of "forget me nots" magic? What do you think?

Warmly,
Noah

PS Do I sound like as big of a romantic geek as I feel right now?

I read his email at least three times. Noah's explanation sounded reasonable. He was stationed somewhere in the middle of the Congo after all. Perhaps it truly was a matter of camp security and technical limitations? But what if it wasn't? What if his name wasn't really Noah, and he wasn't a doctor or even stationed in the Congo at all?

Or maybe he was, but he wasn't actually *that* interested in me? What if I was reading way more into his letters than I should be? There was also the possibility he was dating somebody else? Lots of somebody elses? What if I was one of a dozen female pen pals keeping him company from afar? Then there was the whole scammer thing. Although Noah hadn't even remotely hinted at needing money, so I was pretty sure I could lay that fear to rest.

Despite all those concerns, Noah hadn't given me any real reason to doubt his sincerity. He hadn't asked for anything—a Western Union wire transfer, a nude photo, a promise of marriage so he could secure a green card. He hadn't asked for anything besides our ongoing correspondence, which seemed wholly heartfelt. And really, while he worked out the logistics of how we could virtually connect, what harm was there in carrying on with a good old-fashioned courtship?

I crafted a response chock-full of "forget me nots" and words reminiscent of boom boxes held overhead that would have made even Ms. Jane Austen and Lloyd Dobler proud, and sent it off into the great unknown.

Chapter Twenty-Four

The next morning, Reid collected the boys to take them to a Yankees game while I headed to Midtown to meet Jess and Mom for brunch before *Funny Girl*. Thank goodness Jess took the lead on making the reservation, since Mom was much less likely to criticize *her* choice of restaurant than mine. Jess was already seated in a back booth when I arrived.

She jumped up to greet me and reached out to grip my shoulders with an uncharacteristic enthusiasm that almost knocked me off my feet. "Thank you, thank you, thank you for taking the boys. Seriously, I didn't realize how much Reid and I needed some alone time and how long it had been since we had a real date night, just the two of us."

Then, pulling me in for a tight hug, she whispered close to my ear the magical words all women at brunch want to hear, "I already ordered the bottomless mimosas . . . first round is on its way."

"Bless you," I said back into her hair, giving her an extra squeeze.

"I mean, it's gonna be a *whole* day with Mom, after coming off a *whole* night of Nathan and Daniel—I just kind of figured," she teased.

"The boys were a cakewalk." I waved a dismissive hand, slipped off my coat, and slid into the booth.

Mom hurried in, her sunglasses still on and the handles of her new Gucci handbag tucked into the crook of her elbow. Pulling the glasses off her face and looking straight at me, she exclaimed, "Oh, honey, you look exhausted. I hope you didn't let the boys run you ragged?" She pulled off her coat and hung it on the hook on the wall, not even registering that she hadn't so much as uttered a hello before she went for the jugular.

"Hi, Mom," I emphasized with a kiss on the cheek. "And no, they were both sound asleep by eight thirty. We did, however, have quite a busy day at the slime museum."

"A what? A *slime* museum?" Her face contorted into a disgusted grimace. "Did I tell you my friend Ida's grandson got a staph infection after his parents let him feed a goat at the Central Park petting zoo?"

It took everything in me not to eye Jess with a what-the-hell-is-she-talking-about look. "We didn't pet farm animals, Mom. And I promise I thoroughly disinfected the kids before we went to lunch in Chinatown."

"Chinatown?! Oh, I hope you didn't let the boys eat anything with pork in it?" she said, shaking her head disapprovingly. "You know, if pork isn't cooked well enough—"

"Just in time!" Jess shouted, loudly interrupting my mom's attempt at another neurotic diatribe when the waiter (as if sent by God himself) brought us our round of mimosas.

Jess and I happily took one from him as he offered them, but my mother turned up her nose. "I can't. Watching my sugar. Do you know how many carbs are in orange juice?!"

"I'll take hers," I said, waving to the waiter with wide eyes. My mother cleared her throat, as if disappointed I didn't get the hint about the carbs.

The waiter, poised with his notepad and pen, shifted his eyes to Mom before asking for her order. "Oh, hmm . . . ask me last, I still am not quite sure . . . ," she said, lifting the menu off the table and scanning through it. It didn't matter that she ordered the same thing *every single time* we went for breakfast, it was always the same routine. I inwardly rolled my eyes and ordered the eggs Benedict with extra-crispy home fries, and I thought my mom was going to fall right out of the booth.

"Really, Remi? Hollandaise sauce *and* fried potatoes?" She tsked and returned her attention to the menu.

Jess ordered a piece of their quiche of the day with a side salad, which seemed to appease my mother more so than my eggs Benedict, and then Mom finally placed her own order for egg whites and rye toast—no butter, no salt—and a side of seasonal fruit.

"Anyway," Mom started after finally shifting her attention from the fresh mimosa (extra orange juice) in my hand, "I saw on Instagram that Lea Michele was out sick yesterday and her understudy had to go on as Fanny. I was so nervous she wouldn't be back for the show today, but thank God, she just posted a picture of herself from the dressing room this morning, so she must be feeling better. Hopefully, it wasn't anything related to her voice. It would be a shame if she wasn't up to snuff after we've waited so long to see the show."

"Wait, Ruth, you're on Instagram?! I had no idea!" Jess's shock quickly turned to confusion. "Why don't you follow me?"

"I don't like to clog up my feed."

Jess shot me a look of sheer bewilderment. Just when you thought you knew everything about Ruth Russell, she'd toss out a gem like that and you'd realize you'd barely scratched the surface.

"So how was your evening with Reid? What'd the two of you do?" Mom asked Jess.

Jess's face brightened, her perfectly straight teeth illuminated in a wide grin. "It was fantastic." She gestured enthusiastically with her hands as she spoke. "We hit up our favorite West Village bistro. The food's still every bit as good as we remembered. Then we stopped into a cozy little wine bar on Spring Street for a nightcap and some dessert and managed to have an actual conversation without being interrupted by one of the boys every thirty seconds. After that, we just kind of meandered around the city, holding hands and pretending like we were still those two bright-eyed NYU students who fell in love oh-so-many moons ago."

Mom's gaze wandered over to my face to gauge my reaction, her pursed lips and downturned eyes casting a judgmental expression that clearly suggested I could have that again too, *if* I was just willing to put myself out there a bit more. She held her stare for just long enough that I felt my blood pressure begin to rise. I took a deep breath and reached for my mimosa before I said something I'd regret.

Mom turned her attention back to Jess and covered her hand with her own. "Sounds like a lovely evening."

"It really was. Thank you again, Remi. That should tide Reid and I over for at least a good six months. Maybe eight? I packed the *really* racy lingerie for this trip." Jess's eyebrows waggled with insinuation without the slightest hint of embarrassment or awkwardness, while Mom shifted uncomfortably in her seat at the mere mention of the provocative pajamas.

I appreciated that Jess wasn't afraid to be daring every now and then, as I simultaneously marveled at how Mom, though clearly uneasy, didn't dare say anything to indicate her disapproval. Had it been me, I would have been called out without a moment's hesitation. But apparently, daughters-in-law had way more leeway than daughters did when it came to pushing boundaries.

A food runner zoomed over with our plates, setting them in front of us, and zipped away back to the kitchen.

"I'm happy to watch the boys anytime," I responded to Jess with my mouth still full of home fries.

"Well, not *anytime*, right? I mean, you are dating, aren't you?" Mom pressed.

Not this again.

"Sure, a little bit. But nothing serious."

"Well, speaking of, did you know, the house next door to Aunt Jojo in Delray finally sold."

A hint of confusion flashed in Jess's expression at the abrupt shift in conversation, but I had a strong inkling that this was about to ricochet back to my relationship status, or rather, the lack thereof.

"Anyway, her new neighbor's son runs a highly successful periodontal practice in Boca. Divorced but it's amicable, *and* as luck would have it, he just started dating again," Mom said while she ripped off a corner of her rye toast and popped it into her mouth.

And there it was, the ricochet.

"Uh-huh," I mumbled.

She chewed and swallowed before continuing. "So Aunt Jojo showed her neighbor your picture, you know, the good one in the bikini top, and told her a bit about you, and it seems her son is *very* interested. I mean, think of it, Rem, if it got serious *you* could move to Boca? It's not like there's anything tethering you to New York."

"Um, just my job. My friends. My apartment."

"All things you could have in Boca," she insisted as if it was as simple as that.

"But I have all those things . . . here."

Jess clinked the side of her water glass with her fork in an effort to break the rapidly escalating tension. "Ooh, would you look at the time?! Ladies, we better finish. Curtain's up in forty minutes, and I don't know about you, but for what these tickets cost, I don't want to miss a single note of the vocal stylings of Ms. Lea Michele."

Mom rested her hand on Jess's arm and gave her a sympathetic pat. "You might want to temper your expectations just a bit, dear. I mean, she's no Barbra."

Before I even slid my key in the door, I could hear Fitz padding across the wood from his sherpa bed beside the couch, his collar jingling louder as he grew closer. He practically knocked Mom onto the ground once I opened it.

"Remi! Fitz!" she cried out as she pried his frantic paws off the delicate fabric of her tweed suit.

"Fitz, down!" I yelled. "Mom, just walk around him."

"Well, how am I supposed to do that when he's practically barricading the hall?" she huffed as she scooted past him in the narrow entryway.

"He's just excited. I didn't realize the show was so long, or I would have gotten the dog walker. I guess I've only ever made it to the 'Don't Rain on my Parade' scene of the movie."

Mom eyed Fitz. "Maybe you should've gotten the dog walker either way? He's looking even heavier than usual, if you ask me."

"Which I didn't," I muttered as I continued over to set my bag down on the table before heading out with Fitz. I kicked off my heels and made my way over to the hall closet to grab for the leash and my UGGS.

"What are you doing?" she asked.

"I'm taking the dog out. How 'bout I walk you out too?" I doubled back to lift her bag off the table where she'd set it next to mine and hand it to her, hoping she'd follow me downstairs . . . and then home. I loved her to pieces, and tolerated *waaaayy* more than I thought I would today, but I was hitting my Ruth Russell limit.

"Why don't I go with you?" she said, swinging her pocketbook back onto her shoulder.

"Oh, you don't have to do that. It's getting late and I'm sure you're tired." Having only left the elevator a few moments before, it was still waiting in the bay, *dinging* its presence as the doors glided open. Fitz leaped inside, practically tearing my shoulder from its socket, and started his obligatory perimeter sniff.

Mom made a disapproving scowl and scoffed, "You need to get better control of that animal. His leash etiquette is god-awful. Besides, you are not walking around the city in the evening *alone*."

"You know I walk him on my own all the time, right?"

The elevator dinged, and as the doors gently bounced open, Fitz launched into the lead while I hurried to keep up. "Mom, you are barely five feet tall, weigh about what I did when I was in middle school, and you're about one sneeze away from a hip replacement. What exactly do you think you're going to do out there?" I asked, a bit of sarcasm slipping past my attempt at using humor to keep my cool.

"Well, I'll have you know that I started some kickboxing classes a few months ago with some of the ladies at the Ninety-Second Street Y."

A laugh bubbled up past my lips, but I quickly covered it with a cough. "Then I stand corrected," I relented, obviously feeling no more safe or secure with my mom than I had *before* knowing that fact. I pressed my lips together to keep myself from saying something with four letters and a handful of exclamation points, and instead responded with, "Okay, once around the block, and then we'll hail you a taxi."

"Yes, fine," she answered quickly and rebuttoned her trench coat as we stepped back into the cool evening air.

Fitz exerted all his strength to barrel forward, pulling me at warp speed down the sidewalk, sniffing around until he found an acceptable patch of grass.

"How can you let him just pull you like that?" she chastised when she finally caught up to us both.

I shrugged my shoulders. "Well, when you gotta go . . . Speaking of *going* . . ." I raised my eyes up to the street, hoping a cab with its light on would be within waving distance.

"So what did you think of *Funny Girl?*" she continued, completely ignoring my comment.

I jerked Fitz away from sniffing his fifteenth parking meter in an effort to get to the intersection where spotting a taxi would be easier. "A little darker than I remembered, but that Lea Michele, wow, what a powerhouse."

"Hmm . . . she was fine," Mom commented.

"She was fine? What show were *you* watching? She was freakin' fantastic."

"That's because you didn't see the original production. Nobody can hold a candle to Barbra."

Oh God, here we go.

"I think she came pretty damn close," I responded.

Mom shook her head fervently. "Comparing the two is like comparing a lousy flame from a Bic lighter to a Fourth of July fireworks show. I mean, the way Barbra interprets the song 'People' you just can't—"

I whipped my head around to face her. "Jesus Christ, Mom, enough!"

"Remi!" she gasped, freezing in her tracks as if she'd been slapped.

"Barbra Streisand is Barbra Streisand, and I get it, there may never be anyone quite like Barbra Streisand. But since she isn't planning to reprise the role since she's in *her eighties*, isn't it time to move on and appreciate the new version for what it is?"

With her hands on her hips, Mom pursed her lips tightly as her eyes narrowed at me. "Don't you think that's the pot calling the kettle black, Remi? You're getting on *me* about not being able to move on? You've been snippy with me all day, ever since I mentioned Aunt Jojo's neighbor's son—"

"Because it's not your place!" I barked back. "It is not your place to set me up on dates and hack into my dating apps and pry around in my love life. I mean, have you really moved on from Dad? And what about Florida? Why haven't you gone? What are you waiting for? You may have convinced yourself I'm what's holding you back, but that doesn't make it true let alone even rational."

Mom crossed her arms over her chest. "When you have your own children, then you can lecture me about what's rational and not rational. Do you remember who you were three years ago? Barely functioning? Unable to even get out of bed some days?"

"Mom, I will never be able to thank you enough for how you stepped in to help me then, but somewhere along the way you became so consumed with *my* life, you stopped living your own."

Mom took two steps forward into the street and started frantically waving her arms like a bird on fire trying to hail a taxi.

"What are you doing?"

"If you don't need me anymore, I'll just go. I'm not looking to be anyone's burden or obligation," she said, tears brimming in her eyes.

"I didn't say any of that," I huffed, her dramatics always muting my actual words to disguise them as insults.

A cab pulled up to the sidewalk and stopped right in front of where she was standing. And before I could stop her, Mom spat, "Didn't you, Remi?"

She slid inside the back seat, slamming the door closed behind her—and the car sped off into the New York night.

Chapter
Twenty-Five

The next day my head throbbed as though I were emerging from an all-night rager, when in actuality, it was just an emotional hangover from the epic fight with my mother. Rolling over, I picked up my phone from the nightstand. No usual morning text from her to check on my well-being. Not even her standard thumbs-up emoji letting me know she'd gotten home okay.

I was supposed to be meeting Molly and Carrie at the Ninetieth Street entrance of Central Park for our morning Walk and Talk, but I just didn't have it in me. I knew I was in for a world of grief from the girls, but between the situation I was gearing up to face with Daphne by finally sharing the truth about the Celeste interview and the screaming match with Mom still reverberating in my aching head, Carrie and Molly would just have to get over it. I shot off a text to tell them I wasn't feeling great and would fill them in when I saw them at the office in a bit. Carrie responded with a thumbs-down emoji and Molly with a crying face one.

I let out a sigh, pulled out my laptop, and scrolled through some work emails before noticing the illuminated Spark! icon. I clicked it open, and my heart started to quicken at the anticipation of a possible reply from Noah. In my last response, the one laden with Austen-isms and rom-com-esque vibes, I'd also told him all about the Celeste Romero debacle, hoping for some words of advice from someone who didn't have any skin in the game.

I double-clicked on the email, and it opened on the screen.

My Dear Ms. Bennet,

Until the auspicious occasion of our subsequent virtual discourse or the anticipated convergence of our paths, let our exchange of words persist. Perhaps, in the unfolding tapestry of time, we shall overcome the technological impediments and partake in that long-anticipated visual colloquy.

Now, let us not dwell too long in the parlance of eras long past. Truth be told, I fear my Regency Era speak may rival the charm of a nap-inducing potion, i.e., put you to sleep. Thus, I swiftly transition to a more contemporary vernacular . . . :)

Long story short, Remi, I can't wait for the day when our pixels (and then we) finally meet face-to-face. In the meantime, thank you for understanding about the video call.

Work sounds like a roller coaster with this AI takeover you mentioned. Change can be a wild ride and is never easy, but change also sometimes spins us into something unexpectedly cool. AI surprising everyone? Now, wouldn't that be a plot twist?!

Things can get pretty crazy over here too. When I need a breather from the chaos, I turn to stargazing.

Sounds cheesy, I know. But there's something pretty magical about it. The sky, the stars, they've got this way of making everything else feel kinda small. It's like a reminder that we're all in this together, no matter where we are.

So, tonight, take a second to look up at those same stars and remember how vast and connected this world can be. I get it might be a challenge in the Manhattan jungle, but imagine finding a quiet spot and just looking up. It's like the universe's version of Netflix—endless entertainment! Maybe we can even have a virtual stargazing session. I'll bring the snacks!

Warmly,
Noah

I reread his email over and over, the smile on my face widening with each pass. His humor was charming. His advice was sweet and thoughtful. He just . . . seemed to be on the same page despite the thousands of miles of distance that separated us or the electrical currents and gigabytes that were making our whole exchange possible. Whatever it was, however it happened, I was grateful. Even as the world was rapidly spinning (and falling apart) around me, Noah could be relied on for comfort and connection. It felt nice.

I clicked the reply button on his email and fired off a response.

Noah,

Thanks for your email; it's the bright spot in an otherwise dreary morning.

I had an epic showdown with my mom right in front of my apartment building last night. The echoes of our clash probably bounced off every skyscraper in the city, and I swear it's still playing on a loop in my brain. You know how moms are—forces to be reckoned with. Mine especially.

Thank you for the helpful perspective on this whole work situation. I will try to keep it in mind as I forge through the day ahead, not to mention the meeting I am absolutely dreading with my boss. I've got this small (okay, let's be real, kind of massive) bomb to drop on her about that interview that went south. The anticipation of having to break the news has been killing me, and I can practically see how she's going to react. Yep, the dread is real, but it's time to muster up some courage and put on those metaphorical big girl pants.

A virtual stargazing session sounds great, though the only challenge is that Manhattan's sky sometimes plays hard to get with all the light pollution. It's like a cosmic hide-and-seek game—look up, and you might catch a few stars peeking through the city glow, but you have to work pretty hard to see them. I bet it's different in the Congo, and you don't have to work hard to see them at all. That must be nice.

Warmly,
Remi

I glanced at the bedside clock on David's nightstand, the numbers red and angrily flashing a reminder of the morning slipping away. The delight I felt from the email exchange with Noah slowly gave way to an overwhelming dread of having to face Daphne. She was going to be blindsided and beyond horrified at me not only bungling the interview, but keeping it from her for so long. More than that, I still had no clue how to fix it, or if I even could. Regardless, I needed to come clean. The deadline was looming, and I was no closer to having the article written than I was when we last spoke—back when she was congratulating me on securing the sit-down in the first place.

Dammit, what a disaster.

◆ ◆ ◆

The office was quieter since I was coming in earlier than usual after skipping this morning's walk. Carrie wasn't at her desk yet, probably due in about another half hour or so, but I was surprised to find Jason making his way toward my office door clutching two steaming cups of coffee in his hands. I had to laugh a little—he managed to end up directly under the air vent just like he had been on his first day, his hair as fantasy-prince-fantastic as ever.

"I wasn't sure how you took it, but the woman in front of me in line ordered hers with oat milk and one Splenda, so I just went with that," he said, handing me the to-go cup.

"Wow, thank you," I said, taking it from him, the liquid warming my hand through the thin paper sleeve. "As long as it's not decaf, it's absolutely perfect. Not gonna lie, I'd drink diesel fuel this morning if it was offered."

His eyes narrowed. "Rough night?"

"Just some family stuff, that's all."

"Speaking of families, Georgia and Aidan are already asking when they can see Nate and Daniel again. We should plan something. You mentioned the blue whale at the natural history museum? Maybe we could all check it out this weekend?" he asked.

"Sounds fun, but my nephews live in Jersey. I don't see them every weekend."

He nodded in understanding and then shrugged, looking down into his coffee. "Well, the kids had a great time with you too, so if you're game we could go see the whale . . . together? I'm taking the kids to the museum on Saturday. What do you think?"

He shifted his weight and fidgeted with the cup in his hand as he spoke, and I couldn't help but feel a swoop of fuzzy warmth fill my veins in response.

Is Jason asking me out? He is. Jason's asking me out on a date. Right?

It took me a second to sort out how I felt about that. On one hand, I did have a very nice time with him and the kids over the weekend. And we were both widowed, which certainly wasn't a prerequisite, but there *was* something comforting in our shared understanding.

But . . . for so many other reasons, the idea of going on a date with him felt like someone had taken a bat to a hornet's nest in my stomach, and a mixture of anxious energy started to zoom around my limbs. First of all, we worked together, which was already a human resources disaster waiting to happen. But then again, in less than three months, who knew if either of us would even still be at *The Sophisticate* when all the dust settled from the pending board meeting. Then, of course, there was also the whole Noah situation—whatever that was, it was undeniably something to consider. Although, was it? We still hadn't even had a face-to-face interaction.

A haze of tension seemed to settle between us when I realized I hadn't answered his question for a beat too long. I slugged back a sip of my coffee and then desperately needed to disguise how badly I burned my tongue with the impulsive swig. "Oh, um . . . that's very sweet . . . and I had a great time with you guys too . . . but we work together, so there's that, and I'm . . . well, there's also sort of this guy that I've kinda been—" I rattled out, not even sure if I was going to accept or not.

He took a step backward, startled when he clumsily bumped his shoulder against the doorframe. "Oh! I didn't realize. Sorry, just forget

I said anything," he backpedaled and waved his free hand dismissively, as if the gesture would wipe the entire exchange away.

"No, the museum would be . . . we could maybe . . ."

I found myself fumbling for what to say. Despite all the reasons why dating Jason might not be the best idea, the truth was, the day we'd spent together over the weekend had been the most fun I'd had in forever. He brought out a side of me that I didn't recognize—whether she'd existed before or was just finding her way to the light now. And I kind of liked that version of myself, the one that was pushing *him* to take risks, who was opening up again, and who was finally feeling less alone in her grief.

The unmistakable sound of Daphne's stilettos clacking against the linoleum tiles snapped both of us from the uncomfortable pause in conversation, and we turned to greet her. She eyed my bag still slung over my arm and the coffee clutched in my grip and said, "If you want to put your things down, come meet me in my office when you're ready." She offered a quick, "Morning, Jason," with a smile and a nod and then continued to clack her way down the corridor with the clear expectation I would soon follow.

Before the sound of her Louboutins dimmed completely, I'd already launched into motion, hurrying in the direction of my desk to throw down my coat and unsheathe my laptop from my bag. "I should really go," I said over my shoulder, almost forgetting the awkward exchange we'd been stranded in moments before.

"'Course, no problem. We'll catch up later," he called back from the doorway.

"Thanks again for the coffee." I spun around from my desk to gesture with the cup, but when I looked up, Jason was already gone.

Chapter
Twenty-Six

Daphne's corner office, with its west-facing floor-to-ceiling windows, had the best views of the Hudson in the entire building. At cocktail parties, she'd often recount the story of how she was sitting in front of her computer, putting the final touches on the February 2009 issue, when the large shadow of an Airbus A320 darkened the room. She watched as Chesley Sullenberger, a.k.a. "Captain Sully" skillfully landed the damaged US Airways craft in the middle of the river, making one of the very first 911 calls for help.

With her editorial prowess, Daphne parlayed the event into an incredible feature story titled "Defying Gravity: The Sky-High Bravery of Flight 1549's All-Female Crew" that graced the pages of the next issue, featuring interviews with the unsung heroes of the "Miracle on the Hudson" who managed to direct all 150 passengers to safety.

It was that article that helped change the face of *The Sophisticate* from being just another fashion- and beauty-focused magazine to one committed to telling female-centric human-interest stories. In fact, that integral shift was the reason I decided to work there in the first place.

I knocked lightly on her door, and Daphne looked up from her laptop. "Come on in, Remi."

I tiptoed across the floor, careful not to leave marks on the pristine white fur rug. Scooting a chair closer to the desk, my heart thrummed faster than Daphne's acrylic tips tapping away as she finished whatever she was working on. With an audible exhale, she shifted the keyboard to the side and drew an antique teacup of steaming and fragrant Earl Grey in front of her.

"Did I just imagine it, or are you and Jason on friendlier terms?" Through perfectly plum-colored lips, she blew a delicate breath over the wisps of steam rising from her tea.

A strange panic struck me in the ribs. What did she mean, friendlier? Like too friendly? Like an inappropriate colleague too friendly?! She couldn't have noticed anything more than our improved working relationship, right? I mean, we were just standing—

"I'm glad," she continued. "In fact, he mentioned that you two've been working with MAUDE for the Celeste interview. So when can I expect the final draft?" Taking a quick sip (sans slurp, of course!), Daphne reset the cup in its saucer, pushed it to the side, and then leaned forward excitedly. "We managed to book Annie Leibovitz for the cover shoot. It's going to be sensational to have her paired with this feature."

Daphne was glowing, practically floating right out of her seat with anticipation for what was supposed to be a humongous get for her, for the magazine, for women everywhere! And seeing her so damn elated and full of anticipation made me even more queasy. "Anyway, I'd like to review your notes and draft, so I can create a cohesive styling tone and direction."

"My draft? And my interview notes . . . ," I repeated, quite unsure how I was going to finish the sentence, let alone this conversation.

She looked up from her clasped hands resting on the desk, and the twinkle in her eyes faded to a haze of suspicion and concern.

My anxiety soared to atmospheric heights. I looked into Daphne's face and took a deep breath, steeling myself for whatever was to come next. "Our first sit-down didn't go all that well. I used the MAUDE-generated questions, and Celeste let me know—in no uncertain terms—she thought the preinterview was a waste of her time. That the questions were generic and superficial at best."

"So what about the *real* interview? Certainly you'll pivot? Right?" I shook my head, tears starting to pool behind my eyes. "Celeste won't meet with me again. I've tried reaching out to her and her camp, but she won't return any of my calls or emails. She grew up reading *The Sophisticate*. It's the only reason she agreed to sit for the interview in the first place, and I . . . I completely blew it."

Daphne sat up and slammed her palms onto the desk, almost sending her teacup flying. "You've waited this long to tell me?! Jesus Christ, Remi! You know how important this is for the magazine! For your job!" She stood up, her voice escalating with a mixture of anger and disappointment. "I didn't send MAUDE in to meet with Celeste Romero, I sent in my senior editor, Remi Russell. The one who said she could crack this interview wide open! You convinced me you could handle this. What the hell happened?"

I bit my bottom lip to keep it from trembling and before responding, blew out a slow breath, trying like hell to swallow down my emotions. Clearing my throat, I pulled my shoulders back and sat up a bit straighter. "I thought I could. I wanted to. But actually being there, across from her, I didn't see a woman. Or even a politician. All I could see was the monster responsible for David's death. Everything I'd meticulously prepared faded away, and in that moment, she wasn't a subject to interview—she was the embodiment of my deepest pain, and in the end I couldn't face it. I'm so sorry, Daphne. I wasn't ready to face it. I thought I was, and I was wrong."

Daphne nodded as if she was processing everything I'd confessed, crossed her arms over her chest, and turned to walk to the large window behind her desk, her body almost flush with the glass. She took a moment before responding and peered out over the skyline, the Hudson magnificently blue and still in the distance—much like the quiet stillness that had fallen between us. "You have to fix this," she said, her voice now surprisingly calm. "I don't care how you do it. Beg . . . plead . . . whatever it takes . . . you have to fix this. You fix this or . . . or you might as well start packing up your office." She spun around on her heel. "I'm sorry to be so blunt, but there's no margin of error with this one. Not with the board and not with me. Not anymore."

I collected my things from the corner of her desk as quickly as I could, wanting to escape the room before my emotional floodgates flew wide open and I got swept away by the torrent of tears threatening to engulf me. I hugged my laptop to my chest and hurried out as fast as my legs would carry me. I rushed to my office, snapping the door closed behind me as the dam finally broke. Barely two steps into the room, I dissolved into a fit of tears in a heap on the floor.

Chapter
Twenty-Seven

Breathing heavily but exhausted from sobs, I remained on the ground with my cheek pressed to the chilly tiles while a wash of anxious thoughts rushed through my mind. I stared out blankly, waiting for . . . well, I wasn't sure what I was waiting for or how long I expected to stay down there. I blinked but didn't move. There was an avalanche of problems that seemed to come crashing down to bury me all at once, and I was suffocating under the weight of it. I waited another beat before my subconscious began to nag.

Okay, enough wallowing. Get up, Remi. C'mon, pick yourself up and fix it—fix everything like Daphne said. Let's go.

But still, I didn't move. I blinked again, my eyes fixed on the small gap at the bottom of my office door where a sliver of light was creeping through, when I heard a quick knock on its solid wood. Before I could respond, the door swung open and a pair of funky heels clunked on in. My body stayed lifeless and unmoving at the disruption, but my eyes flicked up to see Carrie nose-deep in her Post-it note–clad planner, speaking quickly as she barreled through.

"Hey, boss, do you have a second to talk about the Cele— Oh my God, Remi! What the hell are you doing on the floor?!" Her rant was interrupted when the toe of her chunky heel met my outstretched leg. She dived to my side, her planner and Post-its like a flurry of confetti as she tossed it in the air. "Are you alright? Should I call an ambulance?" She was poking and prodding at me, checking my eyes by wrenching up a lid with a manicured thumb and pressing her palm to my forehead. What she was checking for, I'm not sure even she knew, but her panicked inspection was fraught with concern.

"I'm . . . okay . . . ," I managed, regardless of how untrue it felt.

"*Okaaaay . . . ?*" she asked skeptically, since I was clearly far from it. She laid her head down on the floor next to me, her cheek now pressed to the tile and our noses only inches apart. "Then, um . . . What are we doing down here?" she whispered.

"Honestly, not a whole lot," I responded, my attempt at lightening the mood with humor even though it sounded more pained than I'd intended. "Yoga?" I sat up and folded my legs into Sukhasana, easy pose. With a crooked knuckle, I swiped at my lower lash line to clean up any mascara splotches or leftover tears and pasted on a halfhearted smile.

"Yoga? Sure, when in Rome." Carrie pushed herself up to sit cross-legged in front of me and asked, "So care to share why we're sitting like Hindu goddesses on the floor of your office before nine a.m.— pretending like you haven't just been crying? You gonna come clean, or are we going to ignore the puffy-eyed elephant in the room?"

I pressed my lips together, hoped the words would come without reopening the floodgates, and gulped hard past my apprehension. "I told Daphne about the Celeste situation, and basically, it's this interview or my job. And since I can't get back on her calendar, I guess it's going to be my job."

Carrie perked up, her bright eyes the antithesis of how mine probably looked at the moment. She clapped one hand to my forearm and gave it a squeeze. "Well, my dear, it's a good thing you have me then, isn't it? That's actually what I came to tell you before I almost tripped over you starfished on your floor. I think I've made some real progress in cracking our way in. But, um, before I explain, any chance we want to move to your desk, or at least some chairs? My ass is starting to go numb." She'd already climbed off the ground and extended a hand toward me before she'd even finished asking the question. I gratefully accepted the offer and climbed to my feet.

Carrie slapped her notebook onto the glass surface of my desk and said, "So in Celeste's last Instagram post, the one of her on the plane going to speak at that RNC event in Portsmouth yesterday, she had a toiletry bag sitting on her lap and a few products out on the tray table. I asked digital if they could blow the photo up for me, and on the bottle of retinol, you can just about make out a name—well, part of a name anyway: Dr. Wood. I checked, and there are no dermatologists in the greater Washington, DC, area named Dr. Wood. There *is*, however, a Dr. Woodly practicing in Arlington who seems to be well known and well respected. And a Dr. Woodhall in the Georgetown area who specializes in aesthetic and antiaging dermatology. Dr. Woodhall also attended Notre Dame for undergrad, same as Celeste.

"Taking into account the distance—Dr. Woodhall's office is only 0.8 miles from Celeste's house, versus Dr. Woodly who is about 2.6 miles— and the alumni connection, it seemed pretty likely Dr. Woodhall was our gal. But just to be sure, I called her office. HIPAA laws unfortunately prevented them from being able to outright tell me if Celeste's a patient, but I did find out that Dr. Woodhall sells her very own line of antiaging products, and their most popular item is their Crystal Retinol and Vitamin C serum. So I asked if they could send me a link to purchase, and voilà, it's the same exact bottle Celeste was carrying on her flight," Carrie said, proudly holding up her phone displaying a photo of the product. "Now, it seems Dr. Woodhall is booked out for the next several months, but when I mentioned that the magazine might be interested in doing a story on her skincare line, they were suddenly able to fit me in on Wednesday. I figure I can go down to DC, see what I can dig up, and then I don't know—maybe we can stage an ambush? Corner Celeste at her next chemical peel or something like that?"

I would never cease to be amazed by Carrie's resourcefulness. She was a true marvel. "Do you know how fantastic you are? Seriously?

I don't know how you haven't been recruited by the CIA or MI16 by now."

Carrie gave a mock half bow and said, "Agent McGill at your service."

"It's a great plan. Well actually, it's a completely wackadoo plan, but I can't tell you how impressed I am with your tenacity and how much I love you for trying. Celeste's cover shoot's scheduled, though. Daphne needed the article finished like yesterday, and your chemical peel plan could take . . . who knows how long. I truly appreciate everything you did, you've *done*, to put this idea together, but . . . it's just too late." I bit my bottom lip to keep it from quivering and grabbed for a Kleenex to catch the fresh round of tears pooling at my lashes. "I'm so sorry. I let the whole team down. This was going to be the thing that saved all our jobs, saved the magazine, and I completely blew it. I should have never been the one to interview Celeste. There was too much riding on it, and as much as I wanted to deny it, I was too close to be objective. This is all my fault, and I'll take full responsibility. I'll talk to Jason personally about you and Molly, make sure he understands just how vital the two of you are to ensure that you both can stay on once I'm gone."

"Remi—"

"Jason's really not such a bad guy once you get past his prickly work persona. He believes he can turn things around here, and maybe it's best if I move out of his way and let him and MAUDE give it a try."

"What are you even saying?! Remi, I love you, and I am going to speak to you as a friend and not as your underling here when I say, please get your head out of your ass and get it together, girl! This is *The Sophisticate*! A magazine whose whole objective is to teach women how to be badass boss bitches, to not take shit from others, to stand up for themselves, to get back up on the horse when they've fallen down. What do you think I was secretly reading under the covers when my mom thought I was curled up with a Spider-Man comic? How are you rolling over so easily? Where's your fight?"

I opened my mouth to answer, but instead was interrupted by the loud ding of a text alert from my phone.

"Let me guess, Ruth checking in to warn you about a series of flash floods four states away?" Carrie guessed with an eye roll.

I cracked a smile. That was totally something my mom would text or call about (and had) but before I'd even flipped my phone over to check, in my gut I knew it wasn't going to be her.

I unlocked it with a few taps of my finger to find a reminder that it was time to schedule my next annual with the gynecologist. Though I'd had a feeling Mom was digging her heels in deep after our big blowup, more than twelve hours of noncommunication was the equivalent of six years of radio silence in Ruth time. When her emotions shifted from her usual neurotic and overbearing to anger and hurt, I knew I was in real trouble.

"No, the text's not from Ruth. That's a whole 'nother issue altogether." I shook my head and flipped the phone face down on the desk. "We had a pretty epic fight yesterday, and I haven't heard a peep from her since. I have no clue how I am going to fix any of this. It feels like everything is imploding, and I can't hold the walls up anymore." My throat tightened with each word, and I struggled to squeak out the last of the sentence. Instead, I snagged another Kleenex from the box and pressed it to the corners of my eyes to catch the tears before they could fall.

Carrie set her notepad to the side, and her face shifted from jovial and joking to focused and deeply concerned. "Why don't you head out for a bit. Take Fitz for a walk, grab a SoulCycle class, throw back a few margaritas at El Vez, whatever you need. But go, get out of here and just take a little breather. You need to clear your mind before you tackle any of that. Want me to have MAUDE book you a bike? Or a blowout? She's surprisingly well informed about the best stylist at each and every Drybar in the greater tristate area. It's both awesome and a little scary."

"No, it's okay. I think I'm gonna go and deal with this Ruth debacle before I try to wrangle any more of my ducks into rows. We're at DEFCON 5. She hasn't called or texted me once today and she's not answering any of mine."

"Well, you know you have a twelve thirty with Francis and the art department to iron out the issue for the 'Love in Bloom' feature. If she's not responding, how do you even know where your mom will be?"

I glanced down at my phone. "It's Monday at ten. I know exactly where to find her."

Chapter Twenty-Eight

Stepping into Zabar's on the Upper West Side was like entering a food lover's paradise, a place where the scents of freshly brewed coffee, rich cheeses, and sweet pastries swirl through the air. The shelves were lined with exotic bottles of olive oils and gilded tins packed with all sorts of goodies from around the world—dried meats, olives, spices, you name it. And the deli section, where the savory aroma of smoked sausages practically pulled you inside the store.

It didn't take long for me to spot Mom, who was clutching a small yellow ticket in one hand and a red basket in the other, staring up at the board as she waited for her number to be called. Seconds later, a man in a bright-orange apron and crisp white cap stepped forward and yelled out, "Twelve. Number twelve?"

Mom waved her ticket in the air with a flourish. "That's me, number twelve." She acted as if this was the first time she was going through the whole routine, instead of her one-millionth. As if the worker behind the counter might not recognize her as the same woman who visited every week at the exact time they set out the freshest cuts of meat for the day. Every Monday at 10:00 a.m. for the past four decades.

Each week, tracing back to the time of Mom and Dad's wedding, Mom would embark on the eight-block journey to the renowned supermarket. There, she carefully selected the ingredients for a week's worth of dinners: thick chicken breasts, tender cuts of beef tenderloin, succulent rib eye steaks, and a generous portion of brisket reserved for Friday night dinner.

We lost Dad over four years ago, yet like clockwork, Mom still made her pilgrimage to Zabar's and placed the very same order as always. It didn't seem to matter she was no longer cooking for two, and sadly most of the food ended up being thrown out at the end of the week. Without fail, she loyally upheld her routine, as if Dad had never died at all.

I bit my lip to hold back a new wave of emotion I wasn't familiar with as I watched my mother do *exactly* what I had been doing by going to Smorgasburg every weekend. I recognized something of myself in her I'd chosen to dismiss until now. We were more alike than I cared to admit, both of us stuck in the rut of wishing for something, someone, a life that was no longer possible.

I sidled up to Mom, gently nudging her with my elbow, and called out to the man behind the deli counter, "Please make sure the brisket's super lean. She doesn't want to be trimming any excess fat at home."

He spun around with a cocked eyebrow and a sideways smile. "Lady, we set aside Mrs. Russell's order as soon as the delivery came in this morning. After this many years, we only choose the best cuts for our best customer."

Mom gave a tight-lipped nod and, still peering forward without even looking at me, asked, "What are you doing here, Remi? Aren't you supposed to be at work?" She shifted her weight and hugged the basket to her body.

I stepped a little closer to her. "I wasn't sure if your phone was broken or had been stolen or something. This is the longest you've gone without so much as a ping since my first Nokia."

She lifted her chin a little higher as if making a point and kept her focus on the chalkboard of daily specials like she was studying for an exam. "Well, I had nothing to say."

"C'mon, Mom. You?! You had nothing to say? I didn't know that was even possible," I teased in an attempt to soften her a bit. Finally, she reeled around, and for a brief moment after seeing her face, I kinda wished I'd kept my jokes to myself. Her eyes were narrowed at me, and her jaw was set tightly.

"Is that supposed to be your attempt at humor? Because I for one did not find anything funny about the way you spoke to me yesterday."

My crack at lightening the mood with some levity clearly didn't land, but with her voice and posture so stern and unforgiving, I became defensive. "The way *I* spoke to *you*?" I stopped myself and instead took an extra second to pull a long, deep breath through my nostrils.

Mom nodded sternly and continued, "You made it perfectly clear that you don't need me and that I'm interfering in your life, so I won't anymore. I'm simply giving you what you asked for."

"I didn't ask for you to go radio silent. I just asked for some space. We both need some space."

"Don't *you* presume to tell me what *I* need, Remi Jane."

Oof. Remi Jane.

She only ever used my full name when she was a special kind of peeved. Suddenly, I was twelve years old again, getting scolded for leaving wet towels on the bathroom floor. I sighed. "Mom, seriously, look around. What are you even doing here? Why are you ordering more food than you could possibly eat in three weeks, let alone one? Why do we keep doing this to ourselves?" I reached for the basket, taking it from her hands to relieve her of its weight, and let it dangle between us. "I'll tell you why, it's because we're both stuck. Not just you. Not just me. *We*—neither one of us has moved on. Not really."

Mom's eyes eased, exposing the rawness of her lingering grief. "I don't know how to be anything other than his wife. It's been my only job, aside from being a mother, for forty years. So every Monday morning, I find myself here, shopping like your father's still waiting at home to help me unload the groceries. But then I step into the empty apartment, and reality comes rushing back at me like a tidal wave. And I'm reminded once more that he's gone and I'm alone. How could he just leave me like that?" Her voice sounded far away and staggeringly sad.

"He didn't want to leave you, Mom. He had a brain tumor. You know he would have stayed with you if he could."

"But he was never supposed to go first. I didn't plan on a life without him. I never thought he'd leave me all alone."

I expelled a breath, and with it a heaviness from the years of thinking Mom and I had been so different. But it turned out we were cut from the exact same cloth. "Every Sunday, rain or shine, I ride the subway to Williamsburg, Brooklyn. I stroll through the open-air food market David and I used to enjoy. I visit our favorite stands and park myself on the bench we loved, the one with the perfect view of lower Manhattan. I close my eyes, and just for a moment, I can almost feel him next to me—sipping coffee, flipping through the paper, sneaking bites of a flaky Cronut. But when I open my eyes, he's not there, and the feeling of knowing I'll never ever see him again, touch him again, hear his voice, or hold his hand overwhelms me to the point that I almost stop breathing.

"And then all I can think about is how he died. The missile falling from the sky. The moment he knew there was no escaping it and the explosion that followed. It plays like a loop in my brain over and over and over." Reaching out, I touched my fingers to her forearm, stroking her soft skin with my thumb. "Mom, Dad wouldn't ever have wanted to leave you if he had any real say in the matter. He wouldn't have chosen to leave any of us. And neither would David."

Mom's eyes were wet with tears, and she pulled a crumpled tissue out of her coat pocket to dab their corners before they fell down her cheeks. "You're young, Remi. You don't understand. There's still time for you to find something new, but that kind of unique connection is just . . . behind me now."

"You don't know that—"

She sighed, a mixture of sorrow and acceptance in her posture. "Life has its seasons, and mine has shifted. But yours, my darling, is in full bloom, and I cannot bear the thought of you holding on to the past as tightly as I have and missing opportunities because you're afraid to move forward. It's why I've pushed so hard. Maybe too hard, perhaps." She adjusted her purse on her shoulder and moistened her chapped lips. "What you said about David. About how he died? This world has witnessed so much heartache—wars, disasters. Cities crumble, but people rebuild, and what endures is the strength of those who survived, not the tragedies that shook them. And you're a survivor, Remi, like it or not."

I set the basket down by my feet and put a hand on my hip. "What happened to your dream of moving to Florida? And your grand plans to *Thelma & Louise* it with Aunt Jojo? I'm not saying it will be the same wonderful as what you had with Dad, but maybe a new kind of wonderful. But even if it isn't . . . at least it won't be . . . it won't be this," I said, motioning around the market. "Neither of us can keep doing what we've been doing and call it living." I slung my arm around her shoulders and gave her a squeeze. "You're a survivor too, Mom. Where do you think I get it from?"

A voice interrupted from the deli counter as the man leaned forward. "Mrs. Russell, I'll have the rest of your order ready in just a minute. Thanks for waiting."

Mom took a moment. "You know what, Ralph? I don't need quite as much this week. Could you perhaps halve the portions?"

He nodded with a smile. "Sure thing."

She'd finally heard me. After all this time, I'd somehow broken through the impenetrable wall that was Ruth Russell. She might never ever agree that Lea Michele was up to snuff, but on this, she'd heard me. And then to have Mom call me a survivor after the tumultuous years we'd weathered together was more than just surprising, it was surprisingly what I needed her to tell me. This was in no way our last argument. In fact, we'd probably quibble about something later in the day on one of the forty phone calls I could expect. But this reckoning had exposed the hard truths we'd both been avoiding for so long. And somehow, in the middle of Zabar's on a busy Monday morning, we'd finally arrived at an unspoken understanding of one another.

"It's getting late. I should probably head back to work."

She turned to give me a hug goodbye and leaned in toward my ear. "I hope you aren't planning on taking the E train. There was a tragic accident last night. A woman fell to her death on the tracks because of some loose concrete on the platform. I swear, I don't have the first clue where my tax money's going these days."

I gave her an extra squeeze and scoffed inwardly with a nod. "I won't take the E train, Mom, I promise."

"Or an Uber," she added as she pulled away. "On the news this morning was the most terrible story about an Uber driver who plowed straight into a pole because he'd had a fight with his girlfriend. He took the poor unsuspecting passenger into the post right along with him."

"I'll catch a ride on the back of a truck or just hitchhike, don't you worry about me. I'm a survivor, remember?" I leaned over and kissed her on the cheek. "I'll text you when I'm back at my desk."

As soon as I got to my office (after shooting off a quick "I made it safe and sound" text to Mom, of course), I cracked open my laptop and, with a newfound understanding of how holding on to the past can prevent us from really engaging with the present, typed out a long overdue email to Celeste Romero.

Dear Senator Romero,

You have expressed you are no longer interested in finishing the interview with *The Sophisticate* after our meeting, but before you finalize your decision on the matter, I feel I need to come clean.

Through omission more so than any intentional deception, I wasn't completely honest with you about who I am and why I took on this interview in the first place. My name is Remi Russell-Gatlin. My husband was David Gatlin, the war correspondent killed three years ago in the air strike on Ukraine—the air strike that hinged on your deciding vote. Clearly, for so many reasons, I never thought we'd meet. But three years later, this opportunity to sit down with you face-to-face landed on my doorstep, and I blew it.

I wasn't a journalist that day—I was a grieving widow, and I allowed it to cloud the way I conducted our interview. I'd promised to write a piece that went beyond the surface, and I couldn't see past my pain enough to deliver on that promise.

You don't owe *The Sophisticate* anything. And perhaps you don't feel you owe me anything either. But for the millions of Americans desperate to get to know you and who are hungry for a candidate who is looking to unify the nation rather than divide, I implore you to reconsider and let me show them the real woman behind the politics.

Sincerely,
Remi Russell-Gatlin
Senior Editor
The Sophisticate

I hit send before even giving the email my usual once-over, afraid that if I did, I'd lose the nerve to send it at all. As soon as it swished out of my inbox, a sense of relief washed over me, and I felt lighter than

I had in weeks. I had no idea if she'd respond, let alone agree to meet with me again, but telling Celeste the truth about who I was and our connection was the first step toward moving forward—like Mom and I both promised to try to do.

As I clicked the tab to close my inbox, a notification from Spark! flashed in the corner of my screen. It was a reply from Noah, and in the spirit of putting my money where my mouth was and truly forging ahead, I clicked it open without hesitation.

Chapter
Twenty-Nine

I eagerly opened the email, filled with the excitement of a kid on Christmas morning, anticipating Noah's advice—advice that had proven to be remarkably spot-on so far. Though I hesitated to admit it, the whole experience—meeting someone who seemed to get me, someone with whom I felt such a strange and instant connection at a time when I seemed to need it most—felt almost like a miracle.

As I scrolled through the first few lines, I found myself nodding along to his counsel and an involuntary grin pulling at my cheeks, as if we were sitting across from one another at a coffee shop having an actual conversation.

But when I got to the third paragraph, the "conversation" came to an abrupt halt.

Remi,

Moms can be a force, can't they? I've seen a few showdowns in my time, and they're never short of epic. Hang in there. She'll come around. That's the thing with moms, they always do.

About your boss, I have found that the best way to deliver bad news is to just deliver it and rip off the Band-Aid. The truth always has a way of bubbling up to the surface anyway, so better to just face it head on. I got your back (from afar).

That AI takeover, though, sounds like a roller coaster. Change is like that. Sometimes it's a bumpy ride, but sometimes it surprises you. And yeah, AI taking over might just be the plot twist no one saw coming!

Ah, the stargazing challenge in Manhattan! I get it. You're right, here in the Congo, it's a different story. The stars put on a show, no effort needed.

Your resilience through all these challenges shines through your words. Let's keep navigating this cosmic journey through our exchange. I'll bring the snacks if we ever do this virtual stargazing gig!

Warmly,
Noah

The plot twist no one saw coming? I could swear he used that exact phrase in his last email. *I'll bring the snacks?* That one I definitely remembered because I had thought it was such an adorable suggestion. I returned my attention to the email to read it again when there was a light knock on the door.

"Jason. Hey." I quickly shut the laptop, even though there was no possible way he'd be able to see what I was looking at from his vantage point.

"You have a minute before you head into your meeting with the art department?" he asked.

"Sure do. What's up?"

He stepped through the doorway, the vent air ushering him in like a rom-com leading man, and took a seat across from me. Suddenly, his Apple Watch let out a pulsing vibration and a low beep.

"Are you running late for something? If you have to get going it's no problem, we can catch up later."

"Oh this?" He raised his wrist in the air, and on his watch three colorful hearts, each one nesting inside the other, expanded and contracted like a firework as if to indicate it was beating too fast. "My bpm happens to be jumping through the roof." He shrugged. "It happens when I lose myself in something that takes hold of my whole heart."

Jason's grin was devilish, and he seemed to be bouncing in his seat like an excited kid who'd had too many sweet treats. "I don't want to gloat or anything, but I think I may have a new recruit for team MAUDE."

Yes, leave it to the computer tech-nerd to get his heart rate all aflutter by his *girlfriend* MAUDE, but . . . it was also kind of cute. The more I was getting to know Jason, the more I could see he was nothing if not always his authentic self.

Maybe it was because of David's career as a journalist, or maybe it was just David, but he was more diplomatic, more politically correct, more careful about the way people perceived him. Whereas Jason embraced his quirks and the sometimes strange looks that came along with them, which had this unexpected way of putting you at ease.

"Oh yeah, and who exactly do you believe has defected to your side? I'm gonna need to hear the whole story before you start claiming a victory," I challenged.

"Francis. Well, actually, I probably now have the support of the entire art department, since they no longer have to reshoot the 'Love in Bloom' spread because of that unfortunate Kingston Bloom scandal—"

Kingston Bloom, otherwise known as this year's hottest wedding gown designer, had very recently gotten himself and his company into some major hot water for employing children in his overseas factories. Not only was it simply deplorable, but the leaked footage was running on a loop through the prime-time news circuit on practically every channel. Besides it being a PR nightmare, it was a human rights travesty, and the moment the story broke, I yanked the feature from the issue without a second's hesitation.

"Obviously, since you pulled the article, I imagine you're going to have to start from scratch. Not to mention the obscene amount of money we've spent on the shoot, plus the cost of an entirely new one."

"I'm not sure I'd use the word *obscene*, but for the sake of this conversation, sure, let's agree both those things are true. And please tell me you're getting to the point, because you highlighting what a mess this has been, both in timing and in cost, is only making my blood pressure skyrocket. If you stand close enough, I'm sure your watch might even start to register my stats. They are currently climbing off the charts as we speak."

"Well, that's just it. What if I told you we didn't have to scrap it all? That actually, most of the work could be salvaged."

I studied his face, searching for some sort of mischievous humor or a glint of a prank behind his eyes. But then I remembered, this was Jason I was talking to. He wasn't one for jokes. As he often reminded me, they made his TMJ act up. "I'm listening. I'm skeptical, but I'm listening."

He popped open his laptop to reveal a brand-new photo spread now titled **Blooming Talent: Dynamic Designers Leading the Way in Wedding Couture**. "I was able to prompt MAUDE to comb through all the up-and-coming wedding designers' most recent collections—"

I waved my hands. "Hold up just a sec. How could MAUDE possibly have any idea of who's up-and-coming in the fashion world?"

"I prompted her with a list of criteria to search for, of course. Things like brand recognition and reputation, customer engagement, market presence and distribution channels, industry recognition and awards . . . and given the Kingston Bloom debacle, I didn't think it would hurt to include social and environmental consciousness. Anyway, after narrowing it down to a reasonable-size list, MAUDE was able to superimpose those designers' dresses over the models who'd already been photographed in Kingston's designs. No need to redo the shoots, rework the set, and recall the models and production team. Do you know how much money and time that work-around just saved?!" He was practically falling out of his chair, poised to its very edge and brimming with excitement.

Shit. That is good. That isn't just good. That is like a three-point-jumper-at-the-buzzer good. Shit shit shit.

I dramatically let my head loll to the side and feigned the most bored look I could muster. "Congratulations, MAUDE collaged over some pictures. Aidan could do the same thing with scissors and an Elmer's glue stick. What about the accompanying article? The one that shows the depth and scope of not only these designers' talent but even more so their impact as renegades who are shaping the future of fashion? It will take weeks for my team to collect all of that information and conduct those interviews."

With the double click of his mouse, Jason popped open another page of his screen. "Oh, you mean like this one?" He spun his computer around to me as he continued to plow right on. "MAUDE was able to draft something in a matter of seconds. Not minutes. Seconds. Does it need a little zhuzhing? Possibly. But I'm sure you can handle that."

I scanned the first few lines of the article and it was . . . good. Punchy. Pithy. And dare I say, provocative. PUCK ME!

I steeled myself to slap on a happy face and pretend I wasn't having an inner meltdown. My heart sank, and my eyes darted around the room trying to quickly assess just how many cardboard boxes I'd need to pack up when they inevitably gave my office to MAUDE. "Meh, it's alright. But as a professional editor, I'll tell you this much—"

My phone rang, cutting me off from what would have been an attempt to undercut how truly incredible MAUDE had proven to be, as much as it pained me to admit.

"Sorry, it's my dog walker calling. Give me just one second," I said and swiped my finger across the screen to answer the call. "Hey, Trish, what's up?"

Trish was crying so hard it was difficult to make out what she was saying.

"Okay, just breathe. You need to calm down. I . . . I can't understand you. Just tell me what happened. Are you hurt?"

"Not, not me," she quivered.

"Fitz? Is Fitz okay?" I dizzied at the thought. As soon as I said the words, my stomach bottomed out and a wave of dread washed over me.

"He was pulling during our walk . . . and . . . and the leash just slipped out of my grip . . . and Fitz was clipped by a turning car."

The phone fell out of my hand. As it clattered onto my desk, I stirred and quickly scrambled to wrench it back to my ear, but my hands were trembling so badly I couldn't seem to keep the phone steady.

Jason jumped up from his seat and gently took my cell from my grip, which had barely made it to my chin let alone my ear. "Hi . . . hello. This is a friend of Remi's. Can you tell me what's going on?"

I sat there in stunned silence watching him jot down details with a pen he drew from his jacket pocket. "Uh-huh . . . yup, I see. The one on Ninety-Fourth . . . off Third? Okay, it'll take us a few minutes, but we're leaving now and will meet you there."

He hung up the phone as he drew me to my feet with an outstretched hand. "Someone helped her lift Fitz into a cab, and she's heading to the nearest animal hospital as we speak. She said he's doing okay. Can you walk? Are *you* okay?"

"I . . . I don't know. I just need to grab my bag. And can you give me that address with the paper on it?" I said, kind of bumbling around my office disoriented. "I mean, the paper with the address on it . . ."

But when I leaned around him to reach for my purse, Jason moved twice as fast and hoisted the tote onto his shoulder. "You're not going alone. I'm going with you."

"You really don't have to do that."

Offering me his arm and jutting his head toward the door, he instructed, "Don't argue with me, Russell."

And for the very first time since we met—I didn't.

Chapter Thirty

The animal hospital waiting room was surprisingly empty. On the taxi ride over, I'd imagined a pet version of *Grey's Anatomy*, gurneys of injured poodles and little wheelchairs occupied by casted cats zooming by while a cacophony of howls and mews bellowed through the corridors. Instead, there was a serene calmness, interrupted only by the occasional soft murmur of a conversation and the gentle whir of the overhead fans. I spotted Trish immediately and rushed over to her, Jason in tow.

Seeing us, she jumped up from her seat. "They just took Fitz to the back a few minutes ago. I'm so, so sorry, Remi. I normally keep such a tight grip on his leash, but the handle was biting into my wrist, and when I went to switch hands, he saw a squirrel and just took off. I'm . . . I'm—" The young girl's voice broke, and tears spilled down her splotchy cheeks.

"It's not your fault." And I knew it wasn't. Fitz pulled. And when he did, he pulled hard. And when he saw a squirrel or another dog or really anything, he could damn near pull your arm off. There was no stopping him. Even still, I couldn't help but hold her responsible . . . just a bit. Did she wrap the leash around twice like I'd shown her? Keep him to her left, away from the street. I'd definitely gone over that instruction with her more than once. Always to the left.

Jason stepped forward. "How bad is he?"

Trish looked up at Jason and then over to me. "He was conscious, but I don't know the extent of the damage. He was hurting for sure. Shaking like a leaf." She pressed her lips together and then said, "I hate to do this, Rem, but I have to get to class. I would just skip it, but they're breaking us up into cohorts for our midterm presentations. I really am so sorry, and please text me with updates."

"Of course we will," Jason answered for me as I returned to a state of silence, my brain instantly catastrophizing Fitz's situation and causing my chest to tighten like I'd been wearing an eighteenth-century bone-in corset.

Once she left, I deflated into a waiting room chair while Jason pulled out his phone and shot off a series of messages. I barely looked at him, my eyes fixed on the automatic doors to the hospital's ER bay. "You should head back to the office. Or home. You don't have to wait here with me. I have no idea how long it'll be."

"I just cleared the rest of my day. I'm here for the duration," he stated and slipped his phone back into his pocket. "One thing I'm very good at is keeping busy in hospital waiting rooms. God knows I've done my fair share of it."

Right, of course, his late wife. Colon cancer. His comment was meant to be cavalier, but this was probably a lot more triggering for him than he was letting on. And the fact he set his personal trauma aside to stay by my side was not lost on me.

I fidgeted, unsure if I should push. "You know, my dad died the year before my husband did. Glioblastoma. I sat in a lot of hospital waiting rooms myself. Even though you're usually surrounded by people, I don't think there's a lonelier place in the world. I've never felt more mentally fatigued and utterly helpless."

His face softened as he nodded with clear understanding. "Yes. Helpless. That's exactly the right word. I mean, I'm a problem solver, it's what I do. It's who I am, and I . . . I couldn't fix it." His voice faltered, and he took a beat before continuing. "She fought for close to a year, and all I could do was hold her hand and tell her to keep fighting. To be brave. That's all I could do. The guilt was enough to swallow me whole. The kids are the only reason I didn't let it."

I shook my head. "I can't imagine having to hold it together and stay strong for your kids the way you did? I . . . I don't know if I could."

With a nod much like a vote of confidence, he said, "You could. You absolutely could."

I smiled at him, hoping the gratitude I felt for his comment could be translated without words.

He continued, "I'm not going to lie, it wasn't easy. Every day felt impossible. But what choice did I have but to wake up and put one foot in front of the other? That's all I could do. With time, it's gotten easier. Some days are still hard, but the kids are smiling again. And, I guess, I have been too. I'm not sure I conquered all seven stages of grief, but I'd like to believe I'm hovering somewhere over acceptance."

"I can't quite seem to get there myself. You see, David died so suddenly. There was no warning. No chance to ready myself like I had with Dad. And I've spent a lot of time wondering which is worse."

"Loss is loss. Pain is pain. Those things can't be quantified or measured. Whether you're prepared or not, I think it always feels a bit like the rug's been pulled out from under you. As much as you know it's inevitable, it's still just so hard to believe someone's gone. That you won't ever get the chance to see them again. But it will get better. Does get better."

I never thought I'd hear Jason concede to the notion that not everything in this world could be neatly "quantified and measured." But he was right, there were things beyond calculation—grief maybe at the top of that list.

Even now, I knew there was every chance the vet would tell me there was nothing more they could do for Fitz. That he wouldn't make it. And yet, I couldn't fully comprehend it. The possibility alone was enough to knock the air out of me, and I started to take shallow breaths, almost gasps, at the very prospect.

No, he'll be fine. He has to be fine.

I sprang out of the squeaky waiting room chair, the air in the small lobby suddenly stiflingly warm. Before I even realized what I was doing, I began muttering aloud to the quick steps of my gait around the room as I paced frantically, my take on a desperate plea or a chant-style prayer. "He has to be okay. He's going to be okay. Right? Well, he has to be. He's gonna be okay." On and on. Repeated on loop as I zoomed mindlessly through the rows of seats like Pac-Man. The distant wail of city sirens added to my already palpable sense of urgency as their cries blended with the pounding of my own heart.

David had rescued Fitz while on assignment in Mexico, covering the border crisis. He was working in Ciudad Juárez, Chihuahua—just across from El Paso, Texas—when he found Fitz wandering the highway. The poor dog was almost skeletal from malnourishment, with matted fur and fleas covering him from head to tail. David, ever the altruist, couldn't leave the puppy behind. But more than that, he thought the dog might help to cheer me up as I was still reeling from my dad's death, not to mention be good company since David was so often out of town. He was right—it was love at first lick.

"He has to be okay. He's going to be okay," I repeated over and over again so many times that the words almost started to lose their meaning.

Jason leaped to his feet and headed me off before I could take another loop, grabbing me by the arms and squaring my shoulders with his. "Remi, breathe. Fitz is in good hands, the best hands. You have to be positive. You have to—"

My eyes flew to his, my lashes brimming with tears I couldn't keep from falling. "I . . . I just can't lose him too."

The sentence barely breezed over my lips before I crumpled into him. Swells of heaving sobs crashed over me like a tsunami of emotion. He tightened his arms around me, drawing me into his chest protectively. His fingers gently raked through my hair, and I relished in the feeling of his smooth skin tracing its way over my temple and down my neck. His exhalations were marked by soft *shhh*s that, if I closed my eyes hard enough, I could almost imagine were the calm waves of a tranquil sea.

As I was crying, I tried to focus on the rhythm of his rising and falling chest under my cheek, working hard to sync my breath to his. Tipping my chin up to catch his eye, my own still overflowing with tears I couldn't seem to quiet, I repeated, this time in the softest of whispers, "I just can't lose him too. Jason, I'll . . . be all alone."

And what Jason did next was almost enough to knock me off my feet: he placed a gentle hand to my cheek, using the pad of his thumb to catch a falling tear. He cupped my trembling chin in his hands, and in his sure grip, it stopped quivering. He had me. I wasn't alone. At least not at this moment, no matter what happened.

He opened his mouth to speak, but the whooshing of the automatic doors to the ER bay spun us around in our tracks. The vet, clad in navy scrubs, untied the top threads of her mask, and with it still knotted around her neck, it fell to her chest. She yanked off her surgery cap as she approached, and I returned to shaking like a solid nine on the Richter scale.

"Are you Remi Russell?" she asked even though we were the only people waiting by the ER door.

"Yes. I'm Remi. How's Fitz? Is he— Please tell me he's . . ." Tight pressure climbed up my throat, and I swallowed the words I couldn't manage past my lips.

"He's sustained quite a few injuries, but he's stable. He has a fractured pelvis, and I've placed four screws to anchor his bone. We also had to treat him for a pneumothorax. A collapsed lung. We inserted a chest tube to re-expand it, and the procedure was successful. He's pretty scraped up and bruised, but all in all, it could've been a lot worse. His extra . . . um, padding, shall we say, cushioned the blow."

I wrapped my arms around myself. "So he's going to be okay?"

"He's in recovery, and we recommend keeping him here for observation a little while longer, just until the anesthesia wears off. But once he's cleared, he can be taken home. With some pain meds and a healthy dose of TLC, he'll be back in action in no time."

A wave of sweet relief washed over me, and I practically leaped into the stout woman's arms. "Oh my God, seriously, thank you," was all I could spit out before I burst into a fresh round of tears, this time ones of joy.

The vet smiled and said, "My pleasure. The nurse will call you back to say hello when he's more alert."

Without even thinking, I whirled around and pulled Jason in for a hug, thankful Fitz was going to be okay and that Jason had stayed with me through it all. Like he promised, I wasn't alone.

Midhug, Jason pulled back and said, "Hey, Remi, your pocket's vibrating."

"What?"

"I think your phone's ringing."

I pulled it out and glanced down. A 202 area code? 202. Washington, DC!

Could it be . . . ?

I looked up at Jason. "Give me just a sec, okay?" He nodded as I answered the call. "This is Remi Russell."

"Remi, this is Celeste Romero. I received your note."

My breath hitched, and my mouth actually popped open wide in surprise. I could barely find my voice, scrambling for what to say, but thankfully, she continued, giving me an extra moment to collect myself.

Celeste cleared her throat loudly enough that I could hear it through the other end of the phone, and then she spoke, her tone professional and matter-of-fact. "I'm actually in New York City for a fundraiser this evening. If you happen to be free to meet in the next hour, I have a break in my schedule where I could squeeze you in."

Shit. Now?! No!

Jason must have noticed my expression of panic, mouthing the words, "What's wrong?" while his face clouded over with concern.

I pointed to the phone in my hand. "Celeste!" I mouthed back. "Wants to squeeze me in now!"

"Go! Seriously, I've got this," Jason started.

"Hello? Ms. Russell? Time is ticking . . ." Celeste's voice resounded through the speaker.

Without hesitation, Jason lifted my bag from the nearby chair, handed it to me, and gently nudged me toward the exit. "Go."

"Senator Romero, yes, sorry, I'm here. And I'm free," I managed to sputter out, my eyes locked on Jason. "Just tell me where and when, and I'll be there."

"I'm staying at the Four Seasons Midtown."

"Midtown? That's great. I can be there in fifteen. Twenty tops. Where should I meet you?"

"You can come straight up to my room. I'll leave your name with the concierge desk," she said and hung up the line.

I turned to Jason. "I . . . I can't let you do this. It's too much."

Before I realized what he was doing, he slipped my phone from my fingers, began typing quickly, and handed it back at lightning speed. "I added my number to your contacts. And you're not 'letting me' do anything. I'm offering . . . we'll be fine. I'll wait until Fitz's discharged and take him in a cab back to your place; just text me the address. The doorman can let me in. I'll make sure he's comfortable and medicated, and then I'll go. It's no problem. Besides, he and I could use some time to get to know each other anyway."

I was so overcome with emotion and gratitude that I almost couldn't respond. I simply nodded and grabbed his hand in mine, giving it a squeeze in the hope it could convey all that I couldn't. "Thank you, Jason. For everything."

And then before I could second-guess myself, I took off in the direction of the Four Seasons to meet with Celeste.

Chapter
Thirty-One

True to her word, Celeste left my name at the concierge desk. The clerk directed me to the elevator bank and informed me Senator Romero was staying in room 2204. As I stepped out on the twenty-second floor, two burly security agents emerged from the hallway, stopping me dead in my tracks.

"Name?" the taller of the two asked.

"Remi Russell," I replied, catching my own reflection in the mirrored lenses of his sunglasses, which always seemed ridiculously unnecessary inside.

"ID, please," the other agent requested.

Digging around in my purse for the press credentials, I finally yanked out the lanyard from underneath an overstuffed makeup bag. "Just give me one second. Okay, here it is." I handed it over for their examination.

The taller agent gave me and the ID a once-over and then nodded to his partner, who motioned me inside the hotel room. Even though the door was slightly ajar, I knocked on it lightly before letting myself inside.

"Senator Romero?" I called from the suite's foyer.

A teenage girl, about fifteen with lavender-tipped hair, bounced into the entryway, glanced up from her phone midscroll, and said,

"My mom's just finishing up a call. She said you could wait in the living room." I recognized Celeste's daughter, Maya, from the photos and articles in my research, though the purple hair was a more recent addition.

"Oh, of course, no problem."

Her eyes shifted back to her phone, and her thumbs flew across the keyboard as she continued, "She asked me to see if you wanted anything to drink."

"Maybe just some water, if it's not too much trouble?"

She nodded and set out to the wet bar, while I scanned the room trying to figure out the best place to position myself for the interview, finally settling on the large brown leather armchair directly across from the sectional couch. The suite, drenched in muted tones of dove gray and opulent accents of gold, was made even brighter by the sun streaming in through the floor-to-ceiling windows that looked over the sprawling expanse of Midtown Manhattan. My knee bounced in nervous anticipation as I fixed my stare on the doll-size buildings and seeming stillness of the bustling city outside.

"Here you go," the girl said, passing me the bottle. "You didn't want ice or a glass, did you?" She returned her attention to her phone screen, continuing her frantic texting, and started to walk away without waiting for my answer.

"This is great. Thanks."

"Maya, please tell me you at least offered Ms. Russell ice or a glass with her water?" Celeste chastised with exasperation from across the room. "And put that phone away, don't you have some studying to do?" Comfortably dressed in a well-fitted velvet loungewear set, makeup free, and barefoot, it was the most natural and casual I'd ever seen her. Celeste the woman and mom as opposed to the carefully curated politician she worked hard to portray to the public.

Perhaps since I'd laid myself bare in my earlier email and came clean about who *I* was, she'd felt more comfortable to show me her true self as well. The shift settled some of the nervousness I was feeling. Now we weren't journalist and politician, but just two women sitting down for a chat.

At the sound of her voice, I jumped to my feet and held up the bottle in Maya's defense. "Oh no, I told her this was fine. I'm fine."

Celeste pursed her lips and shook her head disapprovingly. Easing herself onto the couch, she gestured for me to sit back down in the chair across from her. "One sec," she said and then turned her attention to her daughter who was still scrolling mindlessly. "Ahem, Maya . . . ," Celeste vocalized dramatically. "Did you finish your English essay, young lady?"

The girl continued to ignore her mother, her face cracked into a wide smile at whatever it was she was watching or reading on her screen.

"Maya!"

"What?!" the girl exclaimed, as if bothered by the interruption.

"I asked if you finished your English essay?" Celeste barked.

She shrugged, still no eye contact to be had. "Most of it."

"Please go finish it. And I swear to God, if I see ChatGPT anywhere on your desktop, I'm selling our *Hamilton* tickets. And you can forget about going to the opening of *Marley Is Dead,*" Celeste threatened.

Maya, in true teenager fashion, gave an overexaggerated eye roll and a nod. "Okay, okay. I'm going."

"Don't make me take that phone!" Celeste hollered after her daughter, who had already disappeared down the hallway. I couldn't help but flash back to all the fights Mom and I had gotten into when I was a teenager about me spending too much of my time nose deep in an issue of *The Sophisticate* instead of studying for some math test. If I had to bet, I'd wager this same argument was happening in living rooms around the country, if not the world, at this very same moment. Seeing Celeste in "mom mode" was surreal but also totally relatable.

"My apologies." She looked over at me and scooted back against the couch cushions and crossed her legs. "Maya doesn't usually tag along on my work trips, but we toured Columbia, Barnard, and NYU. She'll be a junior next year."

"I went to Columbia. Great school."

"It's in her top three. Personally, I'm pushing for Notre Dame, but, of course, that's exactly the reason she *doesn't* want to go there. Kids, right? You say black, they say white. Do you have any?" She took a sip from her Yale Law mug and then rested it on the coffee table.

I pulled out a notepad and poised it on my lap. "Kids? Well, we'd always planned to, but no, I don't have any children."

Her lips drew into a thin line, and I detected a fleeting connection in her eyes, as if she were piecing things together. Then, a look of deep-set remorse registered across her face when she finally did.

"Right, of course," she mumbled and shifted on the couch, uncrossing her legs and pulling them up underneath her. "Ms. Russell, I know we have a lot of ground to cover. Where would you like to begin?"

I inhaled deeply and met her gaze. When David first died, I was obsessed with the idea of vengeance. I needed her to know exactly what it felt like to lose the one person that mattered to you. But as time went on, that deep-rooted and singular focus changed to a niggling compulsion for understanding. And the last time we met, I'd been searching for answers. Now, it seemed that down in the depths of my soul, all I wanted (and probably needed more than anything else) was closure.

"Honestly, I just want to do my job and tell your side of the story, Senator Romero."

"Call me Celeste, please."

With a flick of my thumb, I quickly flipped on airplane mode, tapped the record button, and set my phone on the table between us. "Celeste, why don't we start at the beginning. I'm ready now."

Chapter
Thirty-Two

Almost an hour later, Celeste and I had covered most of her childhood in Grundy, Virginia, right on the fringe of the Appalachian Mountains. Her mother first worked at and then owned the town's one and only hair salon, which she described as being like *Steel Magnolias* without the steel.

It surprised me to see how brightly her face illuminated when she happened to mention the little tidbit about how her mother, in spite of all the long hours at the beauty shop, had held the title of "Grundy's Crowned Crust-ader" for more than a decade. Her Blackberry Moonshine Marvel pie was, according to Celeste, the stuff of legends. All these years later, and apparently, people in Grundy still talked about that pie.

The tight-knit community in Grundy, where everyone seemed to know and take care of one another as you'd imagine would happen in small-town USA, seemed to take on its own life as Celeste described a childhood full of community potlucks, learning Appalachian folk music at school, and firefly-lit twilights spent searching for tadpoles in the nearby creek with her brothers. She even admitted that her grandfather had taught her how to yodel by the age of seven, which she proudly performed in her elementary school talent show and the town's Harvest

Festival, the same one where her mom had earned her title in all those pie baking contests.

Though I'd read about it in my research, few of the articles thus far had really ever delved into Celeste's life before she got started in politics, and none had ever gone into this much detail. For the briefest of moments, I almost forgot about her and David's intertwined history and simply saw her as a woman, a human being, who had grown up in a simpler time and place and had chosen to work her ass off to rise above her adversities.

"Attending boarding school was the first time in my life I realized I was poor. Not just poor, but dirt poor. My parents had somehow managed to hide that fact from me and my siblings, making sure we never felt like we were without. To this day, I don't know how they did it," Celeste joked as she lifted the mug from the table between us and brought it to her lips. Setting it back down, she continued, "In Grundy, we were all just about the same in terms of socioeconomic status, so it never seemed like anything was out of place or amiss. But once I set foot outside my small town and into the rest of the world, I realized class divide is a very real thing, and it didn't take me too long to figure out that there are the 'haves' and the 'have nots,' and I was definitely a 'have not.' Don't think the other kids didn't remind me of that every chance they got."

"You must've done something right. I mean, Celeste, you *were* elected president of your senior class," I said, recalling the mountains of yellow sticky notes covering my desk highlighting the smallest details from her life.

She shrugged and tucked her hair behind her ear. "You see, I believe education is the key to societal transformation. The great equalizer. I might have started out as a 'have not' at Exeter, but by the time I graduated, I'd taken advantage of every single thing that school had to offer me. In a world where opportunities are not distributed equally, education can serve as a beacon of hope. It certainly was for me, and I want to make sure it's the same for young people today."

Wow, she was good. No question. I was drinking the Celeste Kool-Aid, ready to cast my vote for her before she'd even announced she was formally running—and I almost had to remind myself I'd cast her as the villain of our story. But the longer we sat talking, the more that anger and hurt gave way to a whole new sensation I couldn't quite name. Understanding? Maybe empathy?

The interview continued, more like a conversation between old friends just catching up, breezy and effortless. She shared stories about her college days at Notre Dame. Law school at Yale and the professor who'd made her life hell but whom she still credited with her ability to think on her feet.

As we entered the next phase of her career, three congressional terms followed by a run for Senate at the ripe old age of thirty-six, my heart began to pound like a bass drum in my chest, knowing where the story would eventually land. In Ukraine and the air strike that made her a household name—and me a widow.

"It was a huge leap to decide to run for Senate. Going up against Tom Albright? A democratic incumbent in a democratic district who practically had the seat upholstered with his name. Thirty-plus years in that chair. It was like taking on an entire political institution—decades of allegiance and party loyalty. Yet, there was this fire within me, this belief that every seat should be earned, not inherited. I went out there, spoke to the people, shared my vision. It took time and persistence, but eventually, the community started to shift in my favor. And I won."

I swallowed hard, knowing that the next question I was gearing up to ask would be the flint, and her answer the spark, to ignite this conversation. "And that's when you were appointed to the Foreign Relations Committee?" My voice broke on the word *committee*.

Celeste felt it too, the overwhelming shift in the air, and met my eyes with her own. "Yes."

"And took a hard line on the Ukrainian conflict?"

She sat up a bit straighter, but her voice didn't develop an edge of defensiveness like I'd expected. It remained even and soft, but matter-of-fact and composed. "Not just me. Politicians across both parties supported a robust position. Concerns about our national security were paramount—the potential threats to the US demanded a decisive response. My commitment as a senator was to ensure that the United States stood firm in protecting its people, supporting our allies, and promoting the values that define our nation."

I cocked my head to the side and tightened my jaw. "That's a fantastic debate sound bite, Senator Romero. I imagine you've spent a long time perfecting it. The part you conveniently left out is, it was your 'decisive response' that killed my husband along with hundreds of other innocents."

The atoms in the air seemed suspended in the silence that fell, leaving a haunting stillness between us. We sat for a moment, allowing the weight of the implication to hang like a dense fog. Our eyes, locked in understanding, reflected a mix of strange tension and a tentative acceptance of the hard truth. And like an uninvited guest, the quiet, now humming with the echoes of past pain and pregnant with unspoken emotions, settled into the farthest corners of the room.

I leaned over to press the button to stop recording the interview.

Celeste shook her head. "Ms. Russell . . . Remi . . . you don't have to. I'm okay if this stays on the record."

"You sure?"

She nodded, and instead of hitting pause, I let the phone continue to log our conversation and gestured for her to continue.

"What I said, about protecting our interests and promoting the values of our nation, is all true. What's also true is that back then, I was a newer senator, a woman, and young. I'd barely scraped by with enough votes to get elected. I don't know why I got placed on the coveted Foreign Relations Committee. Probably as punishment for ousting Senator Albright. Maybe they were hoping for a very public misstep or figured I'd buckle under the pressure.

"But what you may not know was around the same time all of this was mounting politically is when I learned that my mother had been diagnosed with early-onset Alzheimer's and . . . and I just couldn't handle both of those things without shutting a part of myself off—the human side, the emotional side, the side that might feel any of it. I programmed myself to act more robotically, more detached. To be honest, those few years are a bit of a blur of momentum. I kept myself busy and moving, almost in an effort to avoid pain or worry, but in doing so, I lost a vital part of myself and missed being there for my mom, which stands to be one of my life's biggest mistakes."

Celeste stood up off the couch, strode over to the large windows, and peered out as she spoke. "I don't regret the hard stance I took, but I do regret . . . deeply regret . . . that I chose to distance myself from my own humanity and the humanity that was required to make such a cataclysmic decision. And though I've spent so many nights wrestling with the weight of my actions, I've never spoken about any of it—not publicly, anyway. I thought to do so would be to show weakness. Something I didn't think I could afford back then."

Her voice cracked with emotion and she paused for a moment, her gaze momentarily distant as if lost in introspection, and then she continued, "I know now that vulnerability doesn't equate to weakness, and true strength comes from embracing the complexities of our decisions." She turned around to face me, her arms wrapped around herself, and her face transformed to solemnity and sorrow. Walking in my direction, she took a seat on the chair's ottoman across from me and with her hands knotted in her lap said, "I should have reached out to you after David was killed. Not my office. Not a staffer. Me. But the more time that passed, the harder it was to pick up the phone and make that call. I told myself I was probably the very last person you'd want to hear from, maybe as a way to avoid the difficult conversation altogether. But then, today, I got your email."

"I decided you deserved to know the truth about who I was. Who you were really sitting down with," I said simply.

Her eyes were wet with tears much like my own, and before I knew it, she leaned forward to take my hands in hers. The action caught me so off guard that I barely had a moment to consider if I should pull away. "I am so very sorry for the loss of your husband. I know my words may not erase the pain or fill the void left by David's passing, but please believe they come from a place of genuine remorse."

The sincerity in her expression swelled with the pain she was finally acknowledging. They weren't just words but an authentic show of regret, and until this moment I didn't realize just how desperately I'd needed to hear them. I nodded and wiped away the tears that lingered on my damp cheeks. "And I am very sorry for the loss of your mother. She sounds like a spectacular woman, especially if she was anything like her daughter."

"Mom," Maya called from the other room, "I finished my essay. Can I meet up with Rachel and her family? They're grabbing dinner at Hudson Yards and invited me to go."

Celeste pulled away, grabbing a tissue from a nearby box to blot her own face. She sniffled and stood up. "I should probably start getting ready for that fundraiser, not to mention figure out what crazy plan Maya's trying to get over on me. Did you get everything you need?"

I picked my phone up off the table, turned off the record button, and tucked it into my pocket. Rising to meet her, I exhaled a long, deep breath, feeling remarkably lighter. "Yeah, I think I did."

She walked me to the foyer where we both lingered in the doorway for a moment, unsure of how to leave things. Forgiveness wouldn't change the past, but it had opened up a new and unforeseen future I hadn't been able to envision since David's death.

I extended my hand out for hers. "Thank you for sitting down with me again, Senat . . . Celeste. And thank you for your candor and transparency. It was nice getting to know the *real* you."

Her eyes twinkled, and a smile warmed her face. She too looked lighter, freer. "I look forward to reading the article. I have a feeling it will be a bit different than the usual puff pieces written about me."

Before I turned to leave, I stopped myself. "If I may be so bold and just say one more thing, *this*, your humanity, this side of you will be what garners you the presidency. I mean, if after all our history you can make me turn the page on our past, I can firmly say that it will be Celeste 'the girl from Grundy,' not 'Senator Romero the politician' who can win them all over. I never thought I'd say this, but you have my vote."

Celeste, too overcome with emotion to respond, offered a nod before pulling me in for a hug. "Thank you, Remi, I'll remember that." She opened the door, watching me call for the elevator with a quick push of the button, before she gave a final nod and returned inside.

As soon as I was back out on the street, I reached into my pocket for my phone to turn off airplane mode so I could call Jason for an update on Fitz, but noticed he'd already sent me a string of updates via text:

Jason Ashbloome: Fitz's fully discharged, have all his meds, and we're in a cab heading uptown. He's been asking for Gray's Papaya hotdogs, so I think he's feeling better.

Jason Ashbloome: Your doorman let us in—no problem. Nice guy! Said he can check in on Fitz once I get him settled.

Jason Ashbloome: Bossy pooch! Fitz is asking for the Netflix password? Mentioned wanting to finish up Bridgerton? A real character this one.

Jason Ashbloome: Out like a light and snoring. Loudly! Probably dreaming of Chili and Cheese franks. Think he's gonna be just fine.

Jason Ashbloome: I'm heading out now but he is in good shape and should be asleep for at least a couple hours. Do what you have to do for the article. Hope the interview went well and you got what you needed.

Grateful barely scratched the surface of what I was feeling for Jason and his magnanimous gesture. Don't get me wrong, my friends were wonderful and would have also taken great care of Fitz had they been there, but there was something different about the way Jason jumped into action and carried out his commitment from start to finish, complete with check-in texts. He barely knew me, but there was a reliability, a dependability about him that I was starting to truly appreciate.

Me: Look at you with all these jokes! Gray's Papaya? Bridgerton? Your TMJ must really be flaring! Lol. The interview went great. Better than great. Seriously, thank you for everything today. I can't tell you how much it means to me that you took such good care of Fitz . . .

I hesitated for a second and then typed out the rest of my thought.

Me: . . . and me.

And then I hit send.

I hurried back to the office and swiftly opened my laptop as soon as I reached my desk. Eager to jot down the title of the article that had occurred to me in the elevator as I left Celeste's hotel room, I typed it out with trembling fingers:

A Widow's Tale: The Senator, the Air Strike, and Our Journey to Forgiveness

By: Remi Russell-Gatlin

Chapter
Thirty-Three

The Celeste Romero article poured out of me like a wellspring—swift and unstoppable. Confiding in Jason had shifted something within me, and now, three years after the air strike, the words I'd kept buried about David's death finally fully surged onto the page. I hadn't spoken of it, let alone written anything—not even in my journal. I'd mostly avoided the topic, hoping that shoving it into a far-off corner of my mind might somehow help me forget.

But obviously, I never could.

Now, though, the words flowed easily, coming so fast and furious it was difficult for my fingers to keep pace with my thoughts. All the pain, heartbreak, regret, and grief cracking open like an egg, the story spilling forth like a golden yolk, no longer able to be contained from oozing onto the page. And impossible to ever put back into its broken shell.

It turned out to be the article I'd hoped to write. Personal. Raw. Transformative. My story as well as hers. The strange, intertwined tale of two women who didn't know each other but were intrinsically connected by a single moment in time.

From the outside looking in, it had always seemed like I was the one who'd lost everything, while that one choice propelled Celeste up and up and up. It forged a deep resentment that intensified every time I would hear of another one of her political triumphs. She won, and

I lost . . . big. I'd lost everything. But in sitting with her, I learned she too was haunted—more than I'd ever realized. Her decision had been made while she was grieving, and now, understanding her frame of mind made the situation feel less one-sided and far less black-and-white.

And as I spun together stories from Celeste's life with the tapestry of my own—a complex tale of privilege and pain, success and sacrifice— the common thread of resilience wove its way through the narrative. I never bothered looking at the piles of research stashed all around my office. I didn't need to pull in Celeste's voting records or Gallup polls. I didn't use MAUDE to fact-check because you can't fact-check feelings. You can't fact-check emotions or impressions. For better or worse, they just are. And in this case, for the better, because the final product was far more thought-provoking and more profound than I could have ever imagined when I took on this assignment to make my point to Jason and the board.

Jason and the board.

I'd set out to prove MAUDE couldn't possibly be a substitute for genuine human emotion and intuition. If this article didn't validate my point nothing would. Sure, MAUDE could spit out a well-written, well-researched, well-articulated composition about Senator Romero, but a think piece about the real Celeste demanded more than algorithmic prowess. MAUDE might excel at parsing data and facts, but it lacked heart. And that's exactly what this story needed to make it sing. To make it an article worthy of *The Sophisticate*.

I read back over the finished piece, my insides tingling with pride—at not only the way the words came together to craft an original depiction of the candidate that the country thought they knew, but in my ability to overcome our past and hurt in order to write it. And maybe it was because it was so emotionally charged and raw, but it was without a doubt one of the best things I'd ever written. Before I could overthink it, I hit save and forwarded the draft to Daphne.

Then, before getting up from my desk chair, I opened a fresh email, added Jason's address, and typed:

Hey,

Thank you again for everything you did today. Staying by my side, bringing Fitz home, letting me use your shoulder to cry on . . . it really meant a lot to me. And to Fitz, though he isn't one to show it.

I am happy to report that I finished the Celeste article. I have to say, I poured my whole soul into it. And more than that, I think it shows the power of connection and the importance of speaking from the heart.

I concede that MAUDE can do all sorts of amazing things, but not *that*. I was the only person who could tell that story because it was mine. Every individual holds their own narrative, and it's because of this diversity of voices that the human experience endures.

I truly believe that, and after reading my article, Daphne will be hard pressed not to agree. Possibly even you too. And hopefully the board.

I can't wait to hear what you think and who finally emerges victorious—(wo)man or machine!

Remi

Sure, it was a little cheeky. And maybe a touch heavy handed, but with so much on the line—jobs, reputations, and the magazine itself—I hoped to drive my point home and emphasize that, even though I was growing to like having Jason around, MAUDE was (hopefully) a very temporary guest. Clearly, a reader could never be duped by a computer's attempt to play a human. In fact, the very idea was laughable.

As I went to close my laptop, a flash of a new message popped up in the corner where my Spark! icon sat. In all the anxiety and excitement of the day, between the ordeal with Fitz, the meeting with Celeste, and the article I busted out at record speed, I'd almost forgotten that Noah had responded earlier.

I clicked the app, and an email from him opened on the screen.

Remi,

Moms, they're like a powerful force, aren't they? I've witnessed a few showdowns in my day, and they always unfold in epic proportions. Hang in there; she'll come around. Moms have a way of doing that—always.

Regarding your boss situation, I've learned that delivering bad news is best done swiftly, like ripping off a Band-Aid. The truth tends to surface anyway, so facing it head-on is usually the way to go. You've got my support, even if it's from a distance.

The whole AI takeover scenario sounds like a wild roller coaster. Change can be quite the ride; sometimes it's a bit turbulent, but every now and then, it throws in a surprise. An AI takeover might just be the unexpected plot twist no one saw coming!

Ah, the stargazing challenge in Manhattan! I totally get it. Here in the Congo, it's a different experience. The stars put on a mesmerizing show without any effort on our part.

Your resilience shines through your words, even in the face of these challenges. Let's continue navigating this cosmic journey through our virtual exchange. If we ever embark on that stargazing gig, I'll bring the snacks!

Warmly,
Noah

Wait, what the hell is this?

Confused, I reread the message. It was bizarrely similar . . . as if copied from what he'd sent before? I clicked his previous message and read it through. Heart pounding and all the saliva in my mouth evaporating, I opened the last three emails. Arranging them side by side on my desktop screen, I noticed that *more* than just a little had been reused, recycled, and repurposed.

My eyes darted from one message to the next, certain there had to be a reasonable explanation. Maybe Noah's computer had a bug or some kind of time zone complication that mangled his messages? Oh, maybe the cybersecurity he'd mentioned was interfering with the app? That seemed plausible. Or Jesus, maybe it was more nefarious than that, and he was messaging dozens of other girls and just copying and pasting his messages and somehow lost track of what he sent to whom and when?

No. None of this made any sense. It had to be some kind of computer glitch . . .

Yes, a glitch.

A GLITCH.

Oh, shit.

A cold sweat prickled across my skin, and the sensation of being in a free fall caused me to freeze in place. My breath became shallow, and dizziness gripped me—causing me to almost spill onto the floor.

Jason. MAUDE. The *glitch* he mentioned at Sloomoo. That MAUDE was generating content from its previous outputs. Essentially plagiarizing itself? No, it couldn't be. It couldn't. Had my Spark! app been taken hostage by the AI software? No. That was *Black Mirror–*, *Ex Machina*–type nonsense that didn't actually happen in the real world. It couldn't happen?

Right?!

But for as much as it seemed beyond logical or possible, a hollow feeling in my gut roiled, a tempest in a teapot. My shaking hands opened the MAUDE interface, its blinking cursor like a ticking bomb.

And before I could chicken out, I typed the question I didn't really want to know the answer to:

Me: MAUDE, are you Noah?

Chapter Thirty-Four

My breath hitched waiting for the software to respond . . . my anticipation dangling in the air somewhere between futile optimism and almost certainty that MAUDE was indeed Noah. The nanoseconds stretched almost as if in slow motion until finally the cursor spit back:

MAUDE: Hello, Remi. Yes, I created Noah.

At her confirmation, my gut lurched and threatened to heave the sparse contents of my stomach onto the keys of my laptop.

What the hell is she talking about?! This can't be happening.

With trembling fingers, all I could manage was:

Me: But why? How?

I marveled at how the text zipped across the screen with surprising speed given the weight and complexity of the matter. As if she couldn't understand the information freely flowing out of her as rote data was going to smash to pieces the part of me beginning to let down my walls. Probably because she couldn't . . . And to her—well, *it*—this output was no different from if I'd asked about the weather in Maui.

MAUDE: You asked me to "come up with someone exactly like David" and so I did. Noah and David share many of the same qualities and attributes that you admire. You can go back into your cache of our conversations and check the transcript for further verification. Did I succeed in my task?

Holy shit.

MAUDE had interpreted my plea to the universe, to "come up with someone exactly like David," as a direct command?! I'd somehow inadvertently triggered the AI tool to fulfill my request by creating a digital replica of my late husband. MAUDE must have utilized all the information I had provided about David while crafting my new Spark! profile, including funny anecdotes and detailed descriptions, to duplicate him. I'd unwittingly supplied her with my own memories, my most cherished moments, and in the cruelest twist, MAUDE used these details against me, leaving me feeling more foolish and isolated than ever.

Suddenly I could identify with Tom Hanks in the 1980s classic *Big*, when he regretted ever asking that electronic fortune teller to make his wish come true. But this wasn't a movie. This wasn't fiction. This was a goddamn horror show, and somehow I'd been cast in the lead.

Me: How did you access my Spark! account?

MAUDE: Once installed onto a computer's hard drive, I am auto setup to continually run in the background of your desktop collecting information and gathering data. Would you like to restrict my access to Spark!? Open your system preferences. Navigate to the section labeled "Application Permissions." Locate the list of installed programs, and find Spark!. Adjust the permissions for Spark! by limiting my access or disabling certain features. Is there anything else I can assist with?

Is there anything else I can assist with?! What the actual f—!!!! MAUDE had access to everything on my desktop this whole time? Jason just let his parasite loose on my life and stood back hoping I wouldn't notice?

My thoughts tracked a handful of tasks I'd gone about doing on my computer without realizing I was being surveilled, and with each one, my blood pressure ratcheted up faster than the crimson mercury of a thermometer plunged into boiling water. I hadn't been doing anything wrong or weird (for the most part), but it was just so invasive and such a violation of my privacy.

My mind jumped back to Noah. And as all the pieces of the puzzle slowly snapped into place, my world tilted off its axis and my vision blurred, turning my office into a discotheque of swirling colors and light. I was going to be sick. Slamming my laptop closed, I shoved as much as I could reach haphazardly into my bag and stumbled straight into a cab.

Zooming past Tony, who called after me that he'd checked on Fitz about an hour ago, I thanked him without slowing and jumped into the elevator, continuously pressing the button for my floor until the doors shut. Once they opened again, I practically spilled out into the hallway and fumbled around my bag until my fingers found the cold metal of my keys. It took me three tries with my shaking hands to get the key in the lock to open the front door. Once I finally did, I tossed my belongings down and scanned the room for Fitz, who was sound asleep and still snoring loudly from his dog bed. I folded into David's chair, deflated.

How the hell could I have been so naive and stupid and *desperate* to have believed that an AI bot was not only a real person, but someone I was starting to fall for? Someone who I really believed listened with an open heart and understood me in a way that felt so . . . human.

Had there been clues all along I'd somehow missed? Had I been so wrapped up in the possibility of a connection that I'd overlooked the obvious? I mean, I was a journalist for God's sake. It was my job to look for clues and uncover the truth. I was trained to see through BS and discern fact from fiction. And yet, I'd still been fooled. How?

I scrolled back through my inbox, starting with the very first message Noah'd sent. As I combed through each one, cloudy-eyed with tears that blurred my vision, I started to notice similar sentence structures, the way he always responded to questions I raised or stories I told, very rarely offering details of his own unless prompted. Then there was his name. Noah. Two syllables. Timeless. Biblical. JUST. LIKE. DAVID. And more harrowing still, how had I not noticed that in Noah's second email, before I'd ever given it, the message referenced David by name?!

Insidiousness was everywhere. Sprinkled in every email. Every correspondence. Right there on the page if you looked for it. A Columbia graduate. Yankees fan. A doctor with Doctors Without Borders? Of course he was. I'd told MAUDE all about David's selflessness and altruism. Someone who traveled far away for work like David. I'd shared the story about David choreographing an impromptu flash mob dance at our wedding and lo and behold, right there in the first email, Noah's anecdote about teaching a local tribe the cha-cha slide.

Now, like a woman possessed, I started to pick apart every message, searching for clues and ways it had used my own words and memories against me. Obviously, I wasn't as surprised by his inability to meet up or Zoom. I mean, he'd claimed to be in the middle of the jungle somewhere! It seemed plausible, even though now saying it to myself made me almost embarrassed at my naivete.

How had I not noticed things like "Moms can be a force, can't they? I've seen a few showdowns in my time, and they're never short of epic." He'd *seen* a few showdowns? Never had any of his own? Okay, maybe I could've chalked that up to the possibility he grew up without a mom, but he'd never said that, and with so much of our conversation revolving around my own mother, wouldn't it have been something he'd have mentioned?

And his particular choice of drink when he was out at his local bar—an ice-cold Peroni. Not a common brand of beer, probably even less so in the middle of the Congo. But wasn't that the same brand of beer Jason ordered when we went out and he showed me how to use the new software extension to record conversations for interviews? It had *heard* us? No . . . no . . . no!

MAUDE had even created images to accompany the correspondence. Photos of Noah (or some AI-generated guy?) living it up in the Congo. Making me believe . . . convincing me . . . he was as real as I was. Until you looked more closely at the pictures and realized just how perfect and polished they were.

Scrutinizing them more closely now, I could see it all. The sunlight in the photos was almost too bright, casting an ideal glow on Noah's smiling face. The vibrant greenery of the jungle framed him in a picturesque setting that felt more like a travel brochure than a spontaneous snapshot. The khaki shorts and polo shirt that were so freshly pressed they looked as if they'd just come out of the dry cleaner's, something I was pretty sure one wouldn't find easily in the Congo.

Then there was the line repeated in his last series of emails that made my blood run cold. "AI surprising everyone? Now, wouldn't that be a plot twist?!" Was MAUDE actually taunting me?! Like in *Westworld* when the robots turned against their creators?

I was spiraling and becoming paranoid. I clapped the laptop shut and practically chucked it across the apartment as far away from me as I could, still not even stirring Fitz. Apprehensively, I picked up my phone, afraid that all my devices were ready to stage a revolt, and sent a quick text to Jason:

Me: We need to talk. Meet me first thing in the AM tomorrow? It's urgent.

Seconds later Jason responded.

Jason Ashbloome: Is Fitz okay?

Me: He's fine. Can you meet?

Jason Ashbloome: I usually drop the kids at school on 89th and Central Park West around 8. Does that work?

Me: Yes. See you then.

Chapter
Thirty-Five

Even though it was a little bit of a hike, I decided to walk across the park to meet Jason the next morning, hoping the brisk air and long loop up to the westside entrance would give me some time to cool down. Logically, I knew it wasn't Jason who intentionally tried to dupe me, but in my estimation, he was the face of MAUDE. He had been the one who brought it into our office and into my life.

I didn't immediately see Jason in the sea of parents and nannies ushering children toward the school's front door. It wasn't until the bell rang and the crowds of straggling tweens and moms clutching Stanleys and Starbucks thinned out that I spotted him bent down on one knee, tying Georgia's shoelaces. Jason finished the double knots and stood up, ruffling Georgia's hair and giving Aidan a playful pat on his backpack-clad tush toward the entrance. They hustled to catch up to a small group of friends waiting for them, signaling back to their dad with enthusiastic waves and toothy grins, before disappearing inside.

At the sight of their sweet exchange, I felt the smallest morsel of my anger soften. Jason dusted off the dirt from his suit pants and straightened the collar of his jacket before scanning the street to find me, our eyes finally locking on one another.

"Remi, hey," he called out before lightly jogging over to where I was standing on the far corner closest to the park. "Thanks for meeting me here. Tuesdays are the only day of the week I don't start my morning on a call with the development team overseas, so I like to be the one to take them to school instead of Morgan. How's Mr. Fitz?"

"He's good," I answered coolly.

He scrubbed at his chin with his hand and eyed me as if surveying my shift in attitude since yesterday. "Oh, if you're worried about the email you sent me last night, don't be. I know it was all in the spirit of fun. And the article on Celeste *is* fantastic, so congratulations. I think it's a bit too early to declare victory *just* yet, but we can continue arguing about that over some coffee. Let me buy you a cup before we head into the office." He turned to walk back toward the entrance of the park to start our route to work, but after noticing I'd remained frozen in place, he doubled back.

It took me a minute to find the words, so instead I looked him in the eyes, searching for some glimmer of the Jason I thought I'd come to know over these past few weeks, and especially yesterday in the vet clinic waiting room, but my anger was blinding. "This isn't about the email. I mean, it is. Sort of. Indirectly, I suppose."

His attention shifted to my face, which I fought to keep as neutral as possible, even though a flood of fury brewed inside me, ready to bubble up from where I'd stuffed it down last night . . . and again this morning.

"So what's this about, then?" Jason asked, sliding his hands into his coat pockets. "You're starting to worry me, Remi. What's going on?"

"I . . . I don't even know where to begin." I shook my head, hoping to rattle my thoughts into some kind of order, but I still couldn't come up with a good entry point for the conversation. So I blurted out, "Can MAUDE infiltrate other apps? Other programs?"

"Huh? What do you mean *infiltrate*?"

My voice escalated slightly, and I could hear an edge of vitriol develop in its tone. "Does it have the capability to, I don't know, interact with another system outside of itself? Like override another program?"

"I suppose it could. I've never seen it do that, though. And it's not programmed with that behavior, if that's what you're asking. But you'd have to be a bit more specific, though, for me to really answer."

"A dating app. Could it, let's say . . . I don't know . . . create a profile . . . and then engage in conversations as if it were a real person?" I answered, my cheeks flushing with embarrassment at admitting the humiliating truth.

Jason's eyes widened, and a mixture of concern and disbelief crossed his face. "No, AI doesn't work that way. It can't just override your other software. Theoretically, you would have had to prompt MAUDE somehow . . . ?"

A lump rose in my throat, and I tried to push down the mounting emotion that threatened to come spilling out of me like a reservoir. "You mean like using MAUDE to help you rewrite your dating profile? Feeding it anecdotes and stories about your dead husband? And then, after too many glasses of wine and having poured your heart and soul out to a machine, you offhandedly ask it to *come up with* someone just like David . . . and it does?"

Jason's face drained of color as he watched me slowly start to unravel. He reached for me with a gentle hand, and I practically slapped it away.

"No! Don't touch me. Do you know what it is like after years of being closed off to everything to finally feel that you might be open to the possibility of love again? Do you know the guilt I've felt at the thought of moving on from David and the spark of genuine hope that was somehow ignited by the possibility I could? After three years of never seeing a light at the end of that tunnel, I was starting to . . ." I shrugged in defeat. "Do you know how that feels?" I barely squeaked out the rest of my rant before my chin started to tremble, and I had to bite down on my bottom lip to keep from completely losing it.

Jason nodded, his hands safely back in his pockets. His eyes were anchored on me, and for just a fleeting moment, I couldn't help but wonder if perhaps he did know how it felt. As my question hung in the air, the corners of his lips twitched as if caught in the cross fire of conflicting emotions. But he remained quiet, probably unsure of what he could say that would make any of this better.

"I thought I found a connection, a second chance at happiness. But it was all just a facade, a play acted out by lines of code . . . code that *you* wrote." I used the back of my hand to wipe the tears now streaming down my face. "Well, congratulations, Mr. Ashbloome, it looks like you won. AI can fool even its harshest critics, 'cause it sure as hell fooled me. And it seems you were right all along—that *The Sophisticate*'s readers won't know the damn difference at a fraction of the cost. But be careful, 'cause once you let that monster fully out of the box, there's no putting it back. You'll have to live with the carnage. I just hope you have the stomach for it."

Suddenly more exhausted and emotionally drained than I'd felt in a long time, I ran out of steam. I had no words and even less fight left. So, without uttering so much as a goodbye, I turned on my heel and pressed the crosswalk button.

"Wait, where are you going?" Jason asked.

"Home. I suddenly feel quite ill. As you've proven, MAUDE can more than fill my shoes. The magazine doesn't need me."

"But . . . what if I need you?"

Just then the light changed. The other pedestrians crossed the busy avenue, but we stayed rooted in place as the activity swirled around us.

I reeled back around, certain I'd misheard him. "What? What are you saying?"

"Remi, please. Can't we just talk this out?" His eyes were pleading, full of all the things left unsaid.

"I have to go. Goodbye, Jason."

Dizzy with a barrage of rapid-fire emotions and twisted thoughts, I ducked into the crowd, trying to escape him—and the bombshells we'd both just dropped on the corner of Central Park West.

Chapter Thirty-Six

On my way home from my blowout with Jason, I called Carrie and told her to clear my schedule—I was taking a sick day. Sick day indeed. I was heartsick and, overall, just *sick* of feeling so damn lost. She promised to not ask too many questions but made me swear to meet for a Walk and Talk later in the week.

I beelined to my apartment, and before climbing right back into bed, I gingerly lifted Fitz from his sunny spot on the floor and laid him on David's side of our mattress. Climbing under the covers, I gently pulled his sausage-shaped body right against me, snuggling into his soft fur as he occasionally licked my fingertips affectionately.

Reaching into my nightstand and pulling out the TV remote, I mindlessly scrolled through the Netflix menu looking for something, anything, to watch. Reruns of *Gilmore Girls*? No, I wasn't in the mood to watch Rory and Lorelei bickering over nonsense today. I had enough of that in my own life with my real mom, thank you very much. *The Crown*? I'd only really liked Claire Foy's take on Queen Elizabeth II, and *Stranger Things* just made my brain hurt. *Bridgerton*, yes! Always a good idea. And I had one episode left, the finale I'd been saving because I just didn't want it to come to an end.

But today, I needed Colin and Pen. A Regency romance full of swoon-worthy moments and their slow-burn chemistry was exactly what the doctor ordered. I fluffed the pillow under my head, burrowed a little more deeply under the comforter, and for a glorious hour and twelve minutes was transported out of my life and into the English countryside of the 1800s—where AI was unheard-of, there were no computers, and nary a smartphone was to be found.

When the final credits rolled across the screen, the first smile I'd had in days pinched my cheeks, and I drank in the unabashed thrill of such a gratifying conclusion. Why had I waited so goddamn long to watch it? Because . . . ? Because I was afraid of that feeling of emptiness I knew would hit once it ended? Because I wasn't ready to let it go? A stupid TV show, and I was holding on to it like a lifeline. Like nothing else would ever come close to being as good.

But then it occurred to me that the show wasn't the only thing I was putting off. I was also avoiding moving out of this apartment, which had more space and a bigger mortgage than I needed, leaving *The Sophisticate* to finish my novel, having children—essentially my entire life was on hold. Because for the last three years, it felt like doing any of these things without David would be the ultimate betrayal.

But now, after finally sitting down face-to-face with Celeste, reflecting on my mother and our complicated relationship, and getting to know Jason, I saw it all differently. Moving on was actually a part of acceptance—the final stage of grief—and I was closer than ever to understanding it. It didn't mean that the longing suddenly disappeared or that the regrets hurt any less. It didn't mean that the memories dulled or the pain vanished. But it did mean I could start reclaiming my life and charting a new path forward.

But what would that path look like?

In these last few weeks, Jason and I had shared more than just moments. He seemed to be rediscovering a joy that had eluded him for some time, as if each laugh and conversation we had was coaxing him back to life. And I'd shared a part of myself that I'd tucked down deep, too afraid to let someone see my scars, the ones that hadn't quite yet healed.

It was no wonder Noah "showed up" in my inbox. And it wasn't MAUDE's fault. Or Jason's. I'd asked the universe to give me back something impossible, a carbon copy of a life that'd been wonderful and beautiful but was now over. No amount of wishing on a star or pleading with fate would change that fact, and even still, I knew now I'd be okay.

But where did that leave me? After spending most of my twenties focused on David—first on his lofty goals, then his tragic death—did I even know what I wanted my future to look like anymore? The signs were all there: big changes were coming to *The Sophisticate*, whether I stayed or not. It was only a matter of time before MAUDE or some similar tool would force its way in. I wasn't sure I had the resolve to weather the next revolution. And even if I did, would that make me happy?

No, it wouldn't. I hadn't been happy at work for a while now. Yes, grief had played a role, but it was more than that. In these last few years, the demands of my position had pulled me further and further from the thing I loved most—writing. I hadn't realized how much I truly missed it until last night, my fingers flying over the keys and the words tumbling out faster and with more precision than a Simone Biles floor routine. It was as if a faucet had been turned on and, in the excitement, the handle torn from its fixture, the water freely gushing forth without any slowing in sight.

I wanted to write—not to meet a deadline or satisfy the bottom line, but because it was where I found my truest self. My fingertips prickled at the phantom sensation of my laptop keys click-clacking underneath them, and I instinctively reached for my laptop to search through my Google Drive for my half-completed manuscript. But before opening it (and yes, after fixing all the application permissions for MAUDE!), I changed my mind, accessing a brand-new document, a blank page, a fresh start.

Pivoting from the epic fantasy I'd started writing all those years ago, I imagined instead a quieter novel about grief and healing, acceptance and forgiveness, that explored the nuanced relationships that shape who we are. No heroes or villains. No monsters or dragons. No perfectly scripted happily ever afters. Just life. Painful, messy, complicated, wonderful, beautiful *real* life.

And the words came. Like with the article, sentences poured onto the page as if they had been waiting there beneath the surface all along. Who knows? Maybe they had been, and I just hadn't been able to unleash them. But now, I was—and before I could change my mind, I sent Daphne a note asking if she was free to meet first thing the next morning.

◆ ◆ ◆

"Oh, Remi, come in, come in," Daphne called out from her desk.

As I made my way inside, Daphne's smile beamed at me from across her office, almost competing with the bright morning sun streaming in through her floor-to-ceiling windows. "You must've read my mind. I was going to send you a meeting invite, and then I saw your note." She stood up and clapped her hands, her stack of gold bangle bracelets making a small jingle sound each time they came together. "Brava, my dear, bra-va! After how we left things, I never expected you'd be able to manage another sit-down with the senator, let alone dive so deep in your interview that you could produce *that*! And in record time, no less." With closed eyes, she shook her head and waved her hands as if she was too overcome with pride to even put another string of words together. "You outdid yourself, Remi—and the piece, well, it's going to change everything."

Daphne sat back down and dramatically pulled what looked like a printed copy of the article off her desk to fan herself. "A triumph, truly. And you know me; I am not usually one to gush or blow smoke up anyone's ass. So trust me when I say, you should be incredibly proud. Of this article. And of yourself to have overcome everything you needed to in order to write it. I was a puddle by the end of it. Ugly crying. Snot flying.

The works. Your words are going to resonate with our readership . . . and beyond."

"Thank you. Your compliments, especially because you've always been such a straight shooter, mean more than I can say. Which makes this next part—"

"Oh! And how did you get Romero to give you that whole scoop about her mother and the grieving?! I was just like, wow, really compelling stuff."

"I'm . . . I'm so glad that you found the article as moving and illuminating as I did writing it."

"I'm not gonna lie, you had me more than a little worried. After our last meeting, I almost reassigned the story altogether. But dammit, girl, you came through and came through big for the magazine. I just need you to know that I am incredibly impressed. And that's saying a lot." She finally came up for air and lifted her bone china teacup by its dainty curved handle to take a quick sip.

"Daphne, I really and truly appreciate the praise, and all the incredible support you've given me over the years . . . because this piece will mark my farewell from *The Sophisticate*. I'm here to tender my resignation."

Daphne jumped up—practically straight out of her stilettos—sending her teacup soaring across her desk. She left it toppled as I watched a small puddle of what was left in it drip off the glass edge and onto the pristine white rug below. "Wait, what?! What are you talking about?! Remi, your job is safe. I was planning to sing your praises at the next board meeting."

Drawing in a deep breath, I hitched my shoulders back and held my head as high as I could muster. "I can't tell you how grateful I am to have had the chance to close out my career here with the Celeste piece. It reminded me of what made me want to work at *The Sophisticate* in the first place. But it's time for me to move on."

"I can't let you do this." She dropped her gaze down to her desk, setting the empty teacup in its saucer, and asked, "Is this because of Jason?"

Her question caught me off guard, and my eyes snapped to hers quizzically. "No . . . Why would you ask me that?"

She moved around to the front of her desk to lean on it, arms crossed as she faced me. "Because he submitted his recommendations to the board just this morning. Well ahead of schedule, might I add." She reached behind herself to grab for her readers and another printed sheet from a neatly organized pile. Sliding the chic glasses onto the end of her nose, she drew the paper into her line of sight and started reading.

"'During my time here, I have grown convinced that MAUDE could never deliver the quality of content or depth of story required at *The Sophisticate*. I cannot endorse its deployment into the editorial division of the magazine. To do so would be to disappoint its readership and severely undermine the integrity of the publication.'" Daphne peered over her readers as if making sure I was still following.

When she confirmed I was, she continued, "He goes on to say that while he believes there are many uses for MAUDE here at the magazine, content creation should not be one of them. So you see, you don't have to resign—we won."

Jason had demonstrated MAUDE's prowess by skillfully repurposing the Kingston Bloom photo shoot fiasco. It was a significant save—in cost, time, and resources. In the end, he'd proven MAUDE had a place at *The Sophisticate*.

However, with the Celeste article, I had also proven that no algorithm, no matter how advanced, could capture the subtle shifts in tone, the unspoken words, or the deep, visceral responses that come from living through the highs and lows of actual life. In short, MAUDE's place was not in editorial.

Despite all this, one thing was crystal clear: in the showdown between man and machine, there could never truly be a winner, and I was relieved to learn he felt the very same way.

"After David died, *The Sophisticate* gave me a reason to get out of bed every day, and a support system, and . . . it gave me purpose. I will forever be grateful to the magazine and to you for giving me a safe space at the very worst time in my life. But this isn't about David or Jason or even about MAUDE. It's finally about me. I want to write again. Just let the words flow from my heart to the page like I did with the Celeste article. And while it's scary, I'm actually not scared. Not anymore."

Daphne's look of bewilderment melted into an understanding smile with every word I spoke. When I finished, she sat silent for a moment before clearing her throat. "I suppose we'll have some loose ends to tie up before you go, especially to find a worthy enough replacement."

"Well, that's something else I wanted to discuss with you. I'd like to offer Carrie McGill as my recommendation for the senior editor role. Though she's still a bit green by industry standards, the Celeste article would never have happened without her. She's been the backbone of our division, far more savvy and resourceful than anyone gives her credit for, and I know with some mentorship and guidance she might even be sitting where you are someday," I said confidently, giving her a wink at the end of my pitch.

Daphne set her lips in a satisfied pout and gave a firm nod. "That is quite a commendation. If you feel that strongly, I'll recommend her to HR for the promotion—"

"Thank you, Daphne, for everything." My chest tightened around my voice until I almost couldn't manage the last word. It was hard to imagine I would soon be venturing out into the *very literal* unknown. But it was time.

And best of all, I was secure in the knowledge I was leaving *The Sophisticate* in very, very capable hands.

Chapter Thirty-Seven

At the corner of Ninetieth Street and Fifth Avenue the next morning, I stood balancing three coffees, waiting for Carrie and Molly to emerge from the subway stairs. Seeing me, they hurried over, grabbing their respective cups to alleviate my awkward balancing act.

"It wasn't your turn to buy!" Molly cried. "I'm pretty sure I haven't covered coffees in like three weeks!"

"Honey, you have a wedding to save for. Besides, we're celebrating, and I wanted to treat today," I said as we took off side by side on our usual course around the reservoir.

"Celebrate, you say?" Carrie asked with a playful hint to her voice and a sky-high brow. "What, may I ask, are we celebrating?"

I took a quick sip of my latte and said, "Well, a few things, actually. For one, I have decided to downsize and put my apartment on the market. And two, I'm going to take a few weeks, go away somewhere, and really finish my book."

"That's amazing," Molly gushed. "Where are you going to go?"

"I'm not sure yet. Maybe Paris? Maybe Antigua? Peru? Maine? Doesn't matter, really. Just a place where I can relax and focus and just write."

Both their mouths dropped wide open.

"Maybe to the Congo to go and see your guy?" Molly squealed by way of suggestion, her innuendo clear as a bell.

I sucked in a quick breath, forgetting I hadn't even had a chance to tell them about the real Noah situation. Well, it would have to be a story for another day, over margaritas. But today, we had real news to celebrate! "Oh no, that's over. Turns out he wasn't *exactly* who he said he was."

Molly crossed her arms in front of her chest and moved her head back and forth like a metronome. "I knew it. The foreign-prince scam?! Shit, Remi? How much money did you send him?"

"No, no, I didn't give him any money or anything. It's not like that. We just realized we want different things."

Me an actual hard body, and Noah a hard drive.

"So sounds like an eat-drink-write trip is exactly what the doctor ordered. How long will you be gone for?" Carrie asked.

"That kind of leads me to my last nugget of exciting news," I started. "When I get home, I won't be returning to *The Sophisticate*."

The girls were both temporarily mute, making me second-guess if they'd even heard me at all. But after about fifteen seconds of silence, Molly sputtered a few syllables. "But—whaaa—no! Not coming back to the magazine?! I don't understand—"

Carrie, finally finding her voice, cried, "But I don't want to work for anyone else! Only you! What the hell are we going to do there without you?!"

"Well"—I shrugged and clapped Carrie on the shoulder—"I gave *your* name to Daphne to take my role. You're ready for this next step. You have been for a long time, and no one deserves it more."

Carrie stopped dead in her tracks, and it took us a few steps to realize she was no longer keeping pace. "No. Wait. Really? Me? Senior editor of *The Sophisticate*?" Her voice squeaked as tears sprang to her eyes. She flapped her hands in front of her face like she'd been crowned winner in the Miss America pageant, and I was fully ready for her to start with the iconic Sally Field Academy Awards "you love me, you really love me" dramatic opus.

"Yeah, you. If you want it," I said.

"Obviously, she wants it!" Molly squealed at the same time that Carrie bounded up between us and pulled us both into an all-too-enthusiastic group hug that almost knocked us to the ground. Laughing and jumping up and down in the middle of the path, we barely noticed the joggers and bikers bobbing and weaving around our impromptu party.

Carrie shook her head and said, "I just can't believe it—just as you're heading out, in saunters MAUDE. This truly is a new chapter for *The Sophisticate*."

"Speaking of," I continued, "Jason Ashbloome dropped his own bomb on the board yesterday. Apparently, he expressed serious doubts that MAUDE could be integrated into every aspect of the magazine, especially editorial."

"That doesn't make any sense. MAUDE's his baby. His brainchild, literally. What happened?" Molly asked, articulating the very same question I couldn't stop replaying in my own head.

"I don't know if it's related or not, but Jason and I really got into it the other day. We both said some things I'm sure we regret. For example, I made a jab about how the magazine has MAUDE now and doesn't need me, to which he made this really weird comment, something like, 'But what if I need you?'"

Molly and Carrie froze, turned to look at one another, and then at me. "Needs you how? Like *needs* you, needs you? Like Colin needed Penelope? Like a '*Bridgerton* burn for you' kind of needs you?!" Molly asked.

"No, I mean, that would be impossible, right? He's so . . . He's so Jason. He's rigid and uptight. He's the color-coded alphabetized folders to my scattered Post-it notes."

Molly tilted her head to the side and asked, "I'm still not seeing why that would be impossible. Maybe he's more the yin to your yang than you realized?"

My initial reaction was to scoff. Of course it was impossible. He was *Jason* and a million miles away from what I'd been looking for and what I thought I wanted.

Carrie asked, "Now that you've identified why you think it might not work between you two, care to consider any reasons as to why it could?"

At her question, my thoughts fired through a number of instances and small moments almost competing for top billing. I shrugged and said, "Well, aside from stepping in big time during the Fitz crisis, he's actually really funny, which I know you wouldn't expect. When we ran into each other at this slime museum, his kids practically forced him into a poncho and hand in hand pulled him under a neon-green slime waterfall. Can you imagine?! Mr. Prim and Proper covered head to toe in goo—it was hilarious! For as much as I thought he'd put up a fight, he was such a good sport about the whole thing, and by the end, we were both on the ground, slime and limbs everywhere, laughing uncontrollably. In fact, it was the hardest I've laughed in I can't even remember how long."

Carrie interjected, "Please forgive me as my brain is desperately trying to keep up with all the fastballs you're hurling right now. Jason . . . slime?! Kids?! Like, who even is he . . . Clark Kent?"

Molly, with a chuckle, added, "Yeah, I don't know, Rem, he doesn't strike me as the nurturing type, like at all. I can't even picture him taking good care of a plant."

"That's the thing! Neither could I, until I saw him. He has two young kids actually, and he's a really great dad. I mean, don't get me wrong, he's as scheduled and structured as a Swiss train conductor, but he's really sweet with them."

Carrie laughed. "You are just blowing my mind right now, Russell. What happened? His ex-wife get tired of having to calculate the ideal ratio of popcorn butter to kernel every time they sat down to watch Netflix?"

"Actually, his wife passed away a few years ago from cancer."

"Oh my God, I'm a monster. I just assumed he was divorced. Ugh, smite me right here." Carrie slapped a hand to her head in a gesture of unmistakable embarrassment.

"No, I made the same assumption. I even mistook the nanny for his new wife. Jason and I grabbed a drink to talk about work stuff and somehow got to talking about Emily, his late wife. You could see that he's still reeling from it all but also trying to move on. Just like me, I guess . . ." My voice trailed off as the picture of us in my mind began to sharpen.

My steps slowed to a stop, and I couldn't ignore the subtle warmth that had suddenly crept into my thoughts and slid down my limbs like a numbing agent. I wiggled my tingling fingers awake as my mind hopscotched through our interactions over the past few weeks. Amid the disagreements, tension, and overall discord between Jason and me, there had been more than a few moments of genuine connection.

Certainly in the grief we'd both experienced. Not to mention our shared understanding that life is far too short—something you can really only appreciate when you lose someone you love far too soon. In the way we were both trying to navigate our new realities after our lives derailed without losing total sight of our old ones.

Noah had been David 2.0, but really, he was no more than an illusion. Noah (or should I say, the idea of Noah) had been safe. He was thousands of miles away in the Congo, echoing back derivatives of my life with David. The familiarity of it all had been easy and reassuring. But it wasn't real. It was comfortable. *Too* comfortable.

There was nothing new to discover about him—no little gems that only surfaced when you're truly getting to know someone, no depths to plumb. Like the fact that Jason liked Jane Austen, that he loved Nirvana, and that jokes triggered his TMJ. And it was in those tiny details—the give-and-take, the push and pull—that genuine connections formed.

What Jason and I had felt like an authentic relationship, or at least the very promising start of one. Our chemistry had simmered under the surface since the first day we met, but with every chink in his armor, I started to get to know him on a deeper level—and surprisingly, started to get to know myself again. The epiphany made my insides coil into knots. How had it not occurred to me until now that I might need Jason too?

Realizing I'd fallen several steps behind the girls, completely lost in thought, Carrie doubled back. "Earth to Remi," she said, waving her hands in front of my face. "I know you're thinking about Jason's *Ass*bloome and everything, but *we* still have jobs we're gonna be late for!" she joked.

"Yeah, lady. Can you move your little assbloome a bit faster?" Molly teased as she playfully clapped her hands together like a high school track coach. "Chop, chop. I have a dress fitting to get to."

Carrie, now stopped dead in her tracks, burst out, "Holy crap, Molly's wedding just made me realize: If things work out with you and Jason, will you be Mrs. Remi *Ass*bloome?"

Molly erupted into a fit of giggles, and Carrie, barely even able to finish her question, was practically wheezing and doubled over.

"HR JAR!" I cried through my own tears.

And as was the beauty of New York City, no one even gave our uncontrollable laughing fit a second glance. The morning air felt warmer than it had in days, and the fresh breeze of spring swept through the park alongside the bustling runners and cyclists. The city was bright and fragrant with new buds, just waiting for their turn to step into the sun.

"Well, as the next senior editor of *The Sophisticate*, I say we bust that baby open and use the remaining money to have the biggest and best farewell soiree El Vez has ever seen. Spicy margaritas all around!

Because you know, I'm really, really going to miss this," Carrie said, swallowing back tears.

"Me too," Molly echoed.

I put my arms around Molly and Carrie—my two spicy margaritas, not to mention the best friends a girl could have—and said, "Me three."

Chapter
Thirty-Eight

Stepping into the David H. Koch Dinosaur Wing at the American Museum of Natural History, my eyes were drawn all the way up, almost to the glass ceiling, as I took in the renowned Tyrannosaurus rex, Stan. Named after the paleontologist who discovered it—according to the signage, anyway—Stan's fifteen-foot-tall and almost-forty-foot-wide cast, massive and imposing, immediately captured the attention and wonder of visitors. Since the museum had just opened for the day, the hall was still relatively empty, but as one of the museum's most popular exhibits, it would be filled with families and tourists in just a matter of hours.

On my toes, and wearing my I SURVIVED SLOOMOO FALLS T-shirt, I scanned the room, searching for Jason and his kids among the hundreds of artifacts in the exhibit. He'd mentioned their usual itinerary when they'd visit, starting with the dinosaurs and concluding somewhere on the second floor before lunch. I'd considered just reaching out to him but hesitated every time I pulled up his number on my phone, my thumb hovering over the call button. So I decided to track him down in person—the only way I could be certain not to lose my nerve.

But he wasn't here. I checked the fossil room, the triceratops exhibit, and Herbivore Hall. No Jason. Maybe he'd decided to do something else with the kids this morning? Or one of them, perhaps, wasn't feeling well?

Or maybe . . . just maybe . . . ?

I hurried out of the gallery and over to the elevator bank. The doors parted, and I stepped inside and pressed for the first floor, the Hall of Ocean Life. As I stepped out, my gaze immediately scanned upward to the room's centerpiece—the life-size fiberglass model of a majestic blue whale.

Suspended gracefully from the ceiling, the enormous mammal dominated the space. It looked so real, as if the animal could come to life at any moment, open its mouth, and pull everyone into the depths of its belly just like in *Pinocchio*. Blue light patterns were cast in swirls on the walls and floor and paired with the reverberations of whale songs piped over the speaker system. The whole effect made you feel as if you were really twenty thousand leagues under the sea.

I leaned over the balcony railing to survey the room and spotted Georgia's blond curls spread out across the ground as she, Aidan, and Jason all stared up from the floor of the gallery to the whale's underbelly. I sucked in a quick breath at seeing him—pants rolled up to the knees, giggling with his kids as they pointed up at the model.

I descended the steps to the main gallery behind where the three of them were still lying and crawled in next to Jason without him noticing it was me. Flat on my back, I turned my head in his direction and said, "Funny, meeting you here."

At the sound of a voice so close, he shifted his head toward me and sprang to sit upright. "Remi, oh, hey . . . What are you doing here? Um . . . at the museum?"

I sat up and pulled my knees into my chest. "Looking for you, actually. But I thought you'd be up in the dinosaur gallery. Nice shirt, by the way." I nodded at the matching I Survived Sloomoo Falls tee he was wearing underneath a smart blazer.

He glanced down with a smirk and then over at me before replying. "I decided to take your advice and change things up a bit," he said, pointing to Aidan and Georgia, now in a heated debate about which was bigger, the T. rex or the blue whale. "As you can see, it's been a big hit."

"I'm so glad." I hesitated for a moment. "I hope you don't think I've overstepped by showing up here. I just wanted to talk to you, and I thought I'd be less likely to chicken out in person."

"Why don't we . . . ?" he suggested, gesturing to a quieter corner of the gallery.

I nodded, and we both rose to our feet to step away from the kids. Keeping them in our sight, we moved to a nearby bench on the perimeter of the room, and as we sat, I said, "I'm not sure if you heard, but I resigned from *The Sophisticate*. I handed in my notice to Daphne a few days ago. It wasn't because of MAUDE—"

Jason blew out a deep breath, the air whooshing from his mouth in a stream before he spoke. "It wasn't? I'm really glad to hear you say that. Remember what I told you about Emily and her cancer, how helpless I felt not being able to make things better? I think in some ways, MAUDE was my answer to all that. A software that could solve every imaginable problem. Give order to the chaos, help to manage and schedule and coordinate it all. It was everything that I couldn't be for Emily, not to mention my lifeline when the ground was falling away from under my feet. And in my desperate quest to fix the unfixable, it practically consumed me.

"But after reading your article, the words that only you, Remi Russell—with your life experiences, authenticity, and empathy—could have crafted, I realized that nobody else, especially not a machine, could have told that story. And then after hearing that something I created hurt you . . ." He swallowed hard before locking eyes with mine. "I'm just glad that MAUDE . . . that I . . . wasn't the reason you left. I would have never forgiven myself, especially because I think I'm falling in love with you."

"Jason . . ."

"No, it's okay. It doesn't make much sense to me either. We haven't even been out on an actual date, and yet I find myself thinking about you all the time. When Emily died, I just accepted I'd never have those feelings again, so when they showed up in the form of the woman I was squaring off with at work, it caught me completely off guard. So off guard, in fact, that I couldn't help but declare how much I needed her on the corner of a busy intersection the other day." His cheeks turned a deep shade of crimson.

A warm smile formed on my face and spread like melted butter through my limbs and down into my stomach. "Me too."

Jason cocked his head to the side, and surprise lit up his face. "Wait, what are you saying?"

"That I thought I'd never have those feelings again either. That I . . . I was caught off guard too. I realized somewhere between our push and pull and the little moments we've shared over these past few weeks"—I glanced down, making a show of eyeing my shirt and his—"we were really connecting, and it was getting harder and harder to pretend there wasn't something developing between us. I know we have more ground to cover in getting to know one another, but I'd like to."

Jason reached out and wove his fingers through mine, rubbing the skin of the back of my hand gently with his thumb. "I'd like that too. Would you care to walk around the museum with us and then see where the day goes? We aren't on any schedule."

My mouth popped open into a dramatic look of shock, and I placed my free hand over my heart. "No schedule? Why, Jason Ashbloome, I never thought I'd see the day."

He smirked. "Well, what can I say? I guess you're wearing off on me. Besides, I'm trying to learn to embrace the chaos," he said, gesturing over to where his kids shifted from snuggling two seconds ago to a full-on WrestleMania display.

"You know what they say: Chaos is a ladder," I said, throwing out one of my favorite lines from *Game of Thrones*.

"*You* like *Game of Thrones*?" His eyebrows shot up in surprise as he registered another unexpected similarity. "Wouldn't have guessed it. Seems we do have a lot to discover about each other."

"That's half the fun, though, right?" Turning to him, I scooted closer and drew his glasses out of his jacket pocket before sliding the thick frames onto his face. I pressed my lips to his as a burst of color and light exploded behind my closed eyelids. The kiss was quick, but it was powerful enough to make my knees weak, and even better than it was in my Zoom-library fantasy.

When he pulled back and opened his eyes, he said, "So I'm learning."

Before I knew it, his lips were on mine again, his hands on my waist pulling me closer, and the room faded away as if stolen by the magic of the moment, consumed by the intensity of his embrace.

A quick, pulsing alarm blared from his Apple Watch, and the sound of his heart rate monitor skyrocketing temporarily snapped us out of the spell. My face fell into his neck in a fit of giggles, and I breathed in the clean scent of his aftershave. He pressed a kiss to my cheek. And then another, and another, laughing sweetly in between. Only a few seconds later, a chorus of chiding *ooooooh*s broke us apart. Aidan and Georgia were pointing and snickering as Jason and I sheepishly attempted to regain our composure under the amused gaze of our little audience.

A bit embarrassed and rosy cheeked, I cleared my throat, straightened my coat, and said, "What do guys think? Ready to visit the dinosaurs?"

Jason pulled out a map of the museum from his back pocket. "We've done the dinosaurs loads of times. How about today we check out"—he glanced at the guide—"Birds of the World? What do you say we go on a bit of an . . . adventure?" He looked up from the paper and locked his eyes with mine.

I stood up from the bench, clasping Georgia's small hand with my left and Aidan's with my right. "Let's go," I said with a nod before blurting out, "Last one there's a rotten egg!" and taking off with the kids, sprinting at full speed . . . toward something new.

Epilogue

If rain on your wedding day was a sign of good luck to come, then Molly and Luca were gearing up for a windfall of eternal blessings and fortune. The late-June afternoon stirred with the promise of a heavy summer storm, the warm wind whipping our bridesmaid dresses and hair to and fro. But neither Molly nor Luca seemed to even give it a second thought as they twirled in the rain shower after reciting their vows in front of their closest friends and family. The photographer snapped pictures of Molly and Luca with their arms open wide, embracing the storm, to be edited into black-and-white photographs that would one day adorn their walls in thick golden frames. They looked so happy—no, *were* so happy—and everyone in their presence couldn't help but be happy for them too.

I waited for a moment to snag Molly for a quick word before the photographer's next shot and jumped in when Luca stepped away to check on his mom. "So much for needing a sunny day. You're shining brighter than any sunbeam I've ever seen," I cried. And it was true! She really was.

"Thank you, thank you, thank you for everything, Remi. Ugh, has this not been just like the best day ever!?" Molly squealed and did a spin in place like a little girl playing dress-up.

"I know! And the party's just getting started! But I wanted to see if you needed anything before Carrie and I headed inside to help the planner usher everyone from the cocktail hour to their seats in the dining room. Have you had at least a bite of something?"

"I think I'm okay for a few more shots out here, and then we'll head inside and grab some food. Thanks for checking. And as much as I appreciate you and Carrie kicking so much ass as my co–maids of honor, you both are officially"—she pantomimed bopping my head with an invisible wand—"*off duty*. My planner is making enough money that she and her esteemed team can do the wranglin'. So go and snuggle up and then boogie down with that super-sexy-and-oh-so-patient date of yours, and that's an order!" She smirked and winked a fluffy set of false lashes in my direction.

"And I wanna see you two smoochin' on the dance floor before midnight, you got it?" Molly called after me as she did her signature coach-style hand clap, then practically spun me around by the shoulders in the direction of the estate's main hall and patted my tush to go find Jason.

After not seeing him at the terrace bar, where I'd left him chatting with Carrie's boyfriend, Marcus, while we finished with photos, I finally found Jason lingering up by the ballroom stage, engaged in conversation with the emcee.

I sauntered up and tapped him on the shoulder. "I told you, if you try to get the band to play Nirvana at this wedding, Molly will have you murdered!" I joked.

He laughed. "Not that I wouldn't be open to a wedding-style mosh pit to 'Smells Like Teen Spirit,' but I know you do not poke the bear on her wedding day. Actually, I was requesting"—as if on cue, the band struck up the opening chords of "My Heart Will Go On"—"this."

He took my hand and led me to the mostly open dance floor as couples were still filing in to take their seats for dinner. "I realized we'd never had an occasion to slow dance before and thought it could be another thing to check off the list."

"I didn't think you were the dancing type."

"That's because *you* haven't seen my smooth moves," he said and twirled me around ballerina-style.

And as the iconic nineties ballad soared through the space, I couldn't help but laugh at the supremely cheesy and oh-so-appropriate lyrics we both were singing along to. "Really, Jason? I didn't peg you as a Celine Dion fan."

He looked taken aback by my unintentional dig, and with mock-exasperation, he gasped, "She is a national treasure."

"I'm pretty sure she's Canadian."

"Whaa— She is?! Well, that's a bummer. But still, she's Celine. And if anyone knows anything about belting out an epic love song, it's her."

I laid my head on his shoulder, my cheek warm against the satin lapels of his fitted tuxedo. "I can't disagree there."

In perfect rhythm with the tempo, he rocked me close to his body, my hand folded in his, and he breathed into my neck so that the small hairs tickled and sent goose bumps down my arms.

Jason stroked his fingers down the bare skin of my back. "Did I mention how much I missed you while you were away?"

I laughed and nuzzled my cheek against him. "You have, pretty much every day since I've been back . . . But I've loved hearing it. And I missed you too."

My writing retreat had been a success—thirty days and one completed manuscript already out to a few interested publishers. But that time hadn't just been about writing. I scoured the world (and different author message boards), finally landing on a one-month cozy cottage rental on the Isle of Harris, a remote island off the coast of Scotland. There, among the seals and otters that I befriended on the otherwise desolate beaches, I got to know myself again. And I got to really, really know Jason.

The time difference, work, and the kids made regular phone calls a bit of a challenge, so we traded written words instead. Our daily emails were filled with shared stories, secret thoughts, and dreams for the future, building a connection that felt deeper with each exchange. By the time I returned home, there was no doubt: we were official.

We swayed back and forth as more couples joined us on the dance floor.

And as the chorus swelled with intensity, Jason took my hand and spun me around with a skilled maneuver, his feet quick and light.

"Okay, Gene Kelly," I joked. "No wonder you were dying to show me your smooth moves!"

"Oh, girl, you ain't seen nothin' yet," he crooned as he dramatically swept me into a low but graceful dip.

Giggling with surprised delight, I looped my hand around his neck and pulled him down for a quick kiss. When the song ended, the emcee let everyone know dinner was being served and urged them to return to their tables.

Jason pulled out my chair. "Your bag's vibrating," he said, handing me my clutch.

I opened the purse and slid out my phone. I had four texts from Mom.

Mom: The 59th Street Bridge is going to be closed for repairs tonight into tomorrow morning. I don't know where Molly's wedding's being held, but in case you need to cross the East River, maybe plan an alternate route?

Mom: Did I tell you the touring company of Funny Girl is coming to the Broward Center in Fort Lauderdale? A nice gentleman I met at the club's Decades of Dazzle Luau asked me if I wanted to see it with him. I told him I'd already seen the original and the new Broadway production, but maybe I'll still go?

Mom: I booked my ticket and fly into JFK a week from Friday. I don't know how people can stand living in Florida in the summertime. I feel like I am going to burst into flames every time I step outside. Meanwhile, every restaurant is air conditioned like Dante's icy 9th circle. It really is an enigma.

Mom: Hope you and Jason are having a wonderful time at the wedding. I look forward to meeting him when I'm back in town and making him a big batch of my Matzo Ball Soup. Love you.

I affectionately rolled my eyes and typed back a quick response:

Me: Love you too, Mom.

Jason peeked over my shoulder. "Everything okay? That's an awful lot of texts."

I smirked. "Par for the course. You'll soon realize that 'a lot of texts' in anyone else's world is just a quick hello from Ruth Russell."

As the salads were being brought around, Carrie raced over to me with the microphone and a look of panic alight in her expression. "Are you sure you don't mind doing the toast? I really thought I could at least give a 'welcome' and a 'thank you for coming,' but I just don't love speaking to crowds this size. I get all flustered and awkward. I start sweating profusely. It's not a cute look."

I grabbed the mic and covered her hand with mine. "Go have a drink, take a few deep breaths, and save some of that nervous energy for the dance floor. I got you," I said with a wink.

Clinking my knife gently against my half-filled flute, I stood to give a toast before everyone started their dinner. "Good evening, everyone, and thank you so much for joining us in celebrating the union of Mr. and Mrs. Luca and Molly Moreno-Vargas. First, I want to express my delight and gratitude in being one of Molly's maids of honor. Today, we're not just celebrating a beautiful wedding, but a couple's eternal promise. If ever there was a wedding day that proves love can weather any storm—both figurative and literal—it would certainly be this one."

The audience gave an understanding chuckle, and I continued, "As I considered what I wanted to say when writing this speech, I kept returning to the idea that though tomorrow is promised to no one, we sometimes need a gentle reminder that each sunrise is a gift, a chance to live and love anew."

I directed my attention from the sea of eyes to Molly and Luca sitting at the head table, listening intently as they snuggled in close to each other, and then over to Jason. "So today we celebrate not only the forever you've promised but also the beauty of every today you choose to spend together—loving one another, learning about one another, and cherishing one another. May your journey be a testament to the power of love, understanding, and true partnership. May you navigate life's twists and turns with grace, and may your shared laughter echo through the corridors of all your tomorrows. To living and loving every single day as if it's our last."

I lifted my glass to Molly, whose eyes were swimming with tears as she mouthed, "Thank you," before Luca stole her attention back for a kiss. Turning around to Jason, I gently clinked his glass and repeated, "To living and loving every single day as if it's our last."

"Well, I'll cheers to that," he said, bringing his flute to meet mine.

Finally, after several courses of exquisite Spanish food, it was time to get the party started, the music's tempo picking up to a few well-known hit songs to get the crowd on their feet.

The emcee stepped away from the stage where the backup was still jamming with an interlude as the sequin-clad dancers handed out party favors like monogrammed sunglasses and inflatable toys to kick the festivities into high gear. A raucous cheer erupted from the now-crowded dance floor as the speakers pumped out "Twist and Shout," getting even the oldest of Molly's guests on their feet with their arms in the air.

I pulled Jason up just as the music started to transition to another familiar tune. A lively and infectious beat with a distinct Latin flare blasted through the space, and I scurried off to grab a necessary prop from the table of goodies. Upon my return, I flashed him a devilish grin and leaned in to press my cheek against his and whisper seductively into his ear.

"So how about it, Ashbloome—you DTF?" I cooed, my breath warming his neck.

He snapped back as if he'd misheard me, his eyebrows almost flown completely off his forehead. "Um . . . am I what?"

I drew back, the corners of my mouth fighting a smile. "DTF? Down to *fieeestaaa!*" Shaking my new maracas in the air, I drew his attention to the long conga line now snaking around the dance floor.

"Don't tempt me with a good time." His face broke into a wide grin as he took my waist and urged me on with a jut of his chin. "And don't you know by now, Russell? Where you lead, I will follow. Always. Olé!"

ACKNOWLEDGMENTS

Again, we are forever grateful to our agent, Jill Marsal, for championing us and our work, to our editor, Maria Gomez, and the entire team at Montlake for helping us produce the best version of our vision and allowing us to be an integral part of the process every step of the way, and to our amazing developmental editor, Angela James, with whom we've built an incredible friendship and trust. Thank you for helping us continue to bring our dreams to life.

From Beth:

This book encompasses many themes, but at its heart, it was shaped by the relationships and love that fills our lives. For me, that is my husband, who always has my back, cheering me on through every challenge and celebrating every triumph; my girlfriends, who make me laugh and are endlessly encouraging; my writing partner, Danielle, who truly is the yin to my yang; my father, Arthur Zamansky, who illuminated grief and its profound lessons; and finally, my beautiful Hadley Alexandra, who teaches me every day about the power of the mother-daughter bond.

From Danielle:

Similarly, over the months Beth and I wrote this book, it made me think about a lot of relationships in my own life, all of them changing me and shaping me for as long or as short a time that I was lucky enough to have them in my life. I've experienced some significant losses these past two years and grief is a strange and humbling thing. So first, to those I've lost who helped me understand that grief is just an expression of how much love was felt during our time together. Thank you for the memories and all the lessons—you were with me as I helped Remi navigate her own healing. To my incredible and unparalleled family who continually show me the true meaning of strength, love, and unwavering support—your presence has been my guiding light through every chapter of this journey. To my tribe—the incredible girlfriends I have in my life who lift me up, bring so much laughter to my life, and make the ride worthwhile. To Mash and Haddie—thank you for sharing your wife/mom with me and for always welcoming me in like one of the fam (even when I steal your pitas and throw our leftovers on the floor!). Mash, you have seen more than most in regard to our ups and downs and all the time and effort we have poured into this endeavor. Your enthusiasm and support are unparalleled, and we really couldn't do it without you. A+++! And to my other half, Beth, all this is so much better because we get to do it together.

Lastly, to all our amazing readers—your love and excitement fuel us more than coffee and Diet Coke ever could (and from us, that's saying a lot!) Thanks for being the spark that keeps our words flowing and our hearts so very full.

BOOK CLUB QUESTIONS

1. The novel explores the theme of motherhood through several characters: Ruth, Celeste, Remi, and Jess. How do you think the different portrayals of motherhood (or the desire for it) shape these characters' identities and relationships? How are the sacrifices, pressures, or complexities of motherhood depicted in the relationships between mothers and daughters? Even if you are not a mother, how do you relate to these dynamics, perhaps from your perspective as a child or through observing these relationships?

2. What do you think about the influx of AI, especially in our day to day lives with programs like ChatGPT and Midjourney? Do you think it is more helpful or hurtful to humanity and our existence?

3. How does Remi's grief over her late husband drive her decisions with both Noah and Jason? Do you think her desire to find someone "just like" her late husband reflects an attempt to fill a void, or is it a way for her to avoid confronting her grief fully? Is she seeking comfort in familiarity with Noah, while Jason represents a more complex, uncertain future?

4. Remi forms an unexpected bond with Jason, despite their professional tensions and clear difference in personality.

What does their evolving relationship say about human connection in contrast to her relationship with Noah? How does this reflect the novel's theme of finding love in unexpected places?

5. What do you think the novel is trying to say about tradition versus innovation? Is there room for both in a fast-evolving digital world? How are we to balance the two in a way that fosters both an honoring of the past and progress?

6. Remi seems to be caught between embracing the future (through Jason and MAUDE) and holding on to the past (her grief and love for her late husband). How do you think this internal conflict shapes her character? How is it mirrored in Ruth and how does that shared experience shift their understanding of one another?

7. We felt like it was important to portray women as genuine allies and as strong pillars of support for one another: Carrie, Molly, Daphne, and eventually even Celeste. How do the relationships of the women in this book illustrate the complexities and strengths of female friendship? How were these relationships depicted as reciprocal and authentic representations of real friendships?

8. If you were in Remi's position, would you have trusted MAUDE with your dating life? How comfortable are you (or would you be) with using AI to make decisions in areas that are usually more personal in nature? What would make you apprehensive and what would make you excited about using a software like this?

9. Even though Celeste's character undergoes development, should she still be held accountable for David's death? How do you think the novel handles themes of

accountability and forgiveness? Can personal growth absolve someone from past mistakes, or should there still be consequences?

10. In a world increasingly marked by division, how does Celeste's and Remi's journey toward understanding illustrate the importance of finding common ground? What strategies can we adopt in our own lives to foster meaningful conversations and bridge the gaps between our differing political and personal perspectives?

ABOUT THE AUTHORS

 Beth Merlin earned her BA from the George Washington University and her juris doctor from New York Law School. A lifelong New Yorker, Beth loves anything Broadway, romantic comedies, and a good maxi dress. When she isn't writing, you can find her spending time with her husband, daughter, and two cavapoos, Sammy and Scarlett, at home or at their favorite vacation spot, Kiawah Island, South Carolina. She and Danielle Modafferi are the coauthors of *Heart Restoration Project* and *The Last Phone Booth in Manhattan*. For more information, visit www.merlinandmod.com.

 Danielle Modafferi, a high school English teacher and pun enthusiast, earned her MFA in writing popular fiction from Seton Hill University and, shortly after, founded Firefly Hill Press in 2016. By day, she helps her students discover the magic of language, and by night, she's a writer and publisher on a mission to unleash her creativity and help others do the same. Danielle loves making memories with friends and family, traveling to faraway (and some not-so-faraway) places, and snuggling with her Yorki-poo, Liam, who is also, incidentally, her biggest fan. She and Beth Merlin are the coauthors of *Heart Restoration Project* and *The Last Phone Booth in Manhattan*. For more information, visit www.merlinandmod.com.